Tanith Lee was born in England and now lives in South London. She has had a variety of jobs and spent a year at art college before becoming a full-time writer. Her interests include music, painting and reading. She has had two plays broadcast by BBC radio and is also well known as a writer of children's books. Tanith Lee's fantasy novels *The Birthgrave* and *The Storm Lord* are available from Orbit. *Shadowfire* Volume 2 will also be available from Orbit.

Also by Tanith Lee:

Tanith Lee

Shadowfire

Volume 1

Futura Publications Limited
An Orbit Book

An Orbit Book

First published in Great Britain by
Futura Publications Limited in 1978
Copyright © 1978 by Tanith Lee

First published in the United States of
America under the title *Vazkor, Son of Vazkor*

ISBN 0 7088 8039 8

Printed in Great Britain by
Hazell Watson & Viney Ltd
Aylesbury, Bucks

Futura Publications Limited,
110 Warner Road
Camberwell, London SE5

Book One

PART I

The Krarl

1

One summer when I was nine years old, a snake bit me in the thigh. I remember very little of what followed, only being mad with heat and tossing about to escape it as if my flesh were on fire, while time passed in patches. And then it was over and I was better, and running on the green slopes again among the tall white stones that grew there like trees. I learned after that I should have died from the snake's venom. My body turned gray and blue and yellow from it; a pleasant sight I must indeed have been. Yet I did not die, and even the bite left no scar.

Nor was this the only occasion that I brushed with death. When I was weaned I spewed up everything they gave me except goat milk. Another child would have gone no further, for the krarls generously leave their weaklings as a meal for wolves. Being the son of a Dagkta chief by his favorite woman, my mother's pleading no doubt saved me. Presently I got over my delicacy and the forbearance of my father was justified.

I survived by fighting and my days were filled up with it. When I was not fighting for my life, I was fighting every other male child of the krarl. For, though I was Ettook's son, my mother was the out-tribe woman, and I had all the look of her from my very first day in the world. Black-blue hair that was silk on her and a lion's mane on me and her black eyes, like the blind back of the night sky.

One of my earliest memories is of my mother as she sat combing my hair over my scalp, neck, and shoulder blades. She drew the wooden comb through and through those whips with the sensuous possessiveness of all mothers. She was proud of me, and I was proud to have her pride. She was beautiful, was Tathra, and she was like me. I leaned on her knees as she combed me, and even then, I recall, my

7

knuckles were cut open from some battle, someone's teeth I had loosened because they had called her names. From the beginning I was conscious of being unique and out of the herd. I never lived an hour without it. It made me sharp and hard and taught me to keep my thoughts in my head, which was all to the good. My mother Tathra shone like a dark star in among the red and yellow people. It was clear, even to the child I was, they hated her for her glamour and her position, and me they hated as the symbol. When I fought them, I fought for her. She was the rock at my back. My ambition was that I must better all of them so that I should uphold her rights and keep her approbation. My father was not exempt from this ambition, nor my dislike.

Ettook was a coarse red man. A red pig. When he came in the tent, then I was put out. With others he would say, "Here is my son," boast of my height and the muscle growing in me, boast because he had made me, like a good spear. Yet when I displeased him, he beat me, not exactly as a warrior beats his son to tan sense into his hide, or out of it, as the case may be; Ettook beat me with pleasure, because I was his to beat, also something more. I came to see later in my life that each of those blows was saying, "Tomorrow you will be stronger than I, so now I will be stronger than you, and if I break your back, well and good."

Besides, I had no look of him. Somewhere in him, ignored by the pig that ruled his brain, festered the half-suspicion that Tathra had got me from one of her own folk, before he burned their krarl and took her as spear-bride. He had sons by other women, but Tathra he prized. I have seen him stand and look at some plundered bangle he meant to hang on her, and his cock would push out his leggings just from that. I could have killed him then, that red pig grunting for my mother's white flesh. Supposedly it is the oldest hate of man for man, but always new. Truly, Ettook and I were not friends to each other.

The Boys' Rite came due for me when I was fourteen. It fell always in the month of the Gray Dog, the second of the Dog months, during the winter camping.

In spring the tribes went to seek the fertile lands beyond the Snake's Road; in fall of leaf they came back and moved up into the mountains. The high valleys, contained and sheltered between jagged peaks, escaped the worst of the bladed winds and snow. In certain areas the valley bottoms plunged below the snow line; here grass flourished and evergreen, and waterfalls spilled smashing down, too fast to freeze. In these spots the deer and bear came to browse, sluggish, easy prey for hunters' arrows.

Ettook's wintering was shared with other krarls than the Dagkta, with red Skoiana and Hinga and yellow-haired Moi not five miles distant, everyone under a sullen truce. It was too bitter cold for war at that season. The men built long tunnels of packed snow, stone, hide, mud, and boughs, and the tents crouched under them, or in the ribbed caves below the mountain shanks. There was little to do in winter. Storytelling, drinking and gambling, eating and sex were the major pastimes. Sometimes a skirmish between rival hunting bands relieved the monotony. If one man killed another under truce, he must pay a Blood-Price, so the warriors murdered each other carefully and seldom. Krarl ritual was the only other solace.

The Boys' Rite was one of the mysteries of the men's side. No male became a warrior without he had undergone it. Since I could remember, I had known it was ahead of me, this milestone of my life, and I dreaded it, and did not positively know why. But I would rather have eaten my tongue than said so. Even my mother I did not tell. I could not let her see me weaken.

There was a girl I had had in leaf-fall. She was a year or so older than I, and had led me on and then vehemently regretted it when I took her teasing for earnest. She had been at me to shame me, for the women hated Tathra most and passed on their hate to their daughters. The girl thought me unready, no doubt, but she was mistaken. She screamed with pain and anger and bit my shoulders to try to dislodge me, but the shireen—her woman's veil-mask—blunted her teeth, and I was enjoying things too much to let her go just then.

When I was done and found her bleeding I was sorry a moment, but she said, "You out-tribe vermin, you shall bleed too, and yelp when the needles go into you. I hope they may kill you."

Generally the women feared and revered the males of the krarl, but she had some spirit for me because I was Tathra's son. I held her by the hair until she whimpered.

"I know about the needles. That is how the warrior-marks are made. Don't think I shall be squeaking under them like a maiden with the key in her lock."

"You," she spat, "you will writhe. You will swell up and die of it. I shall ask Seel-Na to put a curse on you."

"Ask away. Her curses stink like her person. As for you, you should thank me. I have done your future husband a service, for you were a difficult bitch to get into."

She tried to poke out my eyes then and I struck her a blow to make her reconsider. Her name was Chula, my first wife, as it turned out later, so the rape was in some ways prophetic.

Still, her words oppressed me. The tattooing, which was part of the Rite, troubled me. I think it had been troubling me a long while and she had only brought the trouble out. My body was strange, so much I already knew, from the snake, and other things. I darkened from the sun, I paled in winter as did all the people, yet there had never been a blemish on my skin and nothing left a scar. As if to balance this, my system showed intolerance to any foreign thing taken in, even food. The rich roasted meats of the kill had me sick if I ate more than a shred or two; their beer was like bane to me. I came to wonder at last what the bright inks of the priests would do, and the needles pushed through my arms and breast. It occurred to me eventually that I should probably die of it as the girl had said, and this filled me with a raging anger. To perish for something I held in contempt, and to leave my mother alone in Ettook's tent, was gall for me to swallow. And I could say nothing, having created of my fourteen-year-old self a being of iron.

The day before the Rite fell due I went hunting on my own, up and down the snow-clotted sides of the valleys, in the grinding wind. Even at fourteen there was no one better with arrow or spear.

There were two brown does by a pool. I got them both within a second or so of each other. When I went up to let the blood from them to lighten them, something happened inside me like a stone clicking off from the mountain into the air. It was the first time I had ever killed a thing and realized I had taken its life, something that belonged to it. The deer, slumped in the snow, were heavy as lead and flaccid as sacks from which the wine had been emptied. I wished I had not done it then; we had meat enough. Yet I was trying for something, and soon I got up and, going back with the kill, saw a hare and shot that too, and carried it with me to the tents.

The men stared resentfully at what I had got, and some of the younger women exclaimed. A few of the girls' side were coming to like me a little. Since Chula there had been others, more willing, yet ready to screech and complain after. Still, I had noticed they came back for more.

Ettook was away with various chiefs of the Dagkta drinking on the south side of the camp. He would not be visiting my mother till he returned for the evening meal, or till he was roaring drunk, or both. Tathra sat in her dark blue tent, weaving on a loom got in barter from the Moi. They said they had it from the city peoples west of the mountains, where the great wars had come and gone, leaving only ruin after them.

There had always been war between the ancient cities from time immemorial, but it was a stately war, with rules like a dance. Then someone came who changed things. The tribes had it from scraps and stories blurted by refugees who crossed the mountains to escape the fighting. One tale, discredited at once, was of a goddess risen on earth. More to the tribal taste was the notion of a powerful and ambitious man who drove the old order into battle for his own ends, was slain, and so left the war to blaze on by itself like a fire, unchecked and leaderless. In the first five or six years after my birth, the cities fell on each other like dying dragons, and were torn in pieces. Thereafter the survivors roamed in packs, pirates of their own places, bitter, insane, and bitterly, insanely proud. There were a thousand or more of these bands, each with a different loyalty, under some crazy captain or prince. Sometimes you heard tales of their raiding over the peaks and men of the tribes taken for slaves. The cities' lords had always considered themselves remarkable; no human was their equal. The Moi, however, traded with them, by a burned ruin the krarls called Eshkir. The city warriors were strange, by repute, their faces always masked like the faces of our women, yet in bronze, iron, or even silver and gold, while they wore the pelts of animals and rags on their bodies. From the frayed reins of their horses would drip precious jewels, while the ribs of the horse itself thrust starving through the hide. There was a fable, too, that they never ate, these city men, and they had magic powers. They were never seen in winter, the passes being thick with snow, and seldom far east at any time.

On the Eshkiri loom my mother was weaving a scarlet cloth with an intricate border of black, maroon, and yellow. It would be for him. It made my anger worse to see her thus working for Ettook during my last hours in the world. I felt she should be exclusively mine, for I was sure tomorrow meant an end for me, and I was trying to cram today full of deeds.

Her hair was unbound as she worked, damson-black, her skin winter-white, like a warm snow. Once I was a warrior, by tribal law she would have to cover her face before me, as before all other men except her husband. But that was not yet. She had been old for a tribal bride, she had borne me in her twenty-ninth year; yet she looked no more than a girl in the shadowy tent. Her eyes were half shut from the rhythm of the loom. Only the bracelets chattered faintly on her arms as she moved them.

I stood and watched her a long while and did not think she saw me, but then she said, "I hear he has been hunting, Tuvek my son, and made a kill to last this tent many days."

I said nothing, so she turned and regarded me in a way she had, her head down, gazing up, half laughing. Even when she stood higher than I, by this look she had made me seem the taller. And when her eyes came on to me, they lit up, which was not playacting. You could see to the roots of her when this happened, how she was all pleasure in me.

"Come," she would say, holding out her hand, "come here, and let me see this child of my body, like a god. Can it be *I* that housed you?"

And when I came close to her, she would put her hands on my shoulders, light as a leaf, and laugh at me and her delight in me, till I laughed too.

No other boy of the krarl would have stood for this from his mother, and there were several extra names they discovered for me because I did. From seven years on, the boy is his father's. He apes his father's ways, eats with the men and sleeps in the boys' tent, and scorns the women at their cooking and sewing. If a woman touches him, he brushes her off scowling as if she were the mess of a bird dropped on him from the sky, unless he is eager to take the road between her thighs. However, the other women were not Tathra, their scrawny, clutching paws not her light ones, their faces without the shireen surely not like hers, and their stale female smell rank as a she-cat's. Tathra's scent was always fresh and sweet, augmented with perfumes. Even after the pig had been with her she was clean as clear water.

"Ah, my son," she said now, "my fine son. Tomorrow you will be made a warrior."

I would not even swallow the constriction out of my throat in front of her. I answered, "Yes," as if I had given the matter little thought.

"There is none like you," she said. She tangled her fingers in my hair which had long ago unraveled from its boy's plaits. She could never leave my hair be, a thing I have found in other women since, as if the color or the texture magnetized their fingers. The knot in my throat was growing; I glanced at the cloth on the loom to get my anger back and ease it. She saw my glance. "This is your warrior's cloak I am making."

That undid me.

"Mother," I said, "maybe I shall not be needing it," then bit on my tongue, I was so vexed with myself.

"Tuvek," she said softly, "now we have the truth. What do you think will be done to you?"

"No woman knows the Rite," I said.

"True. But she knows the men survive the other side of it. And am I to think you less than them? You, better than any?"

"I flinch from none of it," I said arrogantly, because she expected too much of me at that moment, "but I think I may die. So be it."

Then I saw that she also was uneasy, that she had only spoken as she did because she was frightened. Her hands tightened on me.

"Kotta," she said, "do you hear this?"

I jerked around, angry again certainly at this. I had thought we were alone in the tent. Now I saw the shadow beyond the loom, the blind healer-woman, resting her great arms on her knees. It was an odd thing with Kotta, though her eyes were sightless, she seemed to see everything there was, as the boys learned early when they tried to steal from among her things. Near big as a man, raw-boned, her blind irises shone blue as slate from her shireen. She was often to be found where you did not think her to be. She helped the women bear, and healed ills and wounds, and she was frequently with my mother. It was common women's talk about the krarl that Tathra would have died of her brat, and the brat too, if Kotta had not aided the birth. I had arrived on a morning of victory after some battle between Ettook's Dagkta and a Skoiana krarl, but Tathra fought harder than any warrior to get me born. She had conceived no other child and some said this was also Kotta's work, as a second bearing would be fatal to Ettook's out-tribe bitch-wife.

Kotta's enamel earrings clinked when she shifted and stared right at me as if she saw every feature.

"You distrust the tattooing," she said.

"I distrust nothing," I said, furious and cold as only fourteen can be.

"You do well to distrust it," she said, making an idiot of me. "As you say, it may be bad for you. Nevertheless, I hazard you will recover from it, as from the snake's bite. But I wonder if they will waste their ink." I did not understand. I was about to throw some harsh sentence to her, and leave the tent, when Kotta added, apparently for no reason, "That loom is from Eshkiri city. There was an Eshkir woman once among the tents."

I would have made nothing of this except that Tathra stiffened into a curious immobile grayness.

"Why do you speak of her?" she presently said. "She was a slave the warriors stole, and she ran away. What more is there to know?"

"True," Kotta said, "yet she saw *him* come," nodding at me. "She kneeled behind you and held you, and you had torn her hands in pain. She was young and strong but she, too, had her child to shed. I wonder how it went with her in the wild."

This was all obscure to me. It held me only because I could see the drawing of my mother's face, like skin about a wound.

Then Kotta said to me, "You won't die tomorrow, young buck. Never fear it. If you are sick, Kotta will see to you."

She had put some sort of spell on me, too. The day's troubles had altered as a shadow alters when the sun goes over the sky.

I went outside to clean my deer, and later, when the cloud roof on the mountains turned all the red, purple, yellow, and black of the warrior's cloak my mother was weaving me, I secured a place by the fire and ate my last meal as a boy.

2

You sleep in a new and isolated place that night, alone with other boys who are to be made men the next day.

At dawn the krarl priest comes to wake you, his face freshly coated with black. He wears a robe tasseled with the tails of beasts and jinking from bronze disks and ivory teeth, the dentition of wild cats, wolves, bears, and men. I had not slept, and I heard him coming before he cuffed me. If he had crept in softly I should yet have known him from his stench.

Seel was the seer of Ettook's krarl. His father had been seer before him, and had slunk in from the forests with only his sorcery to recommend him. Seel's god was the one-eyed serpent, the Treacherous Beguiler, for whom the twists and turns of Snake's Road had been named centuries out of mind. Sometime Seel had taken a wife and got a daughter on her. Shortly, the woman died, which did not surprise me. The daughter, meanwhile, grew up into a bitch. She was her father's handmaid at his conjurings, the lay of half the tribe besides, but her status was mighty. Seel-Na—she had no other name than Seel's daughter, this being the mark of her glory—was ever looking to be Ettook's wife in Tathra's stead. She had one son, a year younger than I, Fid, and she would have liked to claim him as Ettook's, but did not dare. Red Fid had a squint in his left eye, and Jork was the only other krarl warrior who squinted; Ettook's eyes were set straight. It must have rubbed her raw.

When Seel had roused us, we went into the open beyond

the tent. Here we stripped and scrubbed our bodies over with snow. The place was far from the other tents under the tunnels, and there was no sound to be heard in all the valley but the sounds we made, shivering and balking at the cold. The shireens must hide and even the braves keep quiet at this hour of initiation.

The priest came up and looked us over. He prodded and pried at the boys. I was still angry; I had had the company of my anger all night. I thought, *If he puts his talons on me, I shall strike his eyes out through his skull's back.* But he must have sensed me on the boil, for he left my body alone. Then shortly, naked as we were, he herded us up along the valley, running to keep ourselves warm enough to live, past the pool under thin ice that generally the women came to smash for water—though not today, no woman being permitted to take this route on the morning of the Rite—and over the ridge. Beyond lay pines and cedars, black as gashes in the dim flaring yellow of the rising sun. Our path struck through the trees, through the dark shadows to the loom of the great tent of many hides, like death's own house, into which we must run.

Inside the tent it was pitch-black. We fell down gasping where unseen hands pushed us. The floor was rough with rugs, and the air close and hot after our short freezing journey. There were others there ahead of us, and others behind, panting like dogs after the hunt. The darkness seethed with bodies, breath, and terror. I was not the only apprehensive one among them, yet none of them had my fury to season it.

There must have been near sixty youths crushed into that pavilion, males of several Dagkta krarls, while all through the winter valleys the tribes would be holding the rites of this Day of Initiation, each subtly different from the rest.

Soon there rose an odor of smoke, like sweet wormwood.

You took a breath or two of this and half began to choke, but instead the swirling stuff burrowed into the lungs and stilled them. It was a magic incense of the priests. The head seemed gradually to loosen from the body, and float off in the air. My head and I were up in the roof, yet somehow aware of my belly below, with a pit to it as hard and acid as the nut found in a peach.

Next drums started up, either from the corners of the vast tent or in my body, I was not sure. There was a murmuring sound and a sort of disturbance in the blackness, and something squealed out like an animal, but I did not really care.

I lay a long while in the smoke, not caring and at the same moment knowing I should care, should keep hold on my anger, it was all I had.

Suddenly hands fastened on my arms; I was lifted and hauled across the rugs, over the bodies of boys lying in their stupor. I suppose they had been dragging the young males through this way for some time, maybe they had even trodden on me as I now drunkenly trod on others. I had noticed nothing and no one noticed me.

The partition of hides gave on to a cave, and the air turned abruptly dank and white-cold.

There was a light here. I became aware of it in stages. They had dropped me on my back on a hard bed and the chill pierced up through it like teeth. Water wept down walls and someone grunted and someone cried out and the drums muffled and blurred as my eyes were doing.

I was confused enough to imagine I was getting back my senses, and began to shudder with the cold and struggle weakly, for I had discovered they had tied me. I was desperate to be afraid now, for I felt it was my only defense and somehow had been taken from me, but all the mundane images and details—scent, sight, sound—got in the way. Finally death leaned down, black-faced with eyes like bleached iron, and I recognized Seel. This was the time and the place of the tattooing. They were going to make the scars of manhood on me, and I should die.

I think I bit him. He struck me in the face, and I felt the blow and did not feel it. Then the bronze claw scratched me, a delicate smarting itch. It spread across my breast and ribs and arms, preceded by the lascivious lick of the wool tuft, making the pattern. Bronze needle and needle of bone and rasp of the wool thread drawn through under the skin. To begin with it seemed nothing. Next it became unbearable, that incessant twitching-kissing followed by scratching silver pain. I had forgotten biting him, and only recalled after. I had forgotten who he was. I stared into the ebony face, the eyes where the vague glow caught them, and writhed and twisted at each deft stroke.

But from being unbearable, the sensation became stealthily pleasing. I shut my eyes, and a girl was gently raking her nails over me trying to wake me up, and she was waking me in every way, but when I reached for her she was up in a second and running off laughing down a tunnel in the mountains.

I ran after her, but I did not catch her. Instead I came to an area where the walls hugged close toward each other, and I made out a warm light shining ahead in an oval cave. I felt a need to reach the cave, but the way was very narrow. And suddenly a woman's voice flashed clear as diamond in my head. I did not know what she had spoken, but it was a rejection, a command. It brought an agony with it that curled and shriveled me like a burned leaf. I shouted aloud then because, of all things, I had not expected death in such a form.

I was only ill a day or so, but I had some strange dreams. The idea of the ancient cities had got into my fever, masked men and women and one symbol more curious than the rest, a female lynx, salt-white, with a black wolf mounted on her back. Also I had some notion the tribe was stoning me because I had turned a spring of water into blood, to make them afraid.

Eventually I opened my eyes with a mouth full of bone dust, my body like stones, and looked around. I was in the hut of sticks and mud near the boys' tent where the sick ones went. It had been dark, but now a light had come close to me. Behind the light I made out a skinny shadow and recognized its smell as Seel.

By the trembling of the lamp I could tell he was in an ugly humor. He would sometimes froth at the lips and scream like a woman birthing, a thing that alarmed the warriors, who feared his magic. Seeing me conscious, he started gobbling out some curse over me, calling me worm's dung and other tender things. Now and then a fleck of his tepid spittle hit my face. I remembered biting him.

"Greeting, Seel," I said. "Was it your dirty needles that poisoned me, or your dirty flesh?"

He gave a squawk straight off, and some of the hot oil tipped out of the clay lamp onto my chest. I would not have been so forthright with him had I been quite well, I think, for he was a bad enemy and I had unfriends enough. But it seemed funny at the time.

Then I heard Kotta's voice in the far corner of the hut.

"He speaks nonsense, seer, it's only his fever. Take no heed. Such ravings are beneath you."

Seel flung around and the lamp showed her. She was at some healer's work, intent as if she could see all she did.

"He has no fever, woman," Seel rasped. "It is the out-tribe blood in him. He does not bow to the ways of the red krarls. Tomorrow dawn he shall come to the painted tent and I shall judge him, and the One-Eyed." And his gnarled hand crawled around the snake-carving on his breast.

"As you decide, seer," Kotta rejoined politely, "but he is the chief's son."

Seel dashed down the lamp, and strode out like a thin evil wind.

"It is a clever boy," said Kotta, "to enrage Seel."

"Don't lesson me, Kotta," I said. "Tell me how long I've been here."

"The afternoon of the Rite, the night following, the day just gone."

This scared me a bit. It seemed a good while to lose from your life. I said, "Am I better?"

"Better or worse. You, and others, shall reckon it."

"Women always speak in riddles," I said. I sat up and my head rang a little, but quickly cleared. I felt near enough myself, and I was hungry. "Get me some food," I told her.

"I will get you a mirror first," she said, "then see if you still hunger."

This irritated me, for mirrors were women's toys. I did not blame Tathra that she might want to gaze in one, for there was something worth observing, but I hardly knew my own face. Still, Kotta brought me a bronze mirror and held it where I could take note. It was not my face she was showing me but my breast and arms, where the claws of the tattooing needles had patterned the sigils of tribe and krarl.

I thought the lamp was at fault, next, the bronze or my eyes. At length I reasoned the fault was not in any of these.

"Is this so?" I asked her.

"It is," Kotta said.

I touched the muscular body that belonged to me, comprehending it with my hand, and stared down at myself. Even without the mirror, I could see.

There was not a tattoo on me, not even a scar from the needles, and the colors might never have been.

"Did he trick me then?" I said. "Only pretend he worked on me as the other priests did, and the drug-smoke deceived me?"

"Oh, no. The work was done. Many saw it—the spear-pattern of the krarl and the stag-sign of the tribe, and Ettook's mark like three rings. But now it has healed and faded from that hard marble flesh that never has a blemish, oh son of Tathra."

She had predicted well. The hunger had left me.

"Without the tattoos I am not a warrior," I said.

"Just so," said Kotta, "you are not."

3

Once, maybe, the ritual of the Boys' Rite may have been profound and meaningful. Certain of the priests still murmured of gods who came at such times, and the black people of the marsh-towers were said to worship a golden book that spoke to them. But in Ettook's krarl, as with all the red peoples—Dagkta, Skoiana, Hinga, Eethra, Drogoi—the rites were just the husks left over from deeper things, no pith remaining and no mystery, nothing to lift up the soul or go to the brain like wine. And, as generally happens, the more truth the ritual lost the more they bolstered it with significance. There is a saying among the Moi: The chief is clad in gold and purple, only the god dares to go naked.

So they made much of the Rite because it was nothing, and I had failed to be marked by it, as if to prove it nothing. They would be against me now with a wall to back them in all their bewildered savage little pride. And there was something else. Their ways had never meant much to me; to be made a warrior was only a form, I felt no honor in it or glory. I had never been kin with them. To myself I claimed Tathra's blood alone; her obscure krarl, now vanished, I considered mine. Yet to be accounted by the Dagkta as less than

the dregs of the pack, less than the youths I had fought and
bested all my life and scorned to take as equals, wretches that
used certain explicit gestures for my mother's name—to be
reckoned less than *these*, that I would not bear. I bethought
myself at last how I was indeed the chief's son, Tuvek Nar-
Ettook.

When the sun rose I was ready, as I had not been ready
for that other thing. I was concerned with my death, that
morning of the needles, and here I was, alive, and whole.

Ettook's painted tent stood higher than the tunnels, in the
mouth of a vaulted cave. The land ran down from the mountains here on the eastern side to the winter byres of the goats
and horses. There were always a few men moving about there
to guard their livestock from the neighboring krarls of the
campment, since any krarl would thieve from another when
stores got low. Today I could spot only two guards, though
the horses were out in the field, chewing the bark from the
pines.

I soon found where the men had gone.

The slope below the painted tent was thick with warriors
leaning on their spears, their faces, sneering and laughing, I
could see even as I came up from the tunnel ways. They had
scared the women off from the assembly, but big eyes had
been staring all along my route, and fingers pointing me out.
If I went unrecognized today, my life henceforth would not
be easy. I should have the vixens on my back as well as the
foxes' teeth in my throat. I had no mind to be a joke for the
women's side.

A fire gemmed red on the lip of the cave. Ettook was by
the fire, scratching his plaited beard. He had an expression I
had seen before, uncertain whether my trouble angered or
pleased him. Seel was at his elbow and, at his back,
crouching to heat beer for them, Seel's bitch-daughter. That
whetted my mood, to be sure. Her hands glowed from the
heat of the flames, but she was eager to warm herself at the
blaze of my shame. She was younger than Tathra but thin
and stringy except for her breasts, which were heavy,
shapeless, floundering things, not tempting to me in the least;
her faded hair was the color of sour apricots.

I raised my arm to Ettook.

"Greeting, my chief. Your son salutes you."

He looked down at me, glad, no doubt, of the cave's elevation. Already he was no longer able to look down on me when we stood foot to foot.

"Greeting, Tuvek. I hear you are in a wasp's nest once again."

"Wasps are easily disturbed, my chief," I said as sweetly as I could for the feel of vinegar in my guts.

Seel shouted something at me. He was often unintelligible in his rages, though his intentions were transparent enough.

"Seel says you have something to answer for," Ettook said. "He suggests to me you have profaned the Rite, the thing which must not be spoken of."

The Rite was usually given this extra title, implying some mystery that must once have belonged in it. I became aware that Seel had not told Ettook precisely what was wrong. It was to be a grand shock and show for them with me as the focal point.

"My chief," I said slowly and clearly, "maybe the seer forgets I am your son, and that your honor is touched by mine."

Ettook swallowed this down. His eyes narrowed and he glared at me, calculating. I said, "The seer shall say what I have done, then I shall reply, and then you, my chief, shall judge."

"Very well," Ettook said. He looked at Seel. "Say then."

Seel drew himself up and quivered all over. He hawked and dislodged his phlegm in the fire, and cried, "I myself marked him as a warrior is marked. He was not willing, speaking oaths and struggling. When the other boys rose up men, he was groaning and insensible. The herb woman must tend him for a fever. Then I came and witnessed him bare, and saw the One-Eyed had punished him for his cowardice and weakness."

I was dressed in winter gear like the rest, shirt laced and a cloak over it. They would see nothing yet. Seel leane forward, scrabbling through the air at me.

"Take off the garment. Strip, strip and show your wretched shame."

The warriors were rock still, waiting. Ettook grinned and scowled at once. Seel-Na's eyes sparkled through their shireen eye-holes. I made no move and Seel's attitude exploded into a hopping, frothing dance on the ledge.

Having incensed him before, there seemed nothing to gain by holding out any longer.

"Be careful, grandfather," I said to him courteously. "Your old bones must be brittle, you should be more gentle with yourself."

"What is this shame?" Ettook snapped finally, impatience wiping his face over like a cloth. "You must answer, Tuvek."

"Very well. I answer. The old madman there did his work so poorly with the needles that my flesh healed without a sign."

I opened my shirt and showed them, and they grunted and jumped down the slope to get a better view, save for Ettook, Seel, and the fruit of Seel's loins.

They were puzzled, the warriors. They prowled around me, lowering under their ginger brows, then went back toward the cave in a bunch. One said, "He is not warrior." That was all that was needed. Everyone took up the howl.

At this, even though I had been waiting for it, the fury came up in me like a flood tide. My voice had broken early; from my twelfth year I spoke like a man. I filled my lungs and I roared loud enough to drown the lot of them.

"So I am not a warrior? Let each warrior who thinks I am a boy still come here and fight me. That is fair, I think."

That quieted them. They glanced about, wondering whether to gibe or kill me, which was a hard decision for their fleas' minds.

High on the ledge, Ettook laughed.

"My son is valiant," he said. "He has fourteen years and seeks to slay grown men."

"Do you require me to kill them?" I asked him. "Is it to the death? I'm ready."

I had only my boy's knife, but it was to hand, and I had spent some minutes sharpening it before I came.

Ettook glanced about at the warriors, still laughing. Seel cracked his knuckles, and the bitch-daughter had let the beer boil over.

"Yes," Ettook said abruptly, "this matter of the patterns. Maybe there is some mistake; the sweat of the fever has washed out the inks. Let him prove himself. Let him fight. If he can best a warrior, he shall be a warrior. I am the chief, that's my word. You, Distik. Give him one of your own knives and use the other. Don't be easy on him just because he's my blood."

Distik grinned.

"I won't, my chief."

He was the biggest of them, packed with wads of lean muscle and wiry as a young dog. I could see then for sure Ettook wanted my face ground in the snow for me. It occurred to me that if I were beaten, he could simply disown me as a weakling and elect one of his bastards for the heir; he had a couple older than I, already proved. They were thick-witted as he was, and had given me not enough trouble that I should remember them by it, and beware. Of course, if he cast me down, he would cast down Tathra with me, but she would have no say in that. It would not matter to him, he could still go to her and stick himself into her whenever he chose, so she would have all his attention without the honor and safety of the title of wife.

Distik slung the knife to me. It was blunt, I could see, but I did not argue. I was not afraid; I had never feared a fight in my life. There had always been such a bitter snarling somewhere in me that I was only glad of the chance to give it something to bite on. And I had never been bested. Even when Distik came bounding along the slope, red and yelling, I had no doubt of myself. If I was the smaller I was not puny, and I had a brain to guide me.

First off, I could tell, he thought it would be amusing. He could toss me around and make sport of me, and give me a wound or two to insure I regretted my arrogance. After all, he was a man and I a boy, so he did not approach me as he would have done, his peers.

When he came running I waited, then stepped aside and kicked his right leg from under him. It seemed slow to me but it was too quick for Distik. He went down with a shout, hard on his left knee.

I let him slither up and whirl around on me. His face was red as his braids. He made a play with the knife. He was trying to get at my left side, for I had the long knife leading right, but I am agile with both hands, and when he swung in at me I brought up my left fist with my boy's knife folded in it. He had not expected that, nor the sharpness of the blade. I cut his palm to the gristle and his own weapon went spinning down the slope.

Distik faltered there a moment, the blood plopping crimson as beads on the white snow. Then he hurled himself on me like a wolf.

His weight told; we both went plunging over, and rolled downhill after his knife. The hard rock under the ice slammed me in the back, and Distik punched as me hard as he could in the crotch. I had been rather too clever and not expected this of him, as he had not expected much of me. For a second the pain winded me and my sight blacked out, but I had enough of my senses left to kick the ground away, and keep us going on down the incline. While in motion he could not obtain much purchase on me or try to repossess his blade.

The pain in my loins was subsiding to a drumlike ache that made me nearly vomit, and my eyes were full of sparks. He had me by the hair, long as his own; I think he was getting ready to break my neck once we should slow sufficiently; he was past caring who or what I was. With his other arm he had both of mine pinned fast to my sides. I had lost the two knives, I guess when he punched me. I remembered how he had crashed heavily on the left knee and caught it between mine as we fell, squeezing till I heard the bones grind. Distik grunted and his hand slackened on my hair. I went under it and had him by the throat. My teeth met through the skin, and his blood ran in my mouth. I was fighting mad by this time, and the salt of it gladdened me.

He tried to shake me off, and loosened his other arm around me, grabbing to wrench my head back. Just then we tumbled into a soft mound of snow. I released his throat and hit him on the side of the jaw with all my might, and felt teeth snap under the blow. He bellowed, on his side in the snow mound, and I sprang from him and fell back dead-weight on his ribs. The breath went from him in a bloody gust, and he curled together on himself, crowing for it, and done.

I stood up, shivering with hate-lust and triumph, and stared along the slope toward the cave.

It was to be an hour of surprises. I had not anticipated what I saw.

Three of them were coming down to me, making set brutal faces, metal ready in their hands, as they would go to finish off a bear in a trap.

I thought, *This is too obvious. Ettook can't let them take me three to a boy; it shows too much how badly he wants me broken.* But Ettook never stirred and the braves came on.

I glanced around quickly, trying to see a knife, Distik's or mine, in the snow, but there was nothing.

I should have been anxious, but I was too eager to fight; the last bout had sharpened my appetite for it.

Distik had continued lying prone and gasping. I hauled him onto his back and he threshed about, attempting to ward me off. Around his neck hung a great ivory tooth, long as my hand, and perfect save where the hole was pierced for the thong to go through. He found it in some back cave years before and wore it for luck. Seeing his luck had deserted him, it was almost fitting I should rip it off his neck, and perhaps he agreed for he did not offer to stop me. In my grasp the tooth looked nearly as good as a dagger.

The warriors were biding their time approaching me, for the slope was slippery from our fall, and someone had maneuvered ahead of the rest. I saw his squinty eye and recognized Fid's father, Jork. Then I took the slope at a run, going up to meet him.

I went fast, too fast to lose my footing, and slammed into him and plunged Distik's monster-tooth in his neck where the big vein is. The blood jetted over us both; he reeled sideways with a choked cry and collapsed, dragging my weapon with him. Something happened inside me at that, like tough tissue splitting open. A white light sliced through my head. It was like a voice singing to me: *Now the beast is out of the cage.*

I had come up with the last two warriors. I barely noticed who they were. The left-hand man lunged in at me and cut me in the flank, and next moment I ducked and caught at him and was bursting up in a whirl of blood and snow and cloaks, with him held over my head the length of my arms, like an offering to the sky.

He was a big man and I was only a boy. I had always been tall and well-grown and very strong, yet I had never known my strength, and neither had they. It was no bother to me to hold him high and kicking and bawling there, or to swing around with him and cast him off into the other one and watch them go hurtling down together to where Distik lay.

I was meaning to follow them, perhaps to kill them with their own knives, but as sudden as it lit, the white light in my head went out. I stood there in a somber daze getting back my sanity after the fight. And when I raised my eyes to the slope, I ascertained that this time nobody else was coming.

The warriors were very silent, as well they might be.

Seel had prudently combined with the shadows, but Ettook remained by the fire where I had seen him last, and his face was a greenish-white, though he grinned as he jumped down and strode toward me.

"Am I proved, my chief?" I called out to him, loud enough for all of them.

Ettook turned in midstride, shaking his arms at the men.

"Is he proved warrior?" he shouted. "Proved—yes, more a brave than any of my fighters, this, my son Tuvek."

The warriors began to stamp and clack their spears on the rock of the mountain under the cave to show their approval and consent, but not a face matched the noise. Their looks were better suited to a burying, or Sihharn Night when they mount guard against the spirits of the Black Place.

However, Ettook came up to me and clapped me on the shoulder.

I immediately kneeled before him in the snow. I could master as much diplomacy as he.

"If I am a warrior, the strength of my arm is for your service alone, my chief and my father," I said. And he dug his fingers in my hair as any father might, proud of a loved son who had done him honor. I wondered what price he set on this act of his, showing his liking of me after what had gone before. And not for the first time, I wished I had a friend, a single man I could trust my back to.

Ettook took his hand off my bowed head, and I rose.

"The blind woman must bind your hurt," he said, jolly as a grinning death's-head. "First blood from your own people. That's something. I only let so many come at you because I knew you could beat them." I barely kept from laughing myself at that. "The seer shall make the warrior-marks on you freshly," he said.

"No," I said, "that carrion has put his hands on me too often. I must be the Unmarked Warrior of the krarl." We were still speaking loudly for the benefit of the crowd, even some shireens were stealing out now, and a woman had begun mewing for dead Jork; not Seel-Na, I noted. I glared at the warriors and said "Let my deeds speak for me. When I go to battle I shall paint the tribe's colors on my skin, and if any man takes exception, let him tell me so; he shall be answered, as I have answered here."

The woman crying made my spine crawl. I had been thinking of my life and not Jork's death when I slew him. I went to her and lifted her up and hit her in the face, not very hard.

"Don't wail for him in front of me," I said, and she shut her mouth. "I will pay you Blood-Price for him," and I turned to Ettook.

"Yes," he said, "I will see Tuvek gives the Blood-Price for your man. But my son shall also come to my tent and pick out treasure for himself."

When I went to my mother's tent, the news was there ahead of me.

Her face was whiter than Ettook's, and she, too, was smiling, but hers was a smile of victory, though old fear and a confused eternal rancor were mixed in it. When I stooped under the doormouth, she rose and almost ran at me, then stopped, holding herself back. I went to her and put my arm around her, and then she wept.

"Did you suppose I should fail?" I asked her. "I thought their sly needles in the dark might injure me, but never their half-wit's knives. Did you hear all of it?"

"All," she sobbed. Her breath scalded my neck, and she clenched her hands on the conquest she symbolized for herself in my flesh. "How you broke Distik's ribs, and let the life from Jork, and that Urm and Tooni will not go hunting again until the moon has thinned to a bow."

It made me glad to hear her fierceness speak out like this, she was so much more than the other women who could only whine or screech.

"It seems Tathra would defeat the braves of the krarl herself."

She gazed up at me, her eyes shining.

"Tathra has made a son who can."

She put her hand on mine and so she encountered what I had brought in. She had not seen it before, being intent only on me. Now she snatched her fingers away and the brightness in her dulled over.

"What is that thing?"

"The gift of your husband, my mother, the chief's bounty

given to his new warrior. He took me into his tent and opened up the chest there, and told me choose what I had a mind to."

"Why this, of all the treasure?"

"Why not this?"

She turned from me and went away across the tent and sat down where she had been before. She picked up the shireen that lay there and covered herself with it. Although it was the custom, I felt it like the cold.

"You are a warrior," she said, seeing me frowning, "I must hide my face."

"I was a warrior when I entered, but you were unveiled then. Is it this you're hiding from?" And I lifted up the token I had carried here from Ettook's chest of spoils, and held it out at her.

He had taken me into the tent and pushed open the wooden box with its turmoil of glitter inside. There lay the looting of several hundred raids and battles; as much as give me a gift, he had wanted to show me how many men had had their necks beneath his heel. I put my hand in the heap, and he came up beside me and spilled out quantities on the floor so I should see better what he had garnered. There were cups of bronze circled in bright gold, spear hafts of gray hard iron, brazen bucklers set with water-green gems and arm rings of yellow and white metal, handfuls of stones like fires or blood, and collars of ivory strung with blue carbuncles. I had not guessed him so wealthy, and hesitated, wanting the prize of his collection and not certain what it might be. Then my firsts and his had cleared a path, and I found it.

It was a mask, made for a woman for it was small, all pure scintillant silver: the face of a lynx.

My dream came back to me at once—the black wolf mating with the white lynx. I moved my hand and touched the mask, and a shock went through my palm clear up into my shoulder joint. It was like grasping lightning. But I did not shift, and the sensation dwindled and was gone. I lifted the mask and showed it to Ettook.

"I will have this, if my chief permits."

He nodded, sullen as a child whose toy has been stolen. I had got the best from him as I had hoped to. The mask was of value, besides its curious beauty, and obviously it had come from the workshops of the ruined cities. At the back, long yellow cords hung down to decorate the hair, and on the end of each was a little perfect flower of translucent yellow amber. It pleased me and set the crown on my combat, for I was still a boy. I had some notion that I might give it to Tathra to wear in place of the shireen, and let the women chew on that.

Now I saw this was not to be. Tathra shunned the mask, shunned it as something known. I recalled the shock from the metal when I grasped it in its sleep, some old magic locked in the silver, some ghost thing.

"I will give it back to him," I said to her. "Is it cursed?"

"No," she said. I could no longer read her emotions behind the shireen. "There was an Eshkir woman among the tents; the warriors captured her. She was my slave, but she ran away after you were born. The mask was hers."

I recollected Kotta speaking of this the night before the Boys' Rite, and how Tathra had cringed in on herself.

"Did she work you ill, the Eshkir woman?"

"No," Tathra said, "but the women of the great cities are evil, and where they pass they leave a trail like burning."

"I will take this object and be rid of it," I said.

"No, it is what you chose; it was meant for you. The sorcery is long spent; it will not harm you." Tathra sighed behind her veil as if she had been holding her breath, mistaking it for something that must not escape. "It was meant for you," she said again. "It will not harm you."

4

That year, as ever, the winter truce ended on Snake's Road in the month of the Warrior, and I had my first mans' battles.

The fighting was haphazard and bloody. Who won took what he liked from the vanquished—metal, weapons, women, drink. Most often there would be a pact made next, squeak-

ing females returned to their own tents, and vows sworn between the men. Nevertheless, outside truce and pact, krarl
fell on krarl indiscriminately. The Dagkta sometimes feuded
among themselves and continually with the Skoiana, the Moi,
the Eethra, and all the rest. You might barter and share meat
with someone winter or summer, and have to shear off his
limbs in the spring. This was the custom of the tribes, and
perhaps, in the fogs of their past, the scheme had had its reasons. Yet like many of their ways, only the peel remained,
the fruit was long gone. I served it—since it fitted my nature,
giving me a chance to spend my hate lavishly—but I never
thought it noble or wise. Only the black marsh tribes did not
fight. It was said they reverenced a book rather than a deity,
and they were reckoned strange. Having no horses or wealth,
however, they were spoken of with scorn and left in peace.

Naturally, the little wars were dressed up in ritual and significance. War spear challenge was followed by war dance,
and invocation of demons, the one-eyed snake and diverse totems. I bowed to none of these, having seen early the vulgar-
ity and impotence of the tribal pantheon. Generally men
create gods in their own image.

Besides, I had already a kind of belief in myself, in my
own body and what it could do, which was not amazing after
what had gone before. Now I saw braves hang themselves
with amulets, leave tidbits for spirits, and still take an arrow
in the neck. I, worshiping nothing and bribing nothing with
prayers, rode among an enemy unscathed, scything them like
summer wheat. It was a virtue among the krarls for the men's
side to glory in butchery, but I outdid them, and I noticed
several mark my eyes as I came on at them, and their knees
turn to butter.

I had discovered the sweet sharp joy of slaughter. I had not
properly known it before. Learning the lesson, I would have
fought all year round, season to season. As it was I had killed
upward of thirty men by the time we reached the eastern pas-
tures and the summer camping, and got a name among the
krarls with whom we had warred. The Dark Warrior of the
Red Dagkta, the Unmarked One. It was good to see unease
and terror replace the sneers and winks. My own krarl feared
me most but, like Ettook, began boasting of me. I would
paint myself black and scarlet and white in the stead of tattoos, and ride out like a devil in the morning. I wore my hair

loose too, it would never keep in plaits for long; let a man catch me by it if he had a mind, and see how I gifted him for his trouble.

In the final battle before the tenting, a blade went in my thigh and broke off there, and when they came to cut it free, the flesh had closed around it, tight as secrets. The seer showed his teeth about the krarl and told Ettook his son would perish of a diseased wound, but it healed clean, to both their sorrows.

Since the Boys' Rite, Seel had given me his distance, and his words came secondhand. And at the war dance his daughter never offered me her flesh, at which, of course, I broke my heart.

That summer I took a wife. Now that I was a man and out of the boys' tent, I had some need of one to see to my gear. I knew Tathra did not like this. She foresaw girls of the krarl she thought I should value more than her, but presently she and they came to understand there would be no great changes.

Chula's father Finnuk stepped in the painted tent in the marriage month and said she was big with my child and would I acknowledge her. Soon Ettook called for me, and the girl was brought. She looked much altered from the last time we had had dealings, her eyes cast down and the lids painted green, and her shireen embroidered with butterflies of blue silk. Finnuk had loaded her with the family jewels to show me the dowry I could expect, gold and silver and one large emerald of which they were justly proud.

"See," he said, tapping her ripe belly, "this is your planting, Tuvek Nar-Ettook."

"Is it?" I said. "How am I to know that?"

"Chula was unbroken till she lay down for you last fall of leaf."

"I don't deny I had her, but maybe others have been visiting since then."

At that her eyes flashed up, fierce as the emerald, though not as green. I had never seen her unveiled, but there are ways of telling something about a woman's face, even through cloth, and she looked fair enough in the tribal fashion. Her body was pleasing, and her teeth excellent, as I had reason to remember.

"Kotta says the child is from one sowing," declared Finnuk. "She is fertile, a good field, my daughter."

"Perhaps it will turn out a girl," I said. "If she's a breeder of girls, I don't want her." But I was coming around to it. The flash of her eyes had stirred me up a little, as the downcast lids had not. "Take her back in your tent," I said. "If it's mine, she'll bear before the month is run. If she's made me a son, I'll have her." I nearly laughed at the look in her eyes then. I could foresee wild times if we wed. "I'm surprised she's willing," I remarked. "She lost a tooth in my shoulder on the previous occasion."

About sixteen days before the month was done, she dropped her child, and it was indeed a boy. No doubting the father either, for its tuft of hair was black.

A priest of another Dagkta krarl joined us, for Seel would not since there was bad blood openly between us. I imagine he meant to shame me, but he failed. After the fighting ends, the summer truce holds the tribes together again, and there were plenty of other holy men to choose from over the hill. It needs only a few words spoken inside a ring of fire to make a woman a warrior's property.

In my tent, she put things to rights, got out a silver cup I had on a raid, and brought me beer in it for the bride-drink, like a dutiful wife. She had left the child with her mother for our marriage couching. I was fifteen then and Chula two years older, but I stood taller than she, and men would take me for nineteen or more if they did not know my birth-night. When I drew off her shireen, I saw she was pretty and well acquianted with a mirror. Her father had been soft with her, no doubt. She had brought the emerald as part of her dowry, and gold bells were clipped on the ends of her hair, chinking. She kept her glance on the floor very meekly. She had not really looked at me beyond that one memorable look in Ettook's tent.

"Well," I said, "what is it to be this time?"

"I am your first wife," she said, "and I have borne you a son."

"Perhaps you will not be my only wife to do that," I said.

"Perhaps," she said, "but I was your first woman, and that can never be altered."

Then she stared at me, hard and bright, and wrapped herself around me tight as grass. I was surprised at her insistence.

Afterward she did not want to let me go. It was a busy night.

Later, I heard she had been boasting of me, the way the women did. She was arrogant, too, of the child, who was a fine, healthy, bawling, kicking brat. I felt no vast interest in him myself, despite my warrior's ranting in the painted tent. Ettook's un-love had not taught me a particular worth in sons. In any case, I got the boy as a weed will grow.

There was not much to do in the summer beyond the hunting. The fruit swelled thick on the trees, and rogue orchards and fields, resown by the winds, spilled across the sloping land. None of these things provided man's work, only tasks of agriculture for the women and children.

There were ruined places north of the pasturing, old towns with broken roofs of pink tile, and broad streets choked by young trees. Each season the hungry forest reclaimed a little more. Here and there thin towers would pierce above the rest, looking high enough to stir the clouds. It made me wonder who could have built them. On the bald green hills the white stones ran like a giant's fencing, but they did not look so tall to me as once, for every year they had sunk I had been growing.

Half the tribes avoided the towns. The Hinga and the Drogoi claimed you would die if you went that way by night, and the dark-haired krarls, Tathra's people, never ventured this far to the east. In my infancy, Tathra had told me of fallen palaces where dragons were guarding treasures and ghosts rattling spears—tales any child will relish. But I had often hunted there since, alone with my dogs at moonrise, and met nothing bad except for a boar or two who offered some trouble for their meat. And once I glimpsed a big cat, as white as milk, which made me think of the dream in the fever, and the silver lynx-mask. I had taken plenty of plunder since then, but nothing finer than that. Even Chula's emerald I valued less.

I would still go to my mother's tent. I would take her a choice portion of my hunting, and sit to watch her at her loom. Yet there had come a sort of silence over us, dark as the veil she wore now always in my presence. I considered my marriage was to blame, but in my heart I knew it was the silver lynx that pushed between us, though she would not speak of it. At length this took away my patience, and after that we were less easy even than before.

On Sihharn Night, when the men of the red krarls mount the ghost guard and the women of the krarls crowd together for their own watch, Chula was sitting among the torches with the child at her breast, brooding that I had recently found another I liked as well, for she had thought she might tether me like a steer. All the women share Sihharn, and Tathra sat spinning by Kotta. Soon Chula rose and, carrying the boy at his drink, she crossed to Tathra and spoke to her. I do not know what words Chula used, but the substance of them was that I would rather lie on my mother than on my wife, and had done so many times.

The women were always ready to make Tathra's road a stony one. Their ears must have pricked up gladly. Kotta said something to the effect that Chula's sour mood would sour her milk too. But Tathra stood and went away to her own tent without a word.

There are always tongues happy to tell any news. When I heard what had happened it was in the morning. I went directly to the fall where the women fetched water. Chula was there, and thirty or more shireens, which was good for I meant them to see. I walked up to her and struck her flat on the ground so the water pot was smashed. The women screamed and cowered away, but Chula was too scared to scream.

"Speak once more to my mother as you did at Sihharn," I said, "and you will be silent thereafter, for I'll break your neck."

Then I reached forward—she anticipated my coming and squealed—and wrenched the blue-green gem off its chain. I shook it in Chula's face.

"This shall be your apology."

She knew better than to argue, though her eyes were starting from her head with fright and fury.

I sought Tathra next, but Ettook was there; I could hear him grunting at his games. This sent me nearly mad with rage. I got my spears and my dogs and went off alone to the forest tracks to hunt the rage down, and anything else I could find.

The dogs were good. I had them at a Dagkta gathering a couple of springs before, two high-legged, tassel-tailed devils, the color of gray sand; you could scarcely tell them apart.

The compunction I had felt on my last boy's hunt, when I had shot the deer by the winter pool, had left me. I had seen death for what it was that day only because I feared myself on the verge of it. Since then I had lived and killed men, unsparing of their blood and pain.

The dogs quickly found the trail of a buck, and ran grinning down the avenues between the trees.

The forest was burned to the ambers, golds, and reds of autumn, and the paths clotted with old magenta leaves already down. The smell of smoke left from the fires and torches of Sihharn had caught there, like the smell of the year itself, smoldering out.

The dogs' feet tacked among the leaves. Presently my rage cooled under the crimson boughs.

We never took the buck. It was a rutting trail, fierce but not fresh, though there was small game in plenty. I lost the day in the forest as easily as I had lost my ill temper. At sundown, having no mind yet for my wife and my tent, I made a fire with flints and scorched the meat from the kill. I ate sparingly as ever, giving the best bits to the dogs to growl over.

The dusky sky glowed and poured away like wine through the trees, leaving the forest serene as a lake, just the fall wind to speak in it. I kept my knife to hand, but was not wary to lie down in the open. Few savage things need to go after men in the warm months; even the wolf is fat. If anything came near, the dogs would rouse me.

As I stretched there for sleep, I felt cleaned and cleared, and only what I was, a boy, with no one to answer to, and no squabbles to hinder me. I had a notion of striking off alone at sunup, leaving hearth and tent and krarl and tribe behind, leaving custom and pride, my scratchy wife, and the sneering words and the battle-lust and all the rubbish of my past. Yes, even leaving behind my mother with her black-robed face. It is good to dream, though you feel the anchor hold you back, root-deep in the seabed of your life.

I woke at midnight.

I sat up and looked around, but the dogs lay quiet as gray bolsters with their noses on the meat bones. The sky was many starred and the trees slimly mantled in shadow. Nothing seemed abroad to wake me, yet it was like a charm. I got to my feet and took a step or two, and the dogs slept on, and the forest, and I was left alone with whatever drew me.

I walked light but with no sense of danger. I had gone about eighty paces and had a plan of returning, when I came suddenly on an older part of the wood where the trees were massive as pillars and the air heavy with their craggy scent. Maybe it was the scent that woke me, that stagnant muttering of soil and bark and centuries, on the crisp air.

Among the trunks was an open place, and at its center, something white.

For a minute I had a wild thought or two, recalling stories. Then I made it out. A stream bubbled from the earth here, and some thousand or so years ago they had built a basin to receive it, and put a marble girl on the plinth above. I think she was the goddess of the stream, or of the grove.

The basin was green and growing weeds and the water only a trickle now, hardly that. A briar bound the plinth like dark rope. But she, the goddess-girl, was pure as morning under the moon, which still rained on her between the leaves.

She was just human size, not tall but slender, with sweet secret breasts and a waist that narrowed like the waist of a dancer, and her carved gown gliding like serpents on her thighs. Her face had weathered but was still beautiful, like no woman's face I had ever seen. And her stone hair rayed like a stiff flame outward as if some stony wind lifted it yet.

I had never come on a girl I wanted for more than an hour or so. It was strange to find her like that, locked in marble. It must have been the time and the oldness of the wood, but I half got an idea I should have her, that she would come off the plinth and put on flesh for me.

Then I heard the dogs begin barking as if a bear had roused them. I turned and ran back, cursing, with the spell broken in bits. I guessed they had only been looking for me; nothing else was about, and they rushed forward, wagging their tails like fools, smiling and panting.

I did not retrace my steps to the grove, nor in the morning. I knew what I should find, a ruinous scabby statue with a chipped face and moss sprouting inside its lips. She would have a piece missing from her shoulder or her breast. I did not want to see it.

Going homeward to the krarl, I remembered the emerald in my belt.

I seemed to have been away years; something about the night had refashioned time. I partly expected new faces, Et-took and Tathra and Chula long in their graves. A boy's dream indeed. Coming along the slopes I soon observed the smoke of the central fire, and farther off, the smokes of other fires, where other krarls were settled.

I went to Tathra's tent and she was alone, unlike the day before.

I was not inclined to be subtle. I let her see Chula's gem.

"Take this, and wear it. I have told her she'll be sorry if she insults you again."

"No," she said, hesitating, "I don't want her jewel."

So I threw down the emerald by her mirror and her cosmetic pots, and turned to leave.

"Wait," Tathra said, her voice so full of pain, I felt it too. "Oh, Tuvek, do you hate me for what she said?"

I waited with my back to her. When I could master myself, I said, "The girl is brainless. Must I have the same silliness from you?"

"Tell me what I must do. I will do it," she said. "How can I bear your anger? You are all I have."

"I told you what you should do. You will wear her jewel."

"Yes," she said.

Hearing her tone, I was sorry. I had no quarrel with my mother.

"When I come here next," I said, "leave the veil off your face."

"The law of the krarl—"

"Do you think one of their red gods will strike you if you disobey? Obey *me*."

I listened to her movements, knowing I had got my way. She came to me and touched my arm, and she had unmasked herself.

I had not been shown her face for several months. It was not as I recalled. I could not fail to see her age this close. The light seeped through the flap of the tent, and revealed to me the chiselings about her eyes and mouth. Her beauty was dying like a flame. I could have wept for it. I put my head down into her hair like a child so I should not see. She thought it was only love. It made her glad.

PART II

The Warrior

1

Time went by; I never felt it go. The seasons slunk past like people in a mist.

My tent was rich with plunder, and my wives shone and glittered with it. In four years I had wed two more girls in the fire-ring, supposing they might then fight among themselves and blunt their claws before they came complaining to me. Chula bore me sons three summers in a row, but Moka let two out of the gate in one night, and the next winter another two, though Asua seemed intent on sickly girls, most of whom died. At nineteen I have seven legal sons and two bastard boys in Ettook's krarl, with three or four more farther afield.

I had killed so many men in my battles, I had lost count. The magic ritual number in the krarls was forty, meant to appease any spirits who might be listening with its modesty. To say you had killed forty men was to say you had slain legion. Thus Tuvek Nar-Ettook, slayer of forty, master of three women, breeder of thirteen sons, was the creature men hailed when they hailed me, the creature the women looked at so intently, the creature warriors ran from or came at with a spear. Inside the creature, I was. If you put a leopard in a cage and cover the cage against the light, you will never know the leopard is there. It will sleep and pine and die. This is how it was with me, and I never knew it, a beast in a covered cage, asleep, half-dead, and silent.

Ettook was getting old now, grizzled and gray, but still tough and glad to make war. He had a great belly from his drinking; he needed a boost to get him in the saddle, and more often than not, the small horses dropped lifeless under him after a day's ride. Age did not hinder his other riding. He had taken no new wife, but he had a couple of sluts he went to more often now than to Tathra. I was aware this

39

frightened her, imagining he would cast her off. She took pains to bring him back. In the summer and winter truces Moi tracers came frequently right into the krarl, to stand outside Tathra's tent with their curious barter from the ancient cities: perfumes, ointments, even drugs to stoke the blood. Now and then her pale hand, heavy with the rings and bracelets of Ettook's previous lust, would part the flap and signal this or that she would have.

I wished to say to her, "Let him go, and good riddance. I have my own tent, my own wealth, I can keep you safe." But somehow the words would not come. It embarrassed me to speak of his rutting with her. Besides, she was nervous for me, too, as Ettook's heir.

I began to consider Ettook's death, when I should get his chiefdom, such as it was. I was dimly surprised I had not really pondered it before. But the title and the krarl seemed of such small worth, I had hardly dreamed of wanting or coveting it. As it was, my cogitations were desultory and ran in circles. The krarl feared me in battle, but did not like me. Given an excuse, they might finish the out-tribe upstart, and happy to do it. I should have to be so extraordinarily cunning in removing Ettook—who they liked well enough, seeing he was exactly of their species—that I was not certain I might ever achieve anything. Occasionally, over the years, since my boy's fight on the slope with the four braves, I had felt his own hatred of me scorch my back like a hot wind. Being slow and stupid and intent on enjoyment rather than thought, he too had got no workable plan to be shot of me. He would need cunning, as I did, for I was ostensibly a good son to him, courteous always, throwing my decision in with his at the pacts and little councils that sometimes took place krarl with krarl, rendering him gifts from my spoils. No, he could not just strike me down before them all. Doubtless he had been hoping the battles would see to it for him, for I was like a madman then, but my luck held.

The winter of that, my nineteenth year, was bad, the worst I remembered. The snow fell like a curtain days on end, then froze like white iron. The mountain wolves ran in thin, sooty packs. They would come in the camps at night, through weak places in the stockade, regardless of spears and fires, drooling at the scent of men. There was no other game.

The truces were broken, too. In the month of Gray Dog,

fifty Skoiana raided Ettook's krarl at black of night. They got a herd of goats and some horses—we had begun to eat the horses by then—and pushed a way with them over the knife-backed ridges, and were three valleys distant before dawn. Ettook gave me twenty men and some followed from neighboring Dagkta krarls the Skoiana had visited, and we tracked them down. We had a fight in a narrow gully where the spines of mountains clawed up on three sides, bottling us all in with each other. The white ground was soon red, and next morning there were forty or so red heads staked up along the Dagkta camping line, each with its Skoiana tattoos to warn off any others of like mind.

The Moi sometimes robbed us too, but mostly they got by on barter. That winter silver necklets and iron city daggers went for a leg of goat flesh or half a horse's liver. We heard something of their friends also, the city men, tales of riders on the passes even in thick snow, aglint with jewels, starved as the tribes were, but whether after meat or slaves or simply mad, no one knew.

Neither did the weather break in Black Dog, as it generally did. Nor in the month of the Whip when the big winds and first rains should come. A few old men began to say there had been a winter like this when they were warriors, and that it was a year of catastrophe and disappointment. But old men will ever spin this wheel. The summers were always hotter and the winters colder in the days of their strength, and the air thick with epic dramas and portents.

The priests, Seel too, went up to some cave in the mountain and stayed there three days, howling and beating gongs, and great good it did us.

There was no hunting to be had it seemed from one end of the valley-chain to the other. Children were falling down and dying, and the tribes were exposing any new female born among the tents. Asua birthed her fourth girl at this unlucky time. Weak as she was, my wife beat with her fists on me when I took the baby from its basket.

"Peace," I said. "It is the law. Your brats die anyway."

"This one will live," she cried. "I swear she will live. She will grow fair and bring you honor by marriage—oh, Tuvek, never take her from me!"

I looked at her face, running with tears and sallow as curd. She had been pretty once, but bearing and death and sorrow and hunger had altered that. I felt sorry for her, poor thing, she had nothing else. The child would die anyway, as I had said, and besides, be damned to their laws; I was my own master.

"Well, then," I said, "keep it."

Two days later, the winds came flashing along the mountains, but no rain. Gusts blew the ice and heaped it against everything that stood. Presently, great avalanches began over on the huge slopes to the north; you heard their thunder day and night.

One morning the blizzard eased, and I shot a couple of scrawny hares foraging among the trees. Their ribs showed as men's ribs were showing, but I was glad enough for what I could get.

I meant to leave a hare at Tathra's tent. Ettook's gifts of food to her were leaner than they had been since he had his two whores to keep plump now as well. But when I came there, she was absent. As usual, there was some woman skulking about nearby, tending a fire pit.

"Where is my mother?"

"She has gone to Kotta," said the woman.

I was uneasy at this, for though Kotta and my mother were often together, the women only went to Kotta's tent when they were in need of help, or ill.

I gave the woman the hares to skin and clean, and told her what she might expect if she stole any part of them, then made my way through the tunnels to Kotta's place.

I did not walk straight in, you never knew what women's business might be afoot in there, but stood outside and called her name.

"A moment, warrior," Kotta said.

I heard the muffled sounds of a woman vomiting, and my belly wrenched into a knot of snakes.

Shortly, the figure of the blind healer went out of the back of the tent, dark against the white light of the snow. She saw to something there, then came around the tent to me.

"Is it Tathra you have with you?" I asked her.

Her blue, blind, seeing eyes looked into mine like two flints.

"It is Tathra."

"Is she sick?"

"No. Not sick. She is carrying another son for Ettook."

The shock of her words hit me like a fist. I knew all the stories—how Kotta kept Tathra free of pregnancy with certain skills, how it would kill Tathra if she bore again, as it had nearly killed her before. I said, "Your magic potions failed her then? Are you trying different sorcery to be rid of it?"

"What?" she said, harder than I. "Do you suppose Kotta fool enough to tamper with the chief's seed?"

"Don't anger me, woman. I know what you've been at. Do you think I want her to bear this child? It will kill her, will it not? She's no girl, and almost died of me. So abort her. The red pig has sons enough."

"I hear you watch your tongue with the braves," she said. "You should watch it now. Maybe I will tell Ettook how his heir speaks of him."

"Tell him. But first, lose her that burden, or we shall have further words."

She laughed, just one syllable of it and, lifting her veil a little, spit. She stood, big and rough, with her head back.

"Don't tutor me, black-hair. I am not your whimpering wives to take your lip and like it."

I would have knocked her flying, but I heard Tathra's voice call suddenly to me from within the tent.

I put the blow aside, and went past Kotta through the flap.

The tent smelled strong of women, of herbs, and burned charcoal from the brazier. Tathra had been lying on the rugs, but had struggled onto her elbow to look at me. She no longer put on the shireen in my presence, and she was paler than Asua had been when she cried for the life of her daughter.

"All is well, Tuvek," Tathra said, smiling at me. "It will do me credit, for I thought myself beyond the age."

I looked at her, her face all shrunken and white, and Chula's emerald green-blue in the hollow of her throat.

"I will kill him for this."

She gazed at me in terror and clutched my wrist.

"No, Tuvek. No. It's good. I am happy. Now he will cleave to me."

Kotta had entered behind me. She said, "He has a loose tongue, the fine warrior, when he lets his wits off the leash. Do you suppose, boy, I did nothing to help your mother? I have given her drafts, and done other things too, but the fruit is lodged. I can do no more or I shall harm her. This being the case, I must see to it she is vigorous enough to bear. The women know nothing. The first child is often difficult, he makes the way. Thereafter it is better."

Tathra's eyes were wild with fear and misery, and she smiled again and told me how happy she was.

2

That night the winter broke. The rain fell in torrents and the lower tunnels were flooded. Then came the sun, pale yellow as bleached brass.

The Moi have it that the summer sun is a golden girl, who blows on a pipe to summon everything living out onto the earth. Suddenly the black-green emptiness of the valleys comes alive with birds and beasts, as if by a spell. And as they go dancing through the grasses, the hungry hunters bring them down. The bird stabs the worm, the big cat breaks the bird's neck, the man casts his spear into the heart of the cat. That is how the world is. Even the man had better look behind him; the wolf may be near, or another man, or fate, the hungriest hunter of them all.

In the Arrow month, the trek began down from the mountains to the Snake's Road, and the winter truce ended. Just before the tents were struck, the men's side of the Dagkta krarls came together in an upper valley, for a spring gathering.

Everyone put on his best for the gathering, and I had caught the sickness. Leggings of dark blue wool and a woolen shirt of scarlet patterned with indigo and white from the looms of my wives. High boots and jacket of deer-hide, the jacket pierced and studded by golden rings. The black bear fur cloak I had taken from the bear myself; it was lined and edged with magenta, with clasps of silver. The knife belt was red velvet, Moi barter, a city thing as were the two iron knives in it.

I let Moka shave my face with the bronze razor, for she had a steady hand.

She was already swelling big, another duet of boys probably. The sight of it gnawed on me, reminding me of Tathra. Feeling my powerlessness in that quarter, I had tried to put it from my mind.

I had few enough horses to choose from in my pen; we had eaten most of them in the lean winter. I mounted up and soon rode off with my wives' kin, as was traditional, for marriage was a bond on the man's side too. I knew I could trust Asua's Doki, and Finnuck—Chula's father—as little as any, and Moka's eldest brother was Urm, the man I had thrown in my proving fight as a warrior. I had broken his leg and it had never healed straight, so he had no great cause to bless my name.

We reached the valley of the gathering at noon, when the sun stood like a golden shield directly above the columns of black pines at the track's summit.

The chiefs of the krarls would cursorily meet here, clasp hands, exchange tokens. Families would pay off Blood-Prices, and fresh feuds begin. Presently the warriors would get drunk and stab each other in the guts as they were making water up against the trees.

Down by the fires the chiefs' sons were finding their usual preliminary ways to vie and compete, breaking stallions bareback, hurling spears in a mark, or simply matching cup for cup till they fell prone, or got out knives and fell dead. I did not join the drinking, not being able to hold more than a cupful down. But my pride led me into the other things. Each year they hooted for me to try my bow or spear or this horse or that horse, praying to their demons the while that I should make a fool of myself, but I disappointed and beat them every time. They would never learn. Soon I had won off them a set of fine peeled white-wood arrows with scarlet fletches, ten bronze rings, and someone's wolfskin cloak.

There was nothing in the land or in my mind to tell me how my life should alter through that day, to warn me of the hunter with his shaft aimed at my back.

There was a rill of white water up the slope, where I took my horse to water him, near sunfall. While he was drinking, I stood among the trees, looking first down on the valley, which had become a dish of smoke from the fires, then out over the ridge to the mountain wilderness, west and north.

The pines, like the posts of a dark loom, were weaving the deepening sunset between them. It was the sort of light to catch the heart, red, dying light, yet pure as crystal. The mountains stood upon it in clots of shadow and crests of flame, each like a huge crumbling coal on the hearth of the sun.

Then there came a flash, for all the world like a spark out of that hearth. Then another, and again.

I stared where these sparks were jumping, and I saw that some of the mountain shadows had come alive and were moving in from the west in a jagged surging.

I put my hand between my face and the sun's face. So I made out horsemen riding from the west, sixty, seventy, eighty of them, and the sparks were springing from the gems they wore, and the gems on the bridles of their tall horses. The gems and the horses spurred my brain, and countless stories came back to me.

I left my mount to his drink. Disconcerted, he turned to watch me run down the slope toward the valley of the gathering.

I found my father Ettook quickly enough, among a stand of thorn trees. He had got in a betting game of throw-bones, had just lost a gold nugget, and was roaring at the injustice and drinking like a drain. They were all drunk, but Ettook made them appear sober. Nearby, a thin deer carcass creaked above a fire, spitting its stinking grease on them.

"My chief," I said, "I must speak with you."

He nodded at me, his face congealed in merriment, and his eyes cloudy with dislike and beer.

"My son Tuvek," he said. "Behold, my fine son by my fine black-haired mare, my woman who makes me boys, who even now is making me another fine Tuvek in her belly." He shook his beerskin, and they guffawed, saluting his virility in various ways.

"My father," I said, "take some water to clear your brain. Something is happening. You had better be sensible for it."

This was not the manner in which to give him my tidings. I was too riled to care.

He erupted from the game of throw-bones, spilling the beer down his shirt, his yellow teeth clamped together. For six months his brow had been level with my shoulder, which did not suit him. He swung his sweaty paw at me, and caught me a blow in the face. I did not bother to avoid it, though I could have done so; he was slow as treacle. It never even rocked me—the red pig was simply padding now, no muscle—but my own hand was answering on a reflex. I should have pulped his nose if I had let myself finish.

I got myself still, and said, "My chief, there are riders coming up on the valley. I doubt if they approach in peace, whoever they are, but from their ornaments I think they may be city raiders."

Ettook did not hear. Fury was trying to burst his face open and reach me.

I quieted myself further and said, "I ask your pardon, my chief. It is I who am drunk; I talked rashly. I came in haste to warn the krarls."

Another chief had risen; he bawled, and men trampled between the fires.

Then it was a voice spoke that silenced us all.

The sky overhead seemed to split along a white metallic seam; at the end of this sawing, squealing rent a thunderbolt fell, parting the earth.

The ground shook. There was a smell of burning trees. Everything was altered by a black smoke that twisted and frayed, leaving behind broken red confusion. Out of this red confusion emerged stumbling men without arms or faces. A dog dashed briefly in a circle, shrieking, with half its belly tangled around its feet.

As the bloody wave collapsed, the supernatural ripping of the sky came again. Men flung themselves flat as if before a god. This bolt struck farther off, more to the north. And from that section, a second bloody wave of screaming and horror crashed upward and fell back, spent.

I had known nothing before of city cannon, or the great iron shot that was expelled from them. This initial lesson was thorough. It was the first occasion true terror laid hold on me. Terror, for me, was explicit in this sense of utter helplessness before an engine without laws and without vulnerability.

We lay on the valley floor, awaiting death. Twice more death raked the valley. Finally there was a time it did not come.

A sort of lull, not silence, a kind of stifling of sounds and cries, and through this stew of smoke and smothering, an avalanche rattled on the western slope. No wailing, no whooping of braves in battle. Just hoofbeats, the singing of jeweled harness.

Something made me stir, and start to thrust up blindly, with my teeth bared like an animal.

I became aware I was lying on a mattress of cinders and twigs and blood, others' or my own. At this instant, a beast ridden by a man came flying through the thorn.

It was a burnished horse, oil-black as sharkskin, its serpent-long neck stretched out and mouth flaring wide. The man astride it was a lightning of bright ornaments and gaping ragged furs. He had a golden face, the face of a golden hawk, and behind the hawk-crest a banner of white-saffron hair.

He did not glance aside at me. He judged me dead, probably.

The tangle of thorns splintered. They were gone.

After that, it became quiet. I kicked a corpse off my legs, and got up, gazing about in a stupid state of remembering where I was and who I had been. Presently I pushed through the wreck of the trees. The roasting carcass, fallen in the fire, was augmented by a dead man fallen on top of it. Both now roasted together.

Along the valley you could see the path they had smashed for themselves, the riders, like a trail cut through brush. They had fired their hell-bolts, then ridden the periphery of the confusion, sweeping men before them as clever wolves will do with cattle, next herding them at a pitched run up the far ridges and away. There had been a small fight; not much. None with gold and silver faces had remained to feed the crows, but had raced clear, the devil horses leaping the rocks as if wings were strapped on their feet, into the ruby twilight.

It was a savage madman's raid. Indiscriminate, wasteful, irresistible. They had captured around thirty men, and fifty more would be dead from their wounds by moonrise.

The Dagkta warriors floundered formlessly, as if returning to themselves after a fit. None of us made to chase the enemy. Only an aimless shouting blew through the valley, anger and fear venting themselves. Certain chiefs, Ettook with them, were bellowing and shaking spears in the reeking, darkening air.

There are two clever tricks men know. One is to make much of nothing. The second is to make nothing of much.

The hurt and dying warriors were put together to be tended by the seers. The rest banked up the fire, poured out beer in bowls, and so held a war council. The substance of which was this: You could not fight a mask-faced city man; particularly you could not fight iron tubes that coughed out death. Therefore let him be. True, they grumbled about dogs or horses that had perished in the explosions, and some were silent, thinking of dead friends or kin, while gossips told legends of earlier raids, and a good many curses were minted in the firelight. It was well known that the mask-faces whipped and starved their slaves, no doubt the hard winter had finished them, and this was why their masters had come hunting so early .

Eventually, those who had lost sons, brothers, or fathers took up mementos of the corpses, or whole bodies where they were to be found, and rode silently homeward to their camping valleys. Others, whose comrades had been driven westward by the raiders, scowled and stamped and invoked their gods and totems for vengeance. The dismembered dead were left in a pile with their weapons to be burned like the rubbish in the morning.

This was the sum total of their action.

I was like a man getting back complete use of his limbs after a paralysis. Then all my sinews burning and eager for work, I discovered there was none.

Having been afraid, nonplussed by the raiders' alien weaponry, now I was impatient to redeem myself. It would not be enough to rant and rave and make up oaths. I was dishonored in my own eyes, for what that was worth, for abruptly I had choked down the awareness that the enemy were only men. They were not invincible after all, merely carried some dangerous invention on wheels, which they had created. I had lain on my face in the spring mud, and they had ridden over me, as if they had some right to confiscate free men, and barely a hand had lifted against them, and even that hand had not been mine.

Presently, roaming the pines where the wounded shrilled

and sobbed and expired, I had got myself in a white-hot rage, and went among the fires with it.

I went where Ettook was cursing and eating and drinking with his warriors.

"My father," I said, "they took five of your people for slaves. Give me ten, and I will go after them."

He chewed his meat, his beard gleaming with fat. His eyes gleamed too. They told me I should have known better than to beg of him after what I had said to him before.

"Listen to the puppy bark. He wet his drawers at sunset and cried for his mother. Even so brave a warrior as Tuvek swoons like a maid at city men."

The warriors grunted. A couple laughed, then saw my face and shut their mouths. I was so angry I could not get a word out.

Ettook said, "No, Tuvek. You haven't earned the right to lead my krarl to battle. But wipe your eyes. Never fear, we will not tell your wives how you ran to hide in the mud."

Suddenly my anger seemed to burst and was dissipated like a poisoned swelling.

Surprised by my own coolness, I smiled confidently back at him.

"It is good of you, my father, to tell no one. I am grateful. I shall never forget your own bravery. The priests should make a song of it."

It was too delicate for him, but he labored at the problem and shortly he had puzzled it out. He had himself been hidden somewhere; his gear was muddier than mine, and his knives neither bloody nor newly cleaned.

His face writhed itself into a congestion, and I said, "Your pardon, my father. I am embarrassed by the presence of your valor."

And I walked away before he could recover himself, straight to the horse pens. Here, judging my roan would have run off, I stole a mount.

A small piece of an hour later, I was out of the valley and riding west, on the trail of the slave-takers.

They left a fine trail, the city raiders. Horse dung caked the rocks, and hooves pocked in the soft soils of spring, and the footmarks of men, and in places a bluish dust—powder spilled from their wheeled cannon. In one spot even a golden bead on a ring, from harness or rider, dazzled like a firefly in a bush—as if they had intended me to follow and meant to leave me spoor.

A whole night and day I sought them, and part of a second night.

After twenty miles or so of finicky, careful riding, I saw the mountains begin to level and sink down toward high rocky plateaus. The going was better for horses, theirs and mine. By midnight of the first dark, I was confident enough of the quarry that I took a few hours' sleep, lying in a shallow cave. Their trail ran northward, which was not the way to the old burned city, Eshkir, so I deduced, which lay more west and south of us.

The western heights were yellow as a goat's eyes, bare and treacherous as horns, but the northern steeps were thinly green with a reluctant grazing. Presently I passed the site of a recent bivouac, black fire-pits, the ubiquitous dung of horses and men, the earth churned up and despoiled, and the charred bones of two deer they had roasted. Apparently the city demons needed food, despite the tales.

I myself feasted on cold broiled hare, shot at dawn and half burned in my hurry to get on.

My plan was very simple when I should come up with them. I meant to steal in by night on their camp, and unbind and rouse the Dagkta men they had captured. I and they should then appropriate weapons and fall on the mask-faces, taking them unawares, for they would never expect such treatment, proud and crazy as they were. It did not occur to me either that this plan of mine was nothing if not as proud and crazy as anything of theirs. I never thought to question it. I felt I could no other thing but what I did, as if the road had been especially paved for me, and I had only to walk on it.

It was curious, uncanny almost. When my fury left me in the face of Ettook's jeering, it was as if I had turned some corner of my brain and come on myself. And I was not as I had thought, not angry, fierce, or filled with old hatreds, not even beset by enemies. I had never been so cool in my life.

I found a cast horseshoe in the afternoon, and some broken waterskins an hour later. My city men were moving more quickly; you could gauge it from the formation of their tracks. I had a notion I might come up with them before

Tanith Lee

dawn, because the manner of their progress and the indications they left behind them showed a new slovenly disregard of detail and leisure, as if they were nearing some base or camp where everything could be set to rights in comfort. They were not reckoning on being chased, of course. Had they known the strength of the pursuit, they would have died of laughter and saved me my trouble.

I snatched some sleep at moonrise and had a dream I had gone blind. Being blind, I had fallen into an icy water, a pool or river, and the liquid was biting like a million knives. I came awake to find myself saying, passionless and clear, "I will kill her."

This sent me cold. I could still hear my voice and what I had said echoing around in the air. But it was like another man's voice, speaking words that had a meaning for him, none for me.

The cave where I slept seemed full of ghosts, or the emanations the tribes named ghosts. I got up to be free of them and went outside. I untethered the horse, but did not mount up. The stars were bright as windows cut in a black wall, and the low moon a coin of light.

The slopes folded up in bony shoulders to a thick palisade of larches, branches stripped by the winter's heavy snows. I walked the horse up into the trees. Beyond the larch wood, a mile away, a rock stack gathered itself from the landscape like a high chimney on the roof of the earth. And the chimney smoked. The smoke rose from the fires that crowned it, gilding its crevices in ribbings of black and gold.

Somehow, from the instant of waking, I had guessed they were near me. Now I stared at the tall rock, knowing perfectly what came next. With wary fascination I had realized I would climb the rock and move among the fires, confront the city raiders, looking into the glass eyes of their masks. . . . *Javhovor. So enorr Javhovor . . .* what was this? A piece of their language I had overheard? Part of the dream of blindness, maybe; some gibberish.

Sometimes, if the power of a god is considered needful, certain priests will offer themselves to him, open their souls for him to enter if he will. One does not always believe in the god who comes. Too often he looks like drunkenness or sham. What came to me that night I had not invited, but I never doubted it.

I tethered the horse, there in the wood, and made on.

It was no hard journey up the rock. There was an ancient stepway cut in the stone; close to, you saw the stack itself was barely natural, terraced and bastioned by men a thousand years before. It was an outpost of the cities, of Eshkir probably, topped by a palace-fortress now in ruins. Each city and its might had come to ruin. This made me arrogant as I climbed their hill to find them, the children of that perished glory, in their jewels and rags, still clutching at history like a rotten plank in the river.

There was a man. He stood on the terraced track, by a single pale skeletal tree. The tree thrust wildly sideways from the rock, and he was leaning on it. Everything was shadow there, only his bronze mask gleamed faintly, and white metal on his wrists.

He must have heard or sensed me coming up. He tilted his mask-face, and he said, "Ez et kme?" His voice was laconic, casual. He was expecting no others than his own kind. At first it seemed I guessed what he had said, simply by his inflection ("Who is here?") then I found I could answer him.

"Et so," I said. He grunted. It was a joke, for I had replied merely, "I." Before he could speak again, I went up to him and stabbed him in the side. He was no taller than I, and thinner under his furs. Somewhere in the mask he whimpered, but that was all. He died in gaunt bewilderment, as the krarl men in the valley had died.

I put off my cloak and put on his outer garments, and his weapon belt with mine. I pulled the mask off his face last— his mouth was open as if he would ask me another question. As he was going into the Black Place, I thought, he would be asking them there who had slain him, but he would get no Blood-Price off me for his grave.

Even then I was not afraid, finding, as I had, his language ready in my mouth. It was as if I read the stones and learned the tongue from them. I never queried it. It came the way a bird will fly the instant he leaves the tree. That sure, that easy. At a need.

The mask was a bronze eagle's head. I had supposed it would disturb me, but it did not seem so very ill to wear it. Only the eyepieces of clear blue glass made the strange night stranger yet. A violet moon went down, leaving only the dying fires above, the color of brass, and a sky of stars like flecks of sapphire.

I pulled the dead man's patchy cloak over my head, and went on up the stepway, toward the ruined fort.

3

The man I killed had been a sentry of sorts, but they regarded the watch like a game. At the head of the terraces another two bronze-masks sat against a crumbling arch. I anticipated interrogation, seeing they would assume I was their fellow from the post below, but neither spoke. One was striking soft chords from a hollow wooden case with strings held across it on silver pegs, a pretty noise to herald what was coming to them. The other raised his hand to me; no more.

So I got inside the fortress.

Through the blue eagle's eyes I saw their camping bathed in the transparent auburn glow of flames. Here and there men sat or lay beside their fires, mostly silent, as watchful men are often silent in the moonfall of the night, the hour when all tides are turning.

Not much seemed to remain of the building save the outer shell. Centrally, a marble stair ran up to nothing but space; there had been some great hall there once. Along the west wall stretched the picket line of their lean horses, fretful and unslumbering. The play of their muscles was like light on silk, and each neck like the slender curve of a bow. The warrior in me was thinking he should have three or four of those horses after tonight, but it was a remote greed, like a memory.

On the far side of the marble stair, eastward, about thirty tents were pitched. They were not like the tenting of a krarl, but raised on frameworks that gave them many domed and pointing shapes, the fabrics various, exotic, and decaying.

Torn banners hung before them, fringed with bullion and jewels.

It was as though I had come into the court of Death, skeletons in bright armor and wormwood in golden cups to drink.

Behind me, the man with the stringed instrument began to sing. He had a fine voice, chiming on the stillness. I did not really catch the words, but it was a love song, not like any music the warriors knew.

Between the picket line of horses and the tents, right under the stair, two cannon stood on carts, motionless nozzled tubings of black iron. They smelled incendiary, as though they were dragons. It was their smell rather than their size that warned me of the danger in them, for they were not large. Perhaps, guessing me a stranger, they would spit fire at me of their own volition. But this was a child's fancy, something out of my tribal recollection, not my own. Some men slept, sitting by the cannon. They were unlike the rest, dark skinned and also dark haired as I was, while the others in the camp were very fair. Neither did these drip ornaments. Their faces were like knobs of wood, brutal, ugly, and expressionless, even asleep. They were slaves, no mistaking it.

The other slaves, the red men, lay close by. The north end of the ground roofed over a pit, an old cellar or dungeon, with an oval opening looking into it from above, covered by a grating of green crusted metal. The fires shone dimly now and then into this hole, and I could make out a mass of bodies and shadows, and hear them crooning and groaning their discontent. They were past the bawling stage, and past the fighting stage too, maybe. They had had a night and day of forced marching, a caress or two from gemmed whips like that which I had noted hung from the belt of the sentry, little food, if any, and no hope.

No one had challenged me this far. Now a man stepped out of his pavilion. His mask was an eagle's head like mine, but silver, with a green stone between the eyes. He nodded at the grating.

"The trash are unhappy with their lot," he said. The clearness of his speech shocked me at last, for it could have been a tongue I had had since birth.

"Yes," I said, "I'm sick of their noise."

I was looking for a means to get in the pit, other than the

grating. The last section of the northern wall sloped down into a kind of gully, which seemed a likely entry point. I was formulating some story in the alien language about visiting our prisoners and offering them the whip for their racket, when the silver face strode up to me and grasped my arm.

"You are not Slarn," he said.

The masks of the city men had no apertures at the mouth and the voices that came from them were filtered and changed. I could tell this much, however: he was neither a young man nor a nervous one.

"True, sir, I am not Slarn."

"Who then?"

I had been careless, trusting too much my peculiar luck, the occult demon-guide delivered from me.

"Come," he said. "Unmask. I will know you."

"As you wish," I said.

I hazarded I should have the advantage of him; whatever trick me intended to detect, he would not look for me.

I loosened the cloak first, getting my knife ready to hand as I did so. As he took in my black hair, I heard him catch his breath in his throat. Then I had pulled off the mask.

I had been ready for all manner of things, but not for what he did. He fell back, and his arm went up, weaponless, instinctive, in a gesture of deference and denial. He blurted out two syllables I guessed to be an oath. Yet aware of his speech and still unable to fathom the word, I realized in a moment it was not an oath but a name.

"*Vazkor.*"

Unreasonably, receiving this unknown title terrified me.

A chasm gulped for my feet; I had lost my identity.

I had intended a smooth killing, like the other on the track, but I went at him in a blank panic, and drove in the blade vilely, missing the vital organ so he yelped with agony and fear before he fell. So much done amiss, I did not even have the sense left to lean and be certain he was dispatched. I waited only long enough to hear if an answering hubbub would respond to his cry. When the night stayed peaceful, I ran and jumped down into the northern gully, without another caution.

As I had trusted, there was a low door in the side of the dungeon where the slope abutted on the gully. It was solid iron, but secured only by bolts fastened on the outside. These

bolts I ripped from their sockets with my dagger, and stepped
into the pit.

It was freezing, already fetid, the dark relieved inade-
quately through the oval grating by cheerless pale brown
flakes of light.

A man lay moaning against my feet. His legs were bound
with chains to the legs of two neighbors. I had reckoned on
their being bound, but not on chains. However, the metal was
brittle and green as the grating, and they were tangled in it
rather than fettered. I tried to roll him free, chopping meanwhile at the chain with my knife. He muttered and struggled.

"Are you a man?" I asked him in the tribal tongue. I had
observed that his captors had not even bothered to take his
knife away from him. He flinched and groveled on the soiled
floor of the dungeon, and all about the warrior-heap was
flailing and tossing like a fever-house. I felt contempt, black
and deep as the hole in which they lay. Pride in myself had
brought me here; now my pride urged me away. I was not
one with this mortal wreckage, crawling like insects in their
own filth.

But I had come a distance and would not retreat. If they had
no brain or strength of their own, I must goad them with
mine.

The rusty chain cracked under my blade. The three men,
loosed from it, curled together like disturbed puppies. Their
vacant eyes were enlarged and stupid, and it occurred to me
they had been fed some medicine on their journey here. The
last of the three was a Dagkta from Ettook's krarl. I saw he
knew me and was trying to collect himself. I gave him the
bronze-mask's knife, and put him to work on chains.

The slave-pit grew stealthily alive with staggering, bemused
freedom. Some, less affected, were reviving in violent starts,
snarling, searching out weapons, which in most cases had
been left with them. Their eyes and knives glittered in the
faint light. The tincture that had kept them docile was turning them vicious now that they had an avenue to escape and
vengeance. Many were striped on the face or shoulders with
the raw decoration of a whipping. Each had a score to settle.

None of this took very long, once we were started on it.
Soon there were about twenty standing in the pit, and eight
lying down permanently from the treatment they had got,
poisoned with the drug or beaten out of the world.

In the ruin aloft, it seemed too steadily quiet; the fabric of peace was woven differently.

There was no need to speak to the red warriors. Most of them had recognized me, at last, and recognized themselves, and their blood was up. We stole out softly, two by two, into the gully, and scaled the slope.

The city men were on the dungeon roof, not five yards away, politely waiting for us. Near seventy of them.

The body of the silver-mask who had renamed me was missing—he must have lived long enough to crawl into their camp and warn them. Informed of everything, they had negligently formed their cordon and let us leap into it, like moths into the candle.

The warriors behind me faltered. They had never fought any but their tribal kin. What confronted them had an appearance of sorcery.

I was first onto level ground. The fires were burning behind the city men, making of them black dream figures, with bronze and silver beast-heads, white slanting swords, and green and purple rays spitting from their jewels as if their bodies had been pierced with eyes.

Suddenly one of them shouted. I tried to grasp the meaning, but, like a dream itself, my knowledge of their tongue was leaving me—then I caught once more the name the other had spoken: *Vazkor.*

And speech came in my mouth. I did not know what I said.

"So Vazkor enorr. Beheth Vazkor. Vazkor karnatis."

It was like a portent, some god's jest.

They retreated wordlessly, some slowly drawing off their masks, making men of themselves again. The faces they revealed were disbelieving, transfixed, white. Three knelt on the roof as if to worship, and ten more knelt after them, and another ten. These were all older men, forty or fifty years old. Among the rest there was an altercation, cries of anger and doubt. In the midst of this, understanding nothing but hungry for any chance, we sprang on them and cut them down.

In their obscure confusion, they scattered before us. I hacked the kneeling men away to get at the standing angry men behind. I felt no battle lust; it was a grim task that must be done. Presently, I had a city sword, red to its hilt, and I was bathed with blood. It was like a killing of pigs. Though more than twice our number, they scarcely resisted us, as if some destiny had found them out and we were its instrument.

In the end they were silent, and no others came to challenge us.

During the fight, such as the fight was, the guiding principle left me. I was glad to lose it, once it was gone. I wiped off my new sword on the furs of a corpse, and grinned with no laughter, telling myself, *Well, now, Tuvek, you have been possessed by a demon, in which kind you do not believe. I congratulate you.* I spit on the ground, as if I could spit out the ancient language I had mastered and forgotten, both so quickly.

The warriors were stripping jewelry from the dead. A few had ventured to the tents and were inventing doors in them with their blades, and pulling out threadbare cushions of velvet sewed with pearl and similar mildewed wonders. Now and again they would happen on a rack of swords or a metal dainty worth keeping, and a ferocious yell of acquisition echoed through the broken fort.

I, too, went searching shortly, destructive and covetous as any of them, with a sense of I knew not what gnawing at my spirits.

I walked right through the empty tent homes, and reached the last pavilion, and realized I had selected well.

This pavilion was the largest, set a little back, half hidden, around an angle of the eastern wall, and ten black horses were penned there. By the pen one of the dark-haired slave men was squatting. He was like those I had seen earlier, though this one was wide awake. I had met with none in the fight, and supposed they had run off, so I glared at him, and shook the sword, anticipating a prompt view of his heels.

His face remained blank and wooden as a slat, and, sluggish as muddy water, he stepped aside to let me by. I did not trust his docility and that made me reconsider.

We had dealt with around sixty men in this camp, but the force that had come on the valley had been stronger—seventy or eighty. Likely some had ridden ahead to another destination, but here were ten horses by a large tent. Might there be ten men inside, prepared for me?

I spun about on the dark slave, and caught him by his gray-fleshed neck. I asked him questions, but I had lost the magic speech, and either he did not understand the tribal tongue or had no wish to. Finally I fisted him asleep, having had enough killing and foreseeing more, and went to the pavilion timidly as a bride.

Before it a golden banner, real gold beaten thin as a wafer and painted with a crested bird in white enamel, whistled softly in the wind on its pole, The pavilion was crimson velvet, almost black with age. Tassels of green-tarnished gold cascaded across the drapery of a hidden entrance, artfully showing where the opening might be discovered. I went to another side and stuck the sharp city sword straight in the velvet and tore it up like rotten flax. Then I dashed into the tent, alert to deal instant death on either hand.

No need. He had been there before me, the skull-headed gentleman.

A lamp of amber glass depended from the roof frame, showing the scene in perfect deatil.

There were but three of them, after all. They had pulled aside the elegant rugs with which the floor of the tent was strewn, and fixed their own blades in the craggy floor of the ruin beneath, point uppermost, then neatly fallen on them.

I had often heard the tale of men who preferred suicide to this or that shame or deprivation or terror. However, hearing the tale and seeing the evidence are not the same. It shook me, though. It made me think at once, rationally and with an abject, instinctive loathing, what would be *my* test, my ultimate unbearable burden, that I would choose my own iron in my belly rather than endure?

Each man was golden masked, one in the manner of a hawk, and his saffron hair spilled in his spilled blood—the rider in the thorn wood.

Why this? Lost honor, humiliation that we had come from the slave-pit and beaten them? But these had not even ventured out to fight.

I raised my head. The pavilion was hung with soft dazzling silks, embroideries, and fraying gauzes, which made an effervescence of the amber lamp. Then a gauze stirred and drifted aside like powder. And something stood across from me, silver gleaming, a great dart of fire through a jewel—I leaped back, the sword ready. And lowered the sword like lead in my leaden hand.

It was not a city warrior standing there. I had not con-

sidered women might be with them, there had been no others
we had seen; besides, at first she did not seem a woman but a
sorceress, unheralded, materialized so bright and sudden, and
the three dead between us.

She wore some kind of silver dress of snake scales, and a
bodice of milky emeralds that left bare her breasts. Her waist
was narrow but her breasts were full, a soft tactile whiteness
flushing to warm darkness at their tips, and round as little
moons. Her breasts might have reassured me she was human,
too distracting to be celestial flesh. But her face was masked,
the shape of a silver deer with eyes of apple-green quartz,
and behind it her hair was like another sort of fire, a fire of
glacial gold, burning with coldness.

She spoke to me in the city speech I could no longer inter-
pret. I did not comprehend the words, but her meaning was
exactly conveyed: the contempt of the king for his slave—no,
worse, of the goddess for a piece of human offal spoiling the
pasturage of paradise.

I had never got such a tone from a woman, nor ever considered I should. I was too amazed not to bear it a moment,
like the mule his load, and no doubt my mouth was ajar to
tempt night-flying insects.

Then I saw how her right hand, half hidden in the folds of
her skirt, was clenched on a small shiny star, and I flung myself sideways in the second she threw her dagger at me. It
flashed over my shoulder, and sliced among the draperies of
the tent wall.

At that, seeing her failure, she cried out. It was a mortal
voice, a young voice, rough with grief and fury and fright. It
gave me back my sight and I looked again. Now I saw only a
girl, trembling with her fear, a masked girl with naked breasts
that made my mouth go dry.

"Well," I said, abandoning the sword, "your luck isn't with
you tonight, deer-headed maiden."

I knew she could no more understand the tribal speech
than I hers. The lack of verbal communion reduced our inter-
course to one eternal symbolic channel. I was glad it was so
mundane, glad I had now the excuse to forget how she had
seemed to me a dagger-cast before.

I crossed over the dead men, and, as I came at her, she
turned and tried to run. All her pale topaz hair gushed like a

fall of water over her back. It was easy to grab her by the hair, to bring her to face me and to thrust off her mask.

She was beautiful. I had never seen beauty before, not like her beauty. Her skin was white, her hair white as silver at the roots where it entered her white flesh, her mouth was smooth and shaped, and red as a summer fruit, and her eyes were green as the gems of her bodice. Everything of this I glimpsed like a flame burning up at me.

She did not struggle any longer. Her fight was done. I had her easily.

Her breasts filled my hands and she smelled of youth and womanhood. I did not hurt her, there was no need for she never tried to evade me; nor was she a virgin. I had not expected it, coming as she did out of that camp of men. She was their whore, or someone's, and now she would be mine. The gate between her thighs was golden as her hair, and the road beyond the gate was made for kings. Her green jewel eyes reflected back the lamp in the roof. She never shut them; neither did she look. Despite her heart and mind, her body was good to me.

The lamp glowed less vigorously overhead, and she lay there under me, her eyes open and her body open. I was still pleased with my victory, the shallow victory outside, the shallow victory of her.

I said, at random as she did not speak the tribal tongue, "That was a fine treasure to take in your lord's tent, and his dead eyes watching."

And she answered in a whisper. "Be happy then, you filth, you diseased and verminous rubbish. Be happy and die of it."

I started up. She turned me cold with her surprises.

"Where did you learn krarl talk?"

"From the Moi. Who but, when we barter with them? Are you stupid as well as distusting, oh shlevakin accursed?"

I was confounded. I had raped women on countless raids and tribal wars. They had bitten me, screamed, cried tears, or whined with pleasure. They had not coolly insulted me. Nor had they such eyes.

"Since you follow what I say," I said, "tell me why the men here took their own lives."

She smiled at that.

"The three princes of Eshkorek slew themselves on learning that Vazkor had risen from his tomb."

"Vazkor," I said. My belly turned about in me. "Who or what is Vazkor?"

"You," she said. "Tribal savage, dog, offal. Ask the dead."

"You will tell me tomorrow if you tell me nothing now."

"Am I to be with you then tomorrow, oh my master?" She was shivering, not so much from fear as from denying it.

"I won't hurt you," I said. "I am a chief's son, and will protect you in the krarl."

"Oh rejoice, Demizdor," she said. "The savage will protect you in the stinking den of his idiot people."

"Be civil or the savage shall change his mind. Was it your name you spoke?"

She shuddered all over, and said, "Demizdor is my name."

I could not say it quite. I was eager to forget the city tongue I had used.

"Demmis-tahr," I said. She laughed, more like choking than laughter. I could not make her out, though I meant to keep her.

"Even my name is to be defiled," she said. "But I will call *you* Vazkor."

"Call me that, you bitch, and I will kill you."

At dawn, I and twenty-three red warriors rode out of the fortress. Our tribal dead we had burned with their ornaments and weapons; the city men we left for the carrion birds of the mountain valleys. We took all their riches and all their horses, either riding or leading them. They did not like us much after their former lords, but they should come to it, since they must. I had half dreamed of bringing away one of the tubular cannon on its wheeled cart, but the braves would not touch it. It had been only a whim—I had no idea of their workings, nor much hope of learning—so I let it go.

I had kept an eye out for the dark slave-men but saw none, and we did not seek them. We had one prisoner only and she was mine.

I had clad her in her furs over the finery of emeralds so the warriors should not see them or any other of her treasure, gem or flesh, and grow envious. By day I made her tie her hair in a piece of velvet. Only the deer-mask stared out. She was calmer.

I said to her, "Obey me and you are safe. You found me

rough, but try tricks and you will be at the mercy of others who are less courteous even than I."

"That is a winsome thought indeed," she said. Then, as we were going out, she called to me mockingly, "Vazkor, Vazkor."

I could not bring myself to hit her. I was intoxicated with her body and would not damage it, and this she knew, sensing her power already, and she my slave. I took her shoulders and lifted her off the ground.

"I have been thinking, bitch-lady. Maybe you are right. Maybe your king Vazkor—he was a king, was he not, a golden-mask?—maybe he is in me, as the old men said when they kneeled. So. Call me by that name. I shall beat you if you use another. I am Vazkor. One day I shall steal a golden mask and wear it when I stopper you."

After that she kept quiet, for she was no less contrary than other women.

Still, the thought took root in me. If I resembled their dead prince, his must be the spirit which had guided me, my possession. This made it harder to reason myself from the notion, as I had been attempting to do since the fight. The incidents upon the rock had not declined like the dream that began them, but I told myself I would not dwell on them. And I had other things to consider.

The krarl men bellowed for me that dawn, as they would bellow for the chief after a battle raid. When they observed I had got myself a doxy from the city tents, they shouted the louder. I might have what I liked, they would not grudge it, for this hour at least, for I was the hero who rescued them. Later, of course, they would hate me the more for the favor owed.

I set Demizdor on a horse. Though few women rode among the krarls, my woman should ride. Slave she might be, but she had been valuable in the fortress.

I had not had her since that first coupling. She judged me a savage, a dog, whose sex drove him back to her, and I sensed she imagined she might get the better of me through it. So I did not touch her, though my loins were full of snakes. I had never troubled with diplomacy before in the matter of a woman. Like a boy, silly for some wench who would not, I practiced her name under my breath, striving to get it right. When I offered her food and drink she turned away, as if this were the rape, and she would rather be forcibly bedded than fed. I recalled the weird myths of the cities and let her be.

We holed up that night among the mountain steeps. We had encountered no fresh game to shoot, and drank to mute the hunger. I took her a bowl of city wine—there had been casks of it among their tents—but she would not drink when I was by. I left her the bowl, and coming back I discovered it drained.

I lay by her for her own safety, for my pride too. The warriors would have made a sweet song of it, if I had taken a girl and not served her. I did not sleep well. I lay all the while arguing with myself, whether or not to have her and be done.

Close to dawn I heard her stirring, and told myself I had been wise to keep awake. I recalled the dagger she had thrown at me. Presently I saw her outlined on the lightening sky, standing where the ground jumped away into air. For a second I fancied she meant to throw herself off the rock, as the city men fell on their swords.

I tensed, ready to spring and tumble her back, and she said, "Lie easy, warrior. I am not brave enough for that. Not today, at least."

"You are to call me Vazkor," I said. "Did I not tell you?"

Her hair was like a bright smoke in the dawnlight and I could see every curve of her through the silver dress, and it nearly drove me from my wits.

She said, "There is the rubble of a tower near Eshkorek. That is the grave of Vazkor. Twenty years ago he took up the cities in his hands and ground them to his will, and smashed them. He wed a goddess-witch; she was called Uastis. There is some child's legend that she was slain but recovered from death, that she took on the form of a white lynx, and fled before the soldiers came for her. They say she is living yet, in another land, Uastis Karnatis. But Vazkor is dead."

Her words struck echoes inside me. My spine shivered and I bade her be silent. I could still picture how they had kneeled to me in the fortress, the elder men who could remember him, who maybe had looked in his face, and witnessed it once more in mine.

Late in the morning we reached the valley of the spring gathering. There was some smoke rising; it had misled us. We trotted the fine city horses over the upper ridge, and looked down on the aftermath of the great tribal camp, black from old fires and entirely vacated. Not even a hound to welcome us. Only a few flapping, mottled heaps of wings and beaks, where the big birds were dining on dead dogs and horses and on parts of men. The krarls had meant to burn their dead as we had done, but, impatient at the numbers of the slain, had not stayed to tend the funeral fires. These had presently gone out, and left dainty roasted meats for the scavengers. It was not a pleasing sight and turned my stomach. I had seen corpses in plenty, but had not returned to a battlefield when the crows were banqueting there.

She was sitting beside me. In her silver mask, I could not see her mood, but she faced straight down to the valley, and her hands were motionless and nonchalant on the rein.

"The carrion eaters must bless your princes that provide such dinners for them."

"Do the tribes never kill?" she said, quick as a blow.

"We kill hand to hand, belly to belly. Not with iron phalluses shot from behind a hill."

"With our cannon we have razed our own cities," she said. "Don't think I will pity your little loss."

"For a slave you set up a strident mewing."

"I am not your slave," she said, "though you may play at it. Hang me with shackles, beat me, murder me. I am still no slave of yours."

"None of this is necessary. I will get you with child. Then we will see how much my slave you are."

She had no tune to counter that.

The men behind us were sitting also very quietly, sullen and sour at the deserted camp. Against the odds, they had hoped for better. But their chiefs and their kin had reckoned them lost and discounted them, and when the night of the gathering was done, they had turned homeward for the Dagkta tentings. I wondered how many dying men had been helped across the threshold by the priests' knives. I wondered, too, how Ettook celebrated to himself my death, for he would be sure of my death, knowing where I had gone. I had not sampled this dish before. Too much alive, I could not envisage my alleged slaughter. I visualized instead his bastards squealing for their dues, and widows wailing for their husbands taken captive, and at that I remembered my mother. She also would believe me slain or slave. I had forgotten that.

"So," I said to the warriors, "they would not wait. Let's make on and surprise them. They will piss blood when they see us. But there's half a day's riding yet."

The men growled agreement, turning their mounts along the track.

I set a hot pace for them on my new horse, using its starry spurs, and dragging my silver-faced slave by her bridle.

4

The sun was long down, the night moonless and black, when we picked over a narrow pass between the craggy, pine-bearded heights, and the spoons of the camping valleys appeared below, falling away into the mountains, and scattered for miles with several thousand yellow coals of fires.

The warriors were already breaking into bands, making for their own krarls and their own revelations. Already the bond was snapped that had held the twenty-three as one, and their shout for me was only so much frosty breath left behind. I saw then I should have bound them harder to me, that it might have profited me to do so. They had been ripe for swearing blood-brotherhood; they might have followed me after, strength at my back. It was too late now, the time of action blown away, ridden off over the slopes with them. Even Ettook's five men still with me were champing to get home, the dangerous adventure just a story nagging to be told. I had lost my chance.

It was not so much slovenliness that had made me miss it, either, but the arrogance that had come on me when I entered the fortress, and which had never ebbed from my veins. And she had made it worse, my goddess-slave. Her razor contempt had sharpened mine. I saw them all through her eyes, as she was seeing me, a herd not worth the driving.

As I idled there, the impact of the other grim farce smote me. For not frequently do the dead sit among the mourners at their own burying.

To Ettook's warriors I said, "Once we are over a ridge or two, maybe we should go quietly. It will be pleasant to see how we are missed, and by whom."

And they showed their teeth, tasting the flavor of it, though their loyalty to me was gone.

So we went, delicate as mice, into Ettook's krarl.

As I got closer, I could hear plain enough what they were at.

There was a humming and howling, and sometimes a screaming like beasts in a trap. They had lost the most of any krarl: seven dead from the cannon, five stolen or dead, and one of those the chief's heir. They could not choose but hold a death-watch tonight, the fourth night, as the custom was.

I left Ettook's braves to their own plots, and tethered my city horses on the outskirts of the camp. Whatever else, I did not think the warriors would come back and steal them. Demizdor, however, I kept with me, still mounted.

They had cleared a great square below, I could see it from the pines, and I came down following the trees like a shadow, to watch the fun.

Torches burned at the four corners of the square, and a fire at its center. A couple of young trees had been hacked up and set burning on it. Around that fire they stood, my grief-torn kindred.

On the west side were the women. Chula was foremost, in all her adornments, everything I had ever given her, glittering and gleaming, like a heap of plunder, with her hair tattered and her dress tattered, and her arms and the round tops of her breasts scored by her nails. Her shireen clung to her tears beneath it, but her fists were clenched. Through her weeping, you could see her fury. She had missed her miniature queenship because of my death, and she could have killed me for dying.

At the back of my first wife the other two were sobbing less obtrusively, with their children around them. Big-bellied Moka had her four little sons clasping to her knees, crying too. without understanding, the way children will when the adults set up a dirge. Asua held in her arms the girl baby who had so far surprised me by living, but she was watering it as if she meant to drown it now. Chula's three boys, meanwhile, had been lined up by their mother, parading their sorrow as she did, though the eldest was only just upward of four. They looked like three tiny black bears, still in their winter furs. No doubt she would have begun shouting later that their heritage was denied them, gone to the grave with me.

There was a mass of other women, wringing their hands and lifting their heads occasionally to ululate like she-wolves. They were bewailing the clan totems—the chief's son and braves, rather than the man Tuvek, or their own dead husbands.

I looked for Tathra next, with my heart booming, but she was nowhere. I thought how she had been when I left, and how she might have grown ill from bad news. It took the spice from the meat, and I was going immediately to seek her, when the drums of the men's side east of the fire began.

Out of the press of warriors, Seel came, his tarry face painted like a skull now, white on the black, and in his magic robe of embroidered symbols, the robe of the war dance. He cluthced his hands on the one-eyed snake-carving at his neck, and behind him moved Ettook, bowed as if a mountain of misery sat on his shoulders. It gripped me. They were going to make the death chant for me. These, my best of enemies, were going to exclaim to their gods of my virtues and the joy they had had from me. They were going to entreat the Lords of the Black Place to set me free to return to them.

The people drew back from the fire somewhat, to give Seel room. He started to stamp and flap like one of those birds I had seen feeding on corpses earlier in the day. As he blundered by it, he threw pinches of stuff in the flames, and they spit and hissed.

He screeched the names of the men the krarl had lost; at each one a woman or two shrieked. At my name there was a huge moaning, and the warriors beat their spears together.

"Our master is Death. Death is god," Seel ranted. "Twelve of our sons has he taken, but worse than our sum of sons, the son of the chief, the hope of the krarl, the rising star among the tents, our tomorrow, has he taken."

Chula screamed excellently on the cue. The three tiny bears dived into her skirts in fright, so I felt sorry for them.

Ettook lumbered in the broad firelight. He showed around the spearheads, the gold bangles and bronze knives I had taken in the last war months. In the manner of the ritual he praised my valor and my cleverness.

"Tuvek, the flower of my loins, my son best of all sons. Generous to me as the rain to the pasture, brave as the leopard in his battles. Who does not remember Tuvek's courage when the foe ran before him like rabbits? Who was the young god riding among the warriors? It was my son, Tuvek. He who made the women sigh like a wheat field in the wind, he who rode the men beneath the hooves of his horse, whose arms were stronger than brass, and whose wit was sharper than diamond, whose desire made sons, whose anger made silence. Ah, Tuvek, my son, what is there in death's place which causes you to linger there?" He rubbed his face, which was a healthy jocund color. "When the raiders came," Ettook roared, "who but Tuvek dared to follow them? It must mean death to try blade for blade with the cities, yet still he would go. I forbade him, for his safety, yet he paid no heed. He went to save his brothers, the braves. He died for them. Who will not weep for Tuvek, my best of all sons, lord of all warriors?"

The beasts' threnody gushed up again, the spears rattled.

Seel lifted his arms, and a carmine sun and a white moon staggered on his crow's sleeves.

"Death," sang Seel. "In your dark tent our men are standing. Relent, Death, relent. Return to us our men, return to us the son of our chief." Then, raising his voice, he flung himself at the four points of the world, north, south, east, and west, from any of which the answer might arrive, which is why they allow four nights before they seek it, one darkness for each. "Tuvek," the seer squealed, "come back among your folk, come back from the black tent, the bone-grove, to the warm hearth. Death may give you horses and hounds, but you have horses and hounds in the land of life. Death may give you women, but they bear no fruit and you have women of flesh and blood who shall. All Death can offer, you possess. Tuvek, come back among your folk."

"Say no more," I said, stepping out into the raw red light. "I am here."

Only in legend does the dead man reply to the call, generally ghastly to behold, and without his head or some such thing. On the living earth nobody comes; it is just a piece of the chanting to crave and entreat. Although they bark for it, they do not expect the bone.

For a space long enough for me to repeat my words ten times over, they made not a sound. Their eyes crawled up me like flies. Then a woman fell over in a fit—though even the women drink a good deal before a dead-watch, and I think it was the beer more than the ghost that undid her. At this Seel changed his stance. Leaping upward as though his drawers had caught alight, he whirled at me, beating his arms, squawking, "Away, Undead, away, away! Back to the Shadow Region!"

I was not certain if he truly believed himself confronted by a phantom, but this was such a reversal of his former plaint that I leaned on a tree and laughed.

Seel's eyes rolled. He snatched some more of his magical fire powder and tossed it between us. He conjured me to vanish, and I stubbornly would not, but simply stood laughing at him till my ribs pained me.

Presently he left off these antics, drawing back to where Ettook was, and making motions at me from there.

Ettook's face was now a picture, as might be imagined. The healthy, cheery countenance with which he had mourned my demise had given way to a flushed livid whiteness. He knew me a live creature directly, his curse come back to him. He opened his swollen lips to utter some exquisite idiocy, but there was suddenly a lot of screaming that saved him the trouble.

Chula, my first wife, cast herself against me. She threw her arms about my waist, and clutched me as if she were drowning. Some city man's knife had slit the shirt along my right side, and she fastened her mouth there, and sucked at my skin as if she could get sustenance from me. I tried to pry her loose but she clung like a leech.

"Don't eat me, woman," I said. "I'm mortal, never fear." The three little bears had not rushed after her. They were huddled together, still crying in alarm at their ghoul-daddy shouldered up from hell. "Look after your brood," I said to Chula, and pushed her off me at last. Her eyes glared in the shireen, swirling with hurt, anger, triumph, and sex. Then they went past me, and fixed on the shapes of woman and horse behind me. I said, "I have brought you a gift from my battle. An Eshkir slave."

Everyone murmured, and Chula froze like a post.

Meantime Ettook had recovered himself slightly; my wife's passion had given him the leisure.

"So my son fought the city raiders."

"Yes, my chief. Fought and killed."

It was a mark of my scorn for him that I did not mean to humiliate him in front of his subjects. Besides, enough men knew how he had praised me before I set out from the spring gathering, for such chat always finds legs.

Ettook said hollowly some phrase about how welcome I was, and how worthy of preserved existence. He asked me where our Dagkta warriors were, for surely they had returned to the krarl with me? He was trusting I had boasted and they were lost after all. But his luck was out, for even the few who had perished in the prison pit had not been his men.

I was wondering where the five had gone, and wishing I had kept them by me, but I had no need to be anxious. They had only been waiting, with a sense of theater to equal mine, for just such a prompting as Ettook's query. Pent-up high spirits and pride in their return had made them wild, for all five were as young as I. They galloped into the watch-square, whooping and calling in a huge surge of stolen horses, scattering the women and the fire, and setting the babies bawling.

The warriors went on riding in circles for a minute or so, islands of the broken fire sparking on their grins, and on their hands full of looted knives, and the coats of their city mounts.

Piecemeal, the noise and confusion shrank back into the sputter and flicker of the checkered light.

I said, loud enough for everyone to hear me, "With these braves and eighteen more I took the city raiders' camp. We slew them to a man, and kept only one prisoner, the woman here, who is my share of the spoil."

The five riders hooted and cheered me, keeping me hero; maybe it was lucky.

I turned and went to Demizdor. She might have been blind and deaf for all the heed she seemed to take of anything. I wished I could see her face to know her thought.

"Get down," I said. "Now you are here, you will walk like

the other women. I have shown them you belong to me, so you are safe."

She dismounted without a word. I said, seeing Chula's eyes stuck on her still like beetles to a log, "I am giving you to my wives, Golden-hair. They will perhaps put you in the porridge pot and eat you."

When she stood by me, the crown of her head came just beneath my collarbone. I wanted to pick her up and take her away with me, running through the fire to some secret place. But instead, I told her to walk behind me. She obeyed, like any slave, and the need in me to see her face was like an itch I could not scratch.

So I went to my mother's tent, leaving the rest of them about the fire, only telling Chula, as I passed, to see to my horses in the pines, and to getting me some food.

I was at least sensible that I should not go rampaging in on Tathra when she thought me a corpse; that much I did right. In fact, I had had an inclination to seek Kotta first, and have her carry the tidings before me, but her tent, when I came on it, was full of wailing and groans, some woman's sickness she was busy with and would not leave for me. So I must manage everything by myself.

When we reached my mother's tent, I tethered the horse and left Demizdor beside it, telling her not to stray or the warriors would think her fair game, after all. I was beginning not to like her docility, and the task before me made me uneasy besides.

I went into the tent very softly.

There was a brazier burning by the bed place, no greater light than that. For a moment I did not find Tathra, then I discovered where she sat, in the shadow of the tall Eshkiri loom. There was a cloth on the loom, black and white, the cloth a tribal woman constructed to wrap her dead in, when she had his body. But she was not weaving, and the cloth was barely started on.

She kept as motionless as the night. Black as night, too, with her hair and robe, and her face hidden by the shireen. Yet there was something in her attitude that was as naked as her face was not. Her eyes were shut. She did not weep, but she looked finished and withered as a branch burned in the fire. Her loud crying was inside. Whatever my victory, this I had done, and I was not happy at it.

"Ettook's wife," I said, speaking very low, and addressing her as a stranger would do it, trying to come to her gradually. She never stirred. "Ettook's wife, there is a better tale than you have been hearing."

"Thank you, warrior," she said. "You honor me. But do not tell me now, for I am only a fool of a woman who is too stupid to understand in her grief."

I had disguised my voice too well, I saw. I hooked aside the flap of the tent so some of the light from outside should enter, for the sky had cleared and the risen moon was shining bright.

"Your son lives," I said to her. "That is the news."

At this she woke. Her lids lifted, and I turned a little, letting the moon describe me, bit by bit.

"Tuvek," she said. Her tone was cold and empty enough that it frightened me.

"Yes, Mother," I answered. "I'm flesh, not ghost. Come and touch me to be sure."

She got up, stiff as an old woman, and began to walk to me with slow deliberate steps. I dared not go to her, she seemed so full of disbelief and terror; she was almost terrible herself.

But about four paces from me, she must have sensed, as an animal senses it, the warmth from my body, the scent of something living. She gave a muffled sound and stopped as if the earth had hold of her feet. And then her eyes went away from my face, by me, into the moonlight dark beyond the tent, almost as Chula's had done, except that my mother's eyes widened and became stony as though the sight had gone out of them, and she dropped down on the ground.

I spun around with my heart in my mouth, but nothing was there, just my horse and Demizdor, who could barely be seen against the brilliant sky, only the sheen of her silver mask and her unbound hair bleached by the moon to the pallor of snow.

I gathered Tathra up and put her on her bed. As I set her there, she stirred. She clasped my hand and muttered, "Did I dream it?"

I was leaning close; she could not see the doorway. I said, "Yes. Whatever horror you saw, you dreamed, for I saw nothing. I made you ill by coming in too quickly. I will go for Kotta."

"No," she said, "it was the Eshkir woman, with her white hair. She must have died in the wild valleys those twenty years ago, and be envious of your life. Throw away the lynx-mask, Tuvek, or she will harm you through it."

Then I understood. Something in me shivered, but I laughed and told her of Demizdor. I supposed Tathra would be reassured, shed tears and get better, but her eyes were dry and her hand was like ice when she took it out of mine.

"The city women are not women," she said. "They think themselves goddesses. They eat the soul of a man to get his strength."

"We shall see about that," I said.

Just then Kotta came into the tent on her own. Of course some woman could have told her the news, and she had used her head in regard to Tathra. The healer paid no special attention to me, as if dead warriors rising were a common event among the krarls; she merely courteously bade me go, so I left and was glad to. I had had enough of the fears and conjurings of women. It was not the greeting I had wished for.

Outside, Demizdor still stood against the shining night sky, and yet as dumb as the moon. For a second I entertained the notion she had been witch-sending Tathra, but cursed myself for a fool, and put the scare aside.

Unspeaking, I went to my tent. Unspeaking, she followed.

5

The fire was already roasting meat for me.

Moka and Asua were preparing the food and did not run at me, but seemed glad enough that I was back. A widow's lot is seldom sweet, and they were good women in their way, I now acknowledged, ready to please me, and be satisfied with pleasing me. Some of the men's side was there too, my marriage kin, Doki and Finnuk, and all Moka's brothers, even

Urm Crook Leg. They had supplied meat and the grain for the loaves, and the beer, as they told me instantly. I thanked them, and promised them rewards later from my loot-chests, which no doubt they had been at already, thinking me crow-pie.

Chula, meantime, stalked about the roasting joints, ordering this or that done and doing little herself.

I drank a cup of beer with my kindred to content them, though they would be roaring drunk presently, and I flat sober. Then I took Demizdor across to the hen-tent, where my women lay when not with me and the babies were nursed, and called Chula from her bullying.

"Here is the slave I spoke of," I said to her. Chula's eyes narrowed. "Take her in and give her tribal garb. She has some jewels under her furs, they are mine. But you may keep the silver mask for yourself, if you wish. See she wears the shireen instead."

"My husband is generous," Chula said, greedy and suspicious at once. "After that, what?"

"Whatever you like. The slave is yours; put her to work."

"Has my husband no interest in the matter?"

"None," I said, for Demizdor's benefit.

"Then why not give her to a warrior, to my father, Finnuk, perhaps, in return for his portions of meat to me when you were away?"

"I shan't waste a woman on your father," I said. "He's past his prime for that kind of dance. Don't be hasty, my loving wife. You will find her useful to take some of the load of work off your own bowed shoulders. If she's lazy, beat her, but not enough to mark her, and never let her out to catch children in her belly. In the future I may be able to trade her to my advantage, so take care."

"But I may beat her," she said smartly, "if she is disobedient."

"As you see fit."

Demizdor never opened her mouth that I knew, but I had not imagined she would. Chula came forward to her like a cat stealing up on a bird, then grabbed her by the arm and thrust her inside the hen-tent. I tried to think this funny, but the aftertaste was sour.

Ettook never visited my welcoming feast, though several

men were there who did not much like me, yet considered it expedient.

Later, I gifted Finnuk and the rest, and they took the presents, simpering like maids at a posy, though I could see they would like a city horse apiece as well. Only Urm grumbled, and said he had already had a present from me, and showed his crippled leg.

When the fire tired into crimson, the warriors rolled home. A mound of dogs lay in among the meat bones, and the sleepless city horses shifted their feet along the picket line.

Chula was in my tent. When I had tied the flap, she sprang on me like a panther, winding me with her limbs and her red hair. She went at me as if she would get three more sons in one night.

She took the edge off my appetite, but nothing else. It was another I needed under me.

Somewhere near dawn, Chula woke me. She stood in the indigo dimness of the tent, and she had put on Demizdor's dress of scales and the bodice of emeralds, which was too narrow for Chula at the waist and too large for her at the breast, and she was wearing as well the deer-mask, and her ruddy mane tangled behind. It was such a parody, I lay and stared at it without a word.

"Is this how she looked," said Chula, "when you had her?"

"Did she tell you so?"

"No need," she answered, my astute wife, Finnuk's daughter. "I have seen her naked. You could never have let her be, my lusty husband."

I thought of Demizdor in the women's tent; I thought of her too long. When Chula came creeping to me again, I did not want her.

PART III

White Lynx

1

To fall suddenly sick when you have never been ill is a hard lesson. If it teaches anything, it teaches you that you must not trust to the things you know, that it is better to build on shifting sand than the rock which may confound you on the day it shatters.

To fall sick, or to love. There is not much difference when you are unwilling, or untutored, in the fact. For near twenty years you rage about the earth, blinded in one eye, the eye of the heart. Then the eye is torn open.

I had given her to my wives, my Eshkiri slave. I had imagined they would rend her with their claws and she would run to me as her savior. I had never met pride in a woman before, not true pride, or, if I had, I had not known it.

So I fished the spring streams, and played gambling games with the warriors, or shot at a mark, tended my new horses, took my dogs and hunted, lay with Chula or Asua or with another woman or two about the krarl, and presently the tents were struck and we were on the old road of the Snake going east, and there were spears and arrows to be refurbished, and weapons to be got in trim for the season's battles. And here and there, between these activities and actions of a tribal male, I would catch glimpses of a woman in the black shift and the black shireen, walking with pots to a pool, or bent to wash linen, or at the cook-fire (she was never idle, Chula saw to that), and her hair would fold into the wind of spring like a golden wave.

The krarl had not forgotten my hero's deed as swiftly as I had supposed they would. When the first war challenge came on Snake's Road, the five of Ettook's tents I had got from the fortress crowded around me like old comrades, telling the tale again, vowing I should eat the livers of the Skoiana, who had flung the war spear. Now that I should have some fighting I thought I would work the thorn out of my hide that way. It is not conducive to ponder on a woman's thighs when you are shoulder to shoulder with a battle-wild brave and a band of his spear-brothers flying up on left and right. But the next part of my lesson was to perceive I had lost my fighting madness, lost my joy in killing, lost my hate, or most of it. It was not that I was afraid. It was that it no longer mattered to me, my strength and my youth and my valor had gone for nothing because I could not take my victories to her.

I did not realize any of this, at least, not with my brain, only in my guts and my spirits.

Still, we fought the Skoiana and the Hinga, six battles in twelve days. The last was a hunt, far off the road, with a Skoiana krarl burned at the end of it and a host of prisoners, women and herd animals bought off—there was still the feud of the broken truce between the Dagkta and the Skoi. I was away three days in all on that venture, and returned bone tired and raw with anger. There had been women in plenty and I had not wanted them, only one, and she was in the tent of my wives, that black shireen with her filigree hair.

I rode back with the braves, they half drunk and reeling in their saddles, the dismal train of captives blundering behind. Ettook had gone ahead with his older men to count his spoil on the sly. He was distressed as ever that I had missed death; he never ceased, I think, to wish for it.

But I paid all this small heed. The entire while I was remembering Demizdor, how she had thrown her dagger at me, how I had stabbed her deeper. I had made a pact with my lust, that I would have her with no regard for any effete city-female silliness. I would use her up, and be done with her. There was no other way to cut the arrowhead from my flesh.

It was the Warrior month, and well into it, the margin between spring and summer, a line no thicker than a silver wire. We came through the stockade near evening, and the krarl women ran out of their hiding places to greet us with raucous cries and screams; all tradition, and very stale it seemed to me.

The sky was deep blue, sheer blue, with not a cloud. It was a mild season after the cruel winter, smelling already of flowers from the forest that lay alongside the camp. When the warriors and their wives grew quieter, you could hear the flint-striking of the crickets in the grasses, and the central summer fire was pale as water in the flashing sunlight.

Before I set about the business in hand, I went to the rocky wood-shore where the pines grew in a tangle, and a stream ran bright as a knife. I slung down my gear and washed off the war paint in the stream, and drank there. I was exhausted but not ready to sleep, rather wound up tighter than a spring. I could think of nothing but Demizdor. How she looked, how her face had looked when last I saw it, her walk, her body, her eyes. Something of Tathra's gloomy murmuring came to me, of the goddess-women who ate a man's soul. I knew that if Demizdor resisted me I should kill her, and if she lay like ice and I could not warm her through, then a bit of my manhood would wither in that cold. It was very like a spell, a curse.

When I left the stream I was trembling, and it was not the cool of the water alone.

I rubbed myself dry on my cloak and dressed as the shadows were lengthening, turning to red-amber and purple from the fringe of the pines. If I had had a god, I should have offered to him. For the gentleness of my slave so she should spare me the rod of her scorn.

Then, like a filament of the sorcery itself, I saw a figure coming along the path the women had worn to the stream, carrying a great jar to be filled. And it was Demizdor.

I was almost afra' of her, or of the moment, or of my own self. I had no even at that instant, understood the power of the image, made worse by denial and three nights and days without it. *You have had this bitch*, I thought; *you will have her again. She's yours to take, so take her and have done.*

I leaned on a young pine by the rushing water, and let her come up.

"My wives keep you busy," I said. "That's good. A slave should not waste her time."

I put my hand on her shoulder to wheel her around to me. And she cried out, and the jar fell from her hands.

I knew at once she would never have cried so, simply at a touch. She would have been disdainful, silent, wooden, not this. This was unpremeditated, an expression of shock, or pain. Immediately everything in me was altered. I felt the change but did not recognize its principle.

"What now?" I said softly. "Has my dulcet wife been scourging you as she begged to do?" She did not speak. She stood straight and looked away from me.

Then I discovered a red wetness on my fingers that had met her body, and I took hold of her gently and drew her back and found that the shoulder of her smock was sticky. There was a lacing there; I knew it well, having had occasion to unlace a woman before. Presently I had the garment peeled open.

I had been looking at death and wounds head on for days. This was like my first sight. Her skin, cream and smooth as almond, had been ground into a pulp of blood and flesh on the point of her shoulder.

When I saw, my eyes blackened and there came a roaring white thunder in my throat.

"Who?" I said to her. Somehow, this time, I guessed she would answer.

"My mistress, the wife of my master the warrior," she said, steady as a blade.

"Chula."

Despite her immobility, her tone, she was burning hot under my hands. Her weakness cauterized mine.

"How did the sow do this to you?" I said.

"Oh, she is very just. I broke her enameled comb, your gift as I believe. So she combed my skin for me to remind me in the future to be more careful of her possessions. She said I should always have the scar. She made sure of it."

"Demizdor," I said. I had long since got her name perfect. None of the others could speak it; they called her Demya, when they bothered with a name. I held her against me, and her eyes came up to mine, wide, cloudy with fever, greener than wild grasses. She heard it in my voice; I also. It had needed this to make me see where my path had led me.

I sat her on the bank, tore my cloak and sopped up the water with it to bathe the wound. She whimpered at the cold of the water, and I saw her clench her teeth beneath the veil of the shireen not to whimper again.

"You shall go to Kotta," I said. "She will tend this better than I."

I took her up in my arms; she was lighter than when I had raised her last and she had been nothing to carry then. She had starved as well as all the rest it seemed.

She lay against me, relaxed as death, and said, "Vazkor is generous to his slave." There was still some acid in her tongue.

"Console yourself," I said. "Chula shall suffer worse than you. I will ensure that. When I have lashed her, I shall cast her off, and her brats."

"Only for correcting a slave? You are too harsh," she murmured.

We had reached the tents now, black on the westering glare. The shireens were at the central fire and turned to stare at me; the warriors, lounging over their tackle or captives, stared too.

Through the sea of sunset and firelight and staring, I carried Demizdor. She was the only reality in the world at that hour.

Later, I took Chula to Finnuk's tent.

She did not want to go.

The night had turned chill, blue-black as raven's wings with stars caught in the feathers of it. Finnuk had a fire outside, and sat there with his two sons after his meat. I pushed her to him.

"Here is your daughter," I said. "You may have her back."

At first they were all mute with astonishment, their mouths open, only the flames speaking. Then Finnuk surged up, heavy with his anger as only old men can be, for he was old to be a warrior.

"Have her back? By the snake, I do not want her back."

"Ah!" I roared. "So she was no use to your tent either?"

He floundered around a little, and the sons and their dogs growled and padded up and down, eyeing me. Chula meanwhile crouched there, crying inside her veil in loud, furious crowings. By now others had come to see, having followed our progress through the krarl.

"This is my daughter," Finnuk finally informed me.

"Own her, then," I said.

"I do. I do, by the snake. What wrong has she done? She is a good wife to the chief's son. She has borne him three healthy boys."

"She has borne me *trouble*," I said.

"How has she done so?"

"I had a slave," I said, "valuable, a city woman of great

worth I might have bartered and enriched this krarl thereby. This one, at your feet sniveling, has scarred my slave, my property." I knew very well the tack to take. He frowned and grumbled under his breath.

"If that is so, no doubt the slave was disobedient—"

"This woman, your Chula, is disobedient, and to me. I have done with her. Take her, or let the wolves have her. She is no longer anything of mine. You see, Finnuk, there are many witnesses to hear."

Chula wailed. She buried her face in the dirt and kicked her heels.

"Wait now, Tuvek Nar-Ettook," Finnuk remonstrated. "She has been stupid and you should beat her. But this is not a thing for which to cast her off. What of your sons?"

"They are no sons of mine. I renounce the sons with the dam. Maybe she has been dishonest in this, too. Am I to be her whore-master?"

He trampled around his fire, glaring, at a loss.

"There is the matter of her dowry," he said at last.

I was only too ready for this. I flung down by Chula a leather bag of gold rings, all war spoil, worth more than what he had given me with her, save for her emerald, which Tathra wore now. He was quick enough to point that out to me.

"The Eshkiri slave your slut has ruined brought me a bodice of emeralds. Finnuk may come and take his pick."

He shook his head. He did not want to let it go at this, but could see no way around. Besides, I looked and sounded angry, mad-angry, as a bull shut from the cows. I was not, in fact, as angry as that, only drunk with a host of emotions that were painfully new to me. I was cutting the cloth to fit me, and Finnuk and his daughter getting the edge of the knife.

"Tuvek Nar-Ettook," he said, "she is worthless dross. She has displeased you, and I shall improve her. I will keep her in the tent of my women for a few turns of the moon. Then you shall decide."

I shrugged.

"That is of no significance to me. Keep her and keep the gold. For I shan't want her till the moon falls."

At this, Chula raised herself. She tore at the air with her hands, and screamed, "Tuvek! Tuvek—Tuvek—"

Her eyes were wilder than any I had ever seen. They told

me something of my own injustice to her, and I did not like it. There was no room in my world for anything but one.

"I will wed the Eshkir woman before I claim this mare," I said.

And I strode off from Finnuk's fire, and once more there was silence behind me, only the crackle of the flames.

I went to Kotta's place next. She met me at the flap.

"I have come for Eshkir," I said.

"Have you, warrior?" Kotta said. "I have dressed the wound, but she has fever, your slave. If you take her to your tent and lie with her, you kill her. The city women are for the most part not strong, and she will not bear it."

"Then I will not lie with her," I said. "She shall stay here."

Kotta's eyes, seeing nothing, seeming to see everything, unnerved me.

"This is a new sickness," she said. But, as I ducked inside the tent, she added, "I am thinking Tathra has not met her son this night."

"Her husband will be with Tathra," I answered. "I will go tomorrow."

It was dull in the healer's tent, a tan smoky light. Demizdor lay on the rugs, and her head was turned from me. I saw she was unmasked; only a foam of her bright hair had washed across her face to hide it. My pulses ran so fast the tent leaped before my eyes, but I went to her quietly.

"Demizdor," I said, "when you are well, you shall come to my hearth, but you need fear nothing."

She did not look at me, but the blanket over her breasts moved more swiftly than it had before I drew near.

"Demizdor," I said, "I have taken the woman back to her father. My other two wives will not trouble you. I tell you now, when the fighting is done and we are in the summer camping, I will wed you. You shall be my first wife in Chula's stead."

Very softly she asked, "How shall I support this matchless honor?"

The adder was still under the flower, I saw. I did not reply. I lifted the swathe of blond silk from her cheeks, and turned her face gently with my hand. Her eyelids flickered as if she were sleepy; she would not look at me.

"You shall have a city mask to wear," I said. "Not the silver deer, the other has had that. I have a better one, a silver lynx with amber ornaments for the hair. And I will get you fine weave from the Moi. You will find it kinder on your skin."

"So," she murmured, "why do you bother to woo me, warrior? I am your property. You may use me at any time you wish."

Then I knew somehow—maybe from her eyes and from her talk, which was not like the cold, harsh talk I had had from her before—that she was in the same net with me.

I leaned and kissed her. For all she was ill, her mouth was cool and sweet. She caught my arms and held me to her. I had never dreamed that such a thing could make me glad.

Yet when I let her go, she turned from me and hid her face again, muttering in her own tongue, the language of the cities, which now I could not understand. Her liking for me must have been seething in her some while, fermenting against her will into the wine I had just tasted. It did not occur to me then that it could shame her to face me, shame her blood and her pride, make her doubt her reason almost, that she should hunger for one on whom her kind spit.

I went out of Kotta's tent on fire with the victory, acknowledging my fortune.

Let no man count himself fortunate till his gods brand it on his back.

2

The fighting and the raids of the Warrior month were past, and the green month that comes after was done too; it was the month of the Maiden, the marriage month, and the krarl had settled among the wild fields and orchards and the sinking white stones of the eastern summer pasture, when Demizdor came to my tent.

She had had the fever a long while, and then she had been

fragile as a leaf. So much might have told me how she feared to come to me, but I was a fool still, and finding desire in her eyes and in her touch, believed the battle won. Seeing she was sick, I left her in Kotta's charge and in her tent. Here Demizdor dwelt, communicating with no one save the healer and me. It was as well she had my protection. I knew the women of the krarl hated her for her difference and for her beauty—it was the old story of Tathra all over again. Indeed, Tathra hated Demizdor, too, and about this matter, Kotta and my mother fell out. I do not know what words were spoken or what threats offered and scorned. Certainly Kotta had no choice but to harbor the Eshkir since I had ordered it.

Presently Demizdor recovered sufficiently to ride on a mule behind the mule of Kotta as we traveled—she had journeyed in a litter before that, slung between two horses, with a canopy on a frame to hold off the sun, a conveyance usually reserved for women after childbirth if the krarl was on the move. When camp was made each night, Demizdor would sit outside Kotta's tent, daring to be idle, as no woman of the tribes would dare to be. Later, when the lamps were lit, I would visit her, for I could not keep away.

Our conversations were slight, our touches few. It was less than a crust to my starvation, and her tongue was still sharp. She chid me for a savage, she mocked me; she damned our ignorance, our lack of books or music, our treatment of our women and ourselves. I bore all this because her eyes denied it. Her eyes were now as I had seen other women's eyes. One part of me was glad at my restraint, my waiting for her health before I lay with her, for she was waiting too; this much was clear. She wanted me, for all I was shlevakin—city word for barbarian, scum. So I made her wait as she had made me wait, though almost every night my sleep was full of her. And when I was away for a dark or two on some fight or looting, I would think of her, taking no other to my bed-place with me. I had never before, since I began, been celibate so long, but I knew the feast was coming.

Chula, meantime, I left in her father's tent. I did not formally cast her off before a holy man; after the first rampaging, I had lost interest in the drama. Officially she remained my wife, but not one misunderstood that I had put her aside. Finnuk tenaciously clung to the hope that I would relent, and did not claim the emerald I offered him, though he retained the gold. I never saw her about the krarl. I think they deliberately kept her from my sight.

I have said Demizdor was my world in those months. This made me less aware of other things. Even fighting I got more wounds because of it, growing careless, though never feckless enough to let myself be killed. But I was stone-blind to Tathra. Afterward I cursed myself for my stupidity. By then the hour for cursing and for wisdom was past.

I had gone to see her the day following the Skoi raiding, when I had taken Demizdor to Kotta and thrown Chula back at Finnuk.

Tathra sat straight as a spear, but already her body was thickening, ripening with what was in it. I did not like this look, this infection on her which was of Ettook's making. Her face was hidden by the shireen, and she did not attempt to remove it. Nor did she wear Chula's emerald, which I had given her those years before. Instead she offered it to me in her hand.

"Have you come for this, Tuvek? Since you have disowned her, she had better have the jewel. It was her dowry."

"Now, Mother," I said, "I did not imagine you concerned for Chula's rights."

"If you do not come for the jewel, why come to me?" she said.

"Why, to see you," I said, "to greet you. I have been away, or did you forget?"

"I forget nothing," she said. "It is the mother's agony that she forgets nothing. I remember your birth, I remember you at my breast. I remember how you grew to be my pride. And now I am nothing to you. It is the son who forgets." Her voice was bitter, and old and dry as a husk. I knew the whims of women when they carried a child, and assumed it no more than that.

"Well, I am here. I have come to see you."

"I was here to be seen yesterday," she said. "You did not come. You went in preference to your city whore, the witch with lard-pale hair, who ensorcels you. Do you take no heed of my warnings? Am I so little to you at last?"

It was the eternal cry of mother for son. I might have recognized it and dealt differently with her, but her masked face, her wizened voice, her woman's foolishness angered me.

I had hoped myself done with this dire prognostication of evil spells.

"Don't try my patience," I said. "You know how things are between us, you and me. You know nothing of my way with the Eshkir."

"I know you will wed her."

"Thus, you know."

"Yes, and do you suppose it anything but a witching she has set on you, she a slave and you a warrior, to get you to marry her before the seer?"

"Enough of that!" I shouted. I had never met such foolishness from Tathra, nor such clammy ghost-chatterings. "You also, my mother, were an out-tribe prisoner garnered on a raid, a slave of the spear, Ettook's whore, till he took you in the fire-ring and made you wife. Did *you* witch *him*, Mother? If you did, you made a poor choice. When I am husband to my Eshkiri slave, the women will not *dare* to slander her, or the men's side to teach their sons to call her names, as all my life they have done with you. Your red pig praises you as a sow is praised, and tells how he mounts you before the whole tribe, and boasts that he ruts with others besides. Since I could walk, I have been fighting, boy and man, because I was *your* son, and he gave you no honor and therefore none to me. When Demizdor has sons by me, they shall not have to skin their knuckles to prove they are my heirs." I broke off, breathing fast, having said too much, and cognizant of it.

She sat there, still straight, still masked. She said, very quietly, "You have punished me enough by ceasing to love me. You do not need to punish me with words as well."

I was ashamed. The shame did not couple easily with the mood of gladness and victory I had had before. Of everything, it was hardest for me to forgive her that.

"I am sorry," I said. I was stiff and ungenerous; even I could hear it. "We will say no more of this."

"Too much has been said," she answered. I expected her to cry, as once before. Then she had not, and she did not now. If she had wept I would have gone to her. She did not weep, and I did not go.

"There is a hunt at dawn," I said. "I will bring you something."

She thanked me and I left her.

After that inauspicious meeting, she was bland and almost

dumb with me, which got me into a similar habit. I began to think back over the earlier times when she had been odd and difficult. I started to despise her, as I despised the other women who claimed me without my wanting their claim. Yet I did not truly understand that I despised her. She saw it better than I. I spent less hours with her than ever, more with my girl in Kotta's tent. It no longer bothered me that Tathra kept on her shireen in my presence. I barely noticed. It was Demizdor's face I hankered to see.

So my mother sat alone, swelling with Ettook's seed, the fear which had once shown naked in her eyes now sunk to some cellar of her brain. Kotta brought her the medicines and haughtily she would drink them, without a word. Even her husband did not come to lie with her. He did not want her anymore. If she could give him another boy, then her security would spring up like a blossom, but if a girl or a sickly male, there would be nothing for her. Perhaps she saw her own self mirrored in Chula's fate, and Tathra had no parent to take her in, no friend. As for me, the ties were rent.

In those months of my triumph and my hunger and my fierce anticipation, the shadows must have gathered thicker than Sihharn Night for my mother Tathra.

I married Demizdor in the tribal fashion, in the ring of fire, before Seel. He did not want, but I coerced him. I felt my pride that year, and knew what I could make of it. He rolled his eyes and sputtered his sentences through snarling mouth, but wed us he did.

I made sure it was not like other weddings. I presented many gifts, and much meat I had slaughtered myself, and a cask of strong crimson drink I had carried off and kept from the raid on the city palace-fort. I gave Ettook one of my city-man's horses, too, and he grinned uneasily. Two or three of the mares seemed likely to foal, so it was no great loss to me.

Demizdor I instructed to wear the silver lynx-mask, with its amber flower-heads turned almost red in her topaz hair. The Moi had come by with their eternal barter, and I had got cloth from them, a fine white linen striped through with lines of green and bronze. Moka, selecting the cloth, gabbled to them of Demizdor, proud of the attributes of my new bride as she would have been of a new bronze caldron. Moka was content with what she had, a share of a man, children and hearth and home. Demizdor was a spoil of war, something to increase my prosperity and status. To Moka, maybe, Demizdor was not even human, just another rich possession to grace the tent.

Demizdor's arms were bright with bracelets of bronze and silver and her neck with rings of gold. She walked like a chief's daughter into the circle of fire to me. But behind the open eye-holes of the mask, her green eyes glittered with contempt. And then again, when I took her hand it trembled, and her breast rose and fell inside the moth-wing cloth as if she had been running. She knew well enough what was coming to her.

I was glad I had made her wait, given her the space to burn a little, as I had burned.

The wedding feast is for the men's side, about the central krarl fire. Long before it is finished, the bride goes to the tent and soon the groom gets up to follow.

The jumping firelight, the shouts and toasts and passing cups, had been a meaningless interlude between the departure of my woman and my going in to her. When I rose, the night seemed to gather around me, my head sang, and there was only one road on the whole earth, that which would lead me to her.

The tent lines were dark and empty save for the occasional red glow of a brazier, or a scurrying woman late about her chores. Only Kotta's tent showed a light outisde, and she was sitting there by her lamp. When I passed, without hesitation, the blind woman called to me.

"Tuvek, before you go where you are going, it is best you learn something."

I laughed, I was a little drunk—with sex rather than wine.

"Do you think I don't know my task?"

"I think you know it well enough," she said. "It is another thing you do not know."

"What, then? Come, Kotta, I have waited some days for this. A night has only so many hours, and I don't want to waste them here."

She got up and drew near me.

"In my tent," she said, "the Eshkir spoke to me somewhat, as women will speak to women at a need. Her folk were noble, warrior men and consorts of their kings. She was bedmate to one of the gold-masks who fell on their blades in the fortress: a prince. She counted that honorable, and you took her from it."

"That is the past," I said. "The future is now."

"Maybe. The bird in her breast beats its wings for you, yet her brain rebukes her. I have many essences in my place, liquors and banes. There is a little stone jar in the chest; a drop or two out of it is good for the old men's pain in the limbs, but more than a drop or two and the heart stops. Your Eshkir has questioned me about these things and, since she is to be the wife of the chief's son, I have answered her."

The dark had grown sharp edged, and the wine sour in my throat.

"Well, Kotta?"

"The stone jar has gone with your bride," said Kotta. "She took it. She understands Kotta is blind, and reckoned Kotta would not observe what she was at. But Kotta has her own way of seeing."

I stood still, made idiotic by her news. A white surge came and went across my eyes.

"So she will poison me," I said. "It is she who shall die."

"The stream runs deeper than you think," said Kotta. "I have warned you so you can be wary, but try her before you act."

I was already striding away up the path.

My blood beat like a drum in my head. A million strategies came and went like pigeons flying around in my skull. About six paces from my tent, it came to me how I should find her, that she would change even murder with her looks. And then I knew my scheme as if I had been planning it a month.

I opened the flap of the tent.

The light was soft within. Her hair and her flesh seemed woven from the light. She was masked—it was for me to unmask her on this marriage night—but she had removed her robe, and waited there for me, lying on her elbow, clothed in her body with no need for more. It was a city pose, a courtesan's pose for a prince to come in and find. It showed all, yet made it secret, a mystery. The shadows ran and draped between her thighs; the dip of her waist, accentuated by her stance, was girdled with silver from the lamp. Her hair hid her breasts and did not hide them; as she breathed, the glis-

tening strands parted like plants beneath the sea. In her other
hand, curved back to rest upon her hip, she balanced the silver cup, the bride-drink she must offer me, symbol of herself.

"You see, warrior," she said, "I have obeyed your customs."

If I had walked in there, tipsy with desire, perhaps I should
not have questioned it. Yet now I recognized it was too sac-
charine a fruit, the web too certain to catch me.

My knife rested against my side. _Now we shall see_, I
thought, my lust gone to black night in me. But I went to
her, hot-eyed and eager as she had meant me to.

I did not swallow anything of what was in the cup, but
made believe I took some. It had a strange smell, very faint. I
should never have noticed it if I had had no warning.

"Your city wine is bitter," I said to her. "I have never
found it so before."

Her eyes in the mask were steady. She had schooled herself
for just such a scene.

"Then drink no more," she said.

"And waste good liquor?" I pretended again to quaff it
down. Then I reached and drew the mask from her face.

She was very white, that she could not conceal, and her
mouth flinched. Her eyes had become wide, expectant.

"Demizdor—" I said, as if something had surprised me.
Then I let the cup fall, so the doctored wine ran out onto the
rugs.

She drew herself into a knot and shrank from me.

I had watched men die enough times to be able to mime it.
If she had been calmer, she would have recalled that the
hearts of dead men do not pound as mine was doing, that
you can see a man breathe, however shallowly. Yet she was
so certain she had killed me, she looked for nothing else.

I gazed at her beneath my lids, wondering with a crawling
cold what she would do now, and my hand lay dead but
ready, next to my knife.

She did not move at first. When she did, the light disturbed
a flash of white on her cheeks. She was weeping; I had never
witnessed her tears before, even when her lover slew himself,
even when I took her as a slave, or Chula raked her with the
comb.

Shd came creeping to me, slowly, on her knees.

Women had told me, once or twice, my lashes were thicker

than a girl's. Certainly the thickness did me a service then, for I could watch Demizdor through them with no great effort, and she not guessing it.

She began to speak in her own tongue, yet my name was mingled in it. She rocked herself to and fro, as the shireens did above their dead men, the lamp catching her, so beautiful that another part of me would have betrayed to her presently that life still lingered in the corpse. But suddenly she leaned and snatched my knife, too quick for me to stop her.

For a moment I supposed she had reasoned out my deceit, and meant to kill me again and be sure of it. But in a splinter of a second so brief that I had barely come up with myself, I saw the direction the knife was going.

I moved at that. She did not anticipate it, assuming me dead. I seized the knife and threw it away, and pulled her down and turned her so she was under me.

"What's this?" I said, my voice hoarse as if I were half-dead indeed. "Kill me, then die with me? That would be a fine marriage night."

She did not seem afraid, more stunned, as she had some cause to be.

"Someone warned me," I said. "It was make believe. I am not poisoned. If you wished me slain, why weep for me?"

She was still crying. The tears ran down into her hair.

"I have been twenty nights nerving myself to it," she choked out. "I cannot live with you. But when it was done—"

"You did not cry or die for your man in the fortress," I said.

She shut her eyes. She did not need to tell me. For all her murdering, she loved me, and for all my anger I could not kill her, having stopped her own arm at the work.

I touched her as she lay beneath me, the curves and hollows of her gliding flesh. Her eyes tightened, and her hands fastened on me of their own volition.

"You can live with me," I said. "You will see."

I never feared her treachery after. It could have been all too simple for her to finish me in the nights that followed, when desire was slaked or when I slept. Yet she did not, and I knew she would not. There is one sound way a man can bind a woman to him, the same way she will bind him, and with the same rope. That hour I had the proof of her liking. I thought the feuding was done forever.

So Demizdor became my wife, though never like a wife of the krarls. It was Asua and Moka who waited on me, who saw to the duties of the tent, the food, the washing and mending. Demizdor did not even carry the jars to the waterfall. Demizdor lived as a brave lives, scorning the women's tasks, going with me to fish, riding with me to hunt, for she had ridden with her gold-mask on his wars, though never fought in them; so the city women were, it seemed, half man if not warrior. When the krarl saw her mount the black horse I had given her, their eyes expanded and they muttered. *Choke it down*, I thought. *Though the meat is gristly, there are tougher joints to come.* I gave her saddle gear of scarlet and the bridle had tassels of white silk. She wore a man's breeches too, to ride. That caused a stir. She could cast a straight spear at a need, but generally was content to watch me.

I taught her the bone games of the Dagkta; she taught me stranger ones with bits of stone for the pieces, a thing called Castles, which you must play hating and cool to get it right. She marveled elaborately when I learned it straight off, calling me a clever savage. They had some art for the bed also; neither was I a slow pupil at that, nor did she mock me then.

I think she was happy enough at this time, shutting her ears to the inner voice that stung her. I took her through the old white summer towns with their roofs of broken pink tile, and in the mossy courts we would couple like lions, and later she would tie my hair into the grasses and laugh at me, but she loved me then.

I hoped I should get her with child that summer. It was the first child I had ever wanted. It would have been like a pledge between us, another link in the chain that bound our lives. I see from this that even then I felt the shadow brush me.

She told me something of her life among the city clans, though it was a wild, weird tale, and she was reticent, as if the memory frightened her. A prince of the high class of the gold had fathered her on his mistress. Demizdor had the rank of the silver, which was mighty but not mightiest. She had experienced no passion for her lover, a man twelve years her senior, whom she was given to, according to the ways of form and etiquette; yet he was a god to her, so she had been trained to see him. When the wounded silver-mask crawled into the pavilion with his news of Vazkor's rising, her lover had sent her out. The faces of the princes before they masked them were strange, already deathly. It was as if a plague had entered the fortress. She knew what they intended, but her rank precluded entreaty or even questions. She did not comprehend but she must comply. She stood behind the brocades, listening to the silence of their suicide. It was like the ending of a world to her. The dagger she had thrown at me, she had taken up for herself. Of the legend who caused all this—Vazkor—she knew little, only that they feared his name even now. He had overthrown a dynasty and begun the ruin of the land. The ancient order crumbled before the tramp of his armies, and he had raised a witch-goddess from her grave to aid him. These garbled accounts were all she possessed, for the people of the cities did not boast of Vazkor the magician, and he had been dead for twenty years or more.

Certain of their customs she retained. She would not eat in my presence, but at the back of the tent behind a curtain, as if such a thing were disgusting or forbidden. I questioned this only once. She looked away, and answered that centureis before her folk had been supernatural, having no need for food, and that they were ashamed to have grown mortal. I consoled her with mortal pleasure, and we did not speak of it again.

We had two months, a little less.

The shapes of the year, the seasons, moved about us, changing their tempo and their forms. The mild summer burned gently into the tinder of autumn. The fruits were harvested, the haphazard grain, the leaves were yellowing, everything drawing to its close.

One night I woke to hear her crying softly. We had some hunting in the woods, and slept beside the fire, the dogs near us. I took her in my arms, and asked her why she wept, but she would not answer, and that was answer enough. She had taught me also tenderness, with her at least. It did not irk me anymore that her pride wounded her because of me, but then I did not properly understand it. I thought it should pass, that all would be well.

So I held her, and I spoke to her of how I had found the statue in the trees, that fall of leaf when I was fifteen years, the marble maiden of the grove on her plinth above the spring.

Demizdor lay still in my arms, listening. Somewhere an owl called, sailing the moonlight on his broad wings. Sparks burst purple and golden in the fire, and the dogs twitched dreaming tails through the warm ashes.

"One day you will regret me," she said. On her shoulder the scar of Chula's spite was growing dim, like a pale, dark flower. She filled her hands with my hair and kissed my throat. "You are not of the tribes," she murmured. "You are a prince of the Dark City, of Ezlann, Uastis' citadel."

As I drew her down, I saw the lynx-mask glint at me acorss the fire where she had left it, like a face watching with black hollow eyes. And, for a moment, those eyes seemed filled by life before the fire sank again among the wood.

3

Moka bore me a daughter in the month of Yellow-leaf. She looked guilty when I came in (it had always been boys before), but I was lighthearted and reassured her. I gave her a garnet to hang on the baby's basket, for they were reckoned lucky stones, strengthening to the blood.

Three evenings after this, Tathra's child began to move, some forty days too soon.

There had been one of the little Dagkta tribal councils to talk over this right or that. Generally the warriors met about this time, before Sihharn and the preparations for turning west along Snake's Road. Ettook went and so did I. We were gone two days. When we came back it was to find Tathra already in labor.

A boy brought Ettook the tidings. Ettook showed his teeth and made a great joke of it, saying his son was impatient to get out and be a warrior. He had a gibe for me as well, how I had better leave off riding my yellow-haired man-woman, and remember my brave's war skills or the babe should best me even from his cradle.

As for me, my vitals churned. I had kept sufficient of a reckoning to know it was too early, and now it all came home to me, how I had been with Tathra, how I had neglected her. I recollected she had said, "You have punished me enough by ceasing to love me." I might have shrunk down into a child again. Suddenly I could see her in my mind's eye, her beauty and its loss, her wretched life, that she had needed me and I had found another. The mother is the boy's first woman. And no man had ever valued her but me.

It was the mid of the afternoon, warm and lazy, only bees and crickets buzzing in the grass. I went to Kotta's tent. As a rule the warriors kept away at such a season. A decrepit grandmother or two hovered near, crackling in their old woman's voices. Their teeth were black, their sour hair gray. They played with beads in their fingers and said it was a long while to be waiting, and mentioned gore and pain. Then they noticed me and tutted, drawing aside.

As I came up to the flap, an animal screamed inside the tent.

The blood ran out of my heart. I gripped the flap in my fingers and stood rooted there.

The old women nodded approvingly.

One said, "Listen, warrior. That is how you came."

And Tathra screamed again, and the old women chuckled, and congratulated each other on their predictions of a hard, prolonged travail.

Close to the flap, I heard her pleading now, pleading to her gods, pleading with the pain to let her be. The sweat broke out all over me. I thrust open the flap and was in Kotta's tent.

The old women shrilled with outrage and interest. Inside it was red-dark from the burning brazier, and stank of blood and terror. Then Kotta came between me and the light.

"No, warrior," she said. "This is no hour for you. Men sow and women bear. That is how it is."

"Let me by," I said.

And from the rugs behind her, Tathra called frantically, with her voice broken up by panting and hurt, "Tuvek—go out. Don't stay to see my shame. You must not—stay—" Then she caught her breath and tried not to cry aloud.

I put Kotta aside and kneeled down where my mother lay. Her eyes were sunken but starting from her face and mois-

ture streamed into her hair and a frenzied whining came
from her throat. When she saw me so near, she tried to beat
me away. I caught her wrists.

"Scream," I said. "Let the krarl hear you, and be damned
to them. You are bearing another son, one who will treat you
better than I. Come, tear my hands if you want. Let me feel
your pain."

She fell back gasping.

"No," she said. "You must go."

But the vise seized her again. She drove her nails into my
hands and shrieked.

"Good," I said. "It will be easier soon." But she shut her
eyes and scarcely breathed. Kotta was bending near.

"How long?" I asked her.

"Too long," she said, having forgone dissuading me. "A
night and this day already. It is like the last." But next she
said quietly, "I cannot turn the child. It may die."

"Let the thing die. Save Tathra."

"Hold her, then," Kotta said, "if you are for helping her."

Accordingly, for an hour I held my mother, and Kotta
aided Ettook's son into this world. For it was a son. There was
hair on its head, red hair as his had been, and it was dead.

Tathra lay in my arms as Demizdor had lain not so many
nights before.

"Is it well?" she whispered.

"It is," said Kotta. "You have borne a warrior."

I wondered why she should lie, but Tathra's unmasked face
was showing me. Shrunken and colorless, it had acquired a
silent inward look, as if she had begun listening to some
music in her brain. The look gradually settled on her like a
snow, like dust. It was the look of death.

Kotta meanwhile moved about us, doing what she could.
The blood fled from my mother as if it would be free of her.
We wrapped her in blankets but she was cold. The coals of
the brazier reflected in her open eyes, which presently ceased
to blink, and thus I knew she had died.

I could not even tell in the end if she realized who held
her. Since her remonstrance she had spoken no further word
to me, not even my name.

I felt only emptiness. I thought, *Long ago I came from this
agony, into this tent. Now I have let her go back through the
same gate.*

It is hard or impossible for a warrior to weep; the ease of it is never taught him, rather he must consider it a failing, a weakness. Therefore I could not, through my body was racked. There was no release for me, no purging of my anguish in grief.

At length I laid her down, and went to stare at the child. That pulpy small mess of life with its badge of Ettook's siring.

Kotta came to me with a wooden cup.

"Drink," she said, but I put the cup from me. "You must leave," she said. "There are things to be done here."

"That object is not like me," I said of the dead baby. I scarcely knew what I said.

"Tuvek," Kotta said, "go out now. Go to your woman."

"It was his seed that killed her," I said, "his *red* seed."

Kotta contemplated me with her blind eyes. She took up a salve and applied it to my hands where Tathra had torn me. I let her do this as if I were an infant.

"On the night of your birth," Kotta said, "the Eshkiri woman gave her hands to Tathra and Tathra bit and clawed them. The Eshkir was young, and she was not as other women are. Her hair and her skin were white, and her eyes like white jewels. She carried also, but she was small. I did not guess she would bear so soon, but she bore, here in this tent, at sunrise, when I was off among the warriors to tend their wounds after the battle. She did not leave much trace of it, but Kotta is a healer, Kotta knew. When I returned, the Eshkir and her baby were gone."

I took a dreary interest in her tale, but she had pushed me to the door flap.

"Go," she said, "Return at sunset. There are words that must be said. I have promised Ettook's wife, before you came, to say them."

Abruptly I was outside. The daylight seemed too strong, and I did not see who might be lingering there; it was like trying to gaze through milk. I did not seek my tent or Demizdor. I walked away across the hill, past where the white stones ran, under the face of the low-burning autumn sun.

I came back at sunset, not because of any interest or reasoning in me, but because it was some road to take, some destination to achieve.

It was the night before Sihharn, and the watch-fires were being built through all the krarls across all the green-brown slopes in the dusk. But from Ettook's tenting there came a dismal low ululation, the noise the shireens made at the death of a chief's woman. I thought how they wailed, and how they must be smiling as they did it. Seel's daughter, who would lead the chant for Tathra at moonrise, would barely keep from laughing as she tossed the autumn flowers on my mother's body.

I did not want to meet any of them, Ettook least of all. I climbed in, therefore, like a thief over the stockade, avoiding the central cook-fire, and reached Kotta's tent in the first thick shadows of night.

I called her name, and she replied immediately, bidding me enter.

The tent was much changed, different rugs on the ground, the brazier bright with fire, and the lamp burning, which Kotta lighted for others, not needing it herself. I glanced everywhere before I could stop myself, searching for my mother, but she had been taken to her own place.

"Sit, warrior," Kotta said.

Having no more tempting pastime, I sat and waited.

"What I am to tell you," Kotta said, "Tathra, the wife of Ettook, has charged me to say. Kotta has known these things some while, Tathra, too, in the dark of her heart. Now. Shall Kotta speak straight out to the warrior, or would he rather .c went slowly to the matter?"

"What matter? Speak as you wish," I said.

Kotta said, "Tathra was not your mother, Ettook not your father, the krarl of blue tents not your krarl, the Dagkta not your people."

It was like a sword-flash in my brain; my lethargy ran away. I stared at her and said, too surprised to feel it yet, "Is this some riddle you are making?"

"No riddle. Do you remember I spoke of the Eshkir, the white-haired, white-eyed woman who was brought as a slave into the camp, and fled when her child was born?"

"I remember it."

"Tathra also bore that dawn, a male, but it was sickly. I could gauge from my craft it would be dead within the day. When I left the warriors and came in the tent again, I found this: Tathra sleeping, the Eshkiri woman gone, and in the birth basket a child, as strong and sound as bronze." Kotta leaned toward me. The brazier shone in her veiled face. Her hair was bound in a blue and scarlet cloth, and her sightless eyes, catching the glow, gleamed dully the same blue, the same scarlet from the flames. "Kotta is blind," she said, "but Kotta sees, in her own fashion. The child in the basket might pass for Tathra's child. A son, and healthy; it would bring her honor. But it was not Tathra's child. Her boy was gone; the Eshkir took it. I think it died when I was from the tent. The Eshkir left her living baby and stole the dead; it was her gift to Tathra, the fruit of her own womb, which she did not want. You are that fruit. The Eshkir was your mother. Any might see it now. You have her beauty in you, and the man's beauty of your father, too, that your mother loved and hated and slew."

I began to feel as if I would strangle. My brain was alive with pictures and half-formed words, and my hands shook, but not from weakness.

"If I am to swallow this, then give me the bitch's name, this wild cat who sloughed me, and left me behind like excrement."

"She gave no name to me," Kotta said, "but something of her past I heard two nights before she bore you. Her living had been a rare jumble, not as a woman lives among the tribes; a maze of death and battles and men she had companioned—she had lived several lives in one, it seemed to Kotta, as the snake wears and shed several skins. And in the cities of the mask-faces she had been worshiped as a goddess. The man that got you on her was a king."

"So she would say, no doubt," I answered sharply. "Goddess bedded with king. Yet she was not a gold-mask—the lynx is silver. More probably she was some captain's doxy and he cast her off."

"No. She was no man's doxy. For all she walked bowed among the tents, for all the woman's burden in her womb, she was unlike any women you have seen. Think of the Eshkir you have put by your hearth. She has surprised you. But your mother was to her as the moon to the star. And your father was not a red chieftain but a black-haired lord, master of cities. You have your darkness from him."

"This is very fine," I said. "Why spill the beer now?"

"The one whom it served to keep silent has died. Though,

indeed, Tathra knew her changeling almost from the beginning. Do you not recall how she altered to you when you took the lynx-mask from Ettook's spoil chest? The mask your city wife wears, which was *her* mask who was your mother."

I put my hand to my face to wipe the cold sweat from it.

Kotta said, "That summer we were late traveling, near two months late to reach the Snake's Road, for there was great fighting over the mountains, the beginning of the wars that toppled the cities down, and now and then the braves would go looting ruins. Presently Seel learned of a fallen tower, the tower of an Eshkiri fort to the west, where it was said a king had died with his treasure around him. The warriors rode there, but came back with only one thing, the white-haired woman, your mother. They said she was a witch, or had claimed to be, but they did not believe it in truth, nor did she prove cunning in that way. Ettook let Tathra have her as her slave, and so she journeyed with us till that dawn she ran away, into the wild lands. I think no one ever saw her face but Kotta, and Kotta is blind."

"This king, then," I said, "do you have a name for *him*?"

"Yes. She named him. She was wife to him, yet she had slain him, for he was cold and cruel, and she thought him a sorcerer."

"So do jealous bitches ever," I said. "It is the sum of myth and story. Still I do not have his name, this miraculous father you gift me with."

The name she gave me then seemed to come up from the coals of the fire and set the tent alight. I had not looked for such a thing, and while I had not, I had kept her words at bay, holding them from me. Having his name, my father, it cracked me wide, and let in all the rest like white-hot water.

For she told me I was the son of Vazkor.

4

My life was altered in a moment.

I remembered everything, each of the portents, the signposts that had been there for me, I, who was so unlike the tribes, different in all things, an outcast in the midst of my folk.

I thought of my boyhood dream—the white lynx mating with the black wolf, of the lynx-mask I had chosen, and the shock that had numbed my arm when I set hand to it. There had hung her frigid witch-spell on it still, that cat-goddess, Uastis, who wanted none of me.

I thought of my father, what he had been—the red pig, gross, stupid, snorting at his pleasure, my enemy from a child—and of my father as I found him—noble, a king, my own image painted on the history of all the land. I was back on the fortress rock where I had taken Demizdor. Who but my magician father had risen in me then, given me a portion of his Power, the ability to speak the city tongue as he had spoken it? The masked men had fallen on their knees, seeing his face in mine, hearing his voice in my voice. I remembered, too, the dream I had had before, the knives in the icy water, and the blindness, and waking to say aloud, "I will kill her."

She had betrayed him, my *mother*, so much was clear; betrayed and murdered him, and next been rid of me because I was his seed. It was a wonder she had deigned to let me live at all.

Suddenly the female noise outside the tent rose to an abnormal gray keening. The moon was up, and the women were going to Tathra's dead-couch to make the chant.

And between me and the vision of the dark glory there came the omen of her sunken lifeless face.

Tathra was yet my mother. Though not my flesh, though I had not been shaped in her body, still it was so. Her breasts

103

had fed me, her arms rocked me before ever I knew it. The other, though she had carried me and given me my life, was less mother to me than the beast who eats her young.

I got to my feet and the tent seemed to have shrunk about me; I felt taller than the roof of it.

"Kotta," I said, "I am done with this place. I thank you for opening the cage."

She said nothing, and I went out into the night.

It was the amber moon that follows the ripeness of the year, and the sky was smalt blue about it, veiled at its horizons by the smoke of many hundred krarl fires. I stood on the somber earth, and I sensed him go from me, the man I had been, the warrior, the chief's son, Tuvek Nar-Ettook. Even my bones and flesh seemed changing, and my brain rang.

I turned and walked toward the painted tent of Ettook. I, Vazkor's son.

He was sitting among his elder warriors, and Seel was there in a corner, his eyes like spikes.

Ettook was mourning in his own way, not the death of his wife, but the death of his redheaded son.

"She was too old," he said. "I was too amenable. I should have had done with the mare long since and taken a younger one who would not lose me sons. He was a fine boy, well made, but she killed him. They have little enough to do, these animals of women. Can they not even give us our sons alive?"

This putrid nonsense was volleying out of him like foul air as I opened the flap. When he saw me, he jumped, in the usual manner; then he analyzed me more closely, and he grew very nervous.

"Come, Tuvek," he said. "Share the lose with me. She was a good wife for all that. She shall have a bangle or two to take with her into the earth. A good wife."

The light of the lamps flickered over his face and over the yellow patterns on the blue walls.

I said, "Stand up, you bloody hog, and get on your feet. If you cannot live as a man, you shall at least die as one."

The warriors sprang up instead, cursing. But they were like dogs without a master. My mind went back to how I had bested grown men when I was fourteen years, and I smiled.

Ettook sat quite motionless.

"What is this?" he said stupidly, sweating, knowing too well.

I had meant to knife him, to fight him and knife him if he rose to fight. Then I would cut down any others who came at me. I never dreamed I could not do it.

But, looking at him as he cringed there, showing his dirty teeth, his dirty mouth still sweet from his praise of Tathra, I knew there was another, better way to kill him.

I felt it come, like a slow wave, through my brain.

It was his, my father Vazkor's, skill. He was guiding me as on the fortress rock.

I could kill a man by wanting him dead.

There was a pain in my skull, a splitting, slender, golden pain. And then a pale blotting of light over the painted tent.

The yellow patterns danced and united, the lamps guttered and smoked.

Ettook lunged from his cushions, impaled on a sword of slim lightning, screaming louder even than Tathra had screamed dying of his cockerel's work. I let him sample it to the full.

Then, with no warning, the vital force in me became too great. I could not hold it. I felt my brain seared and bulging, and the arteries of my body were alive with molten heat. I was a man who had devoured fire, and was now devoured by fire from within. Everything seethed in light and vanished in it.

And the light folded into blackness like the turning of a page.

There were no dreams in that blackness, and no guide.

I swam up from the pitchy river to discover myself lying on my back, and over my face a broad sultry sky was swirling.

Not recognizing where I could be, only partially recalling the sequence that had gone before, I tried to raise myself. At once I was capsized by strengthlessness and nausea. Dragging myself over onto my side, I brought up everything that might have been in my belly and, so it seemed, half my guts into the bargain.

This done, I fell back wishing for death.

I ached and hurt as if I had tumbled to the bottom of a

cliff and yet survived it. While I was unconscious, plainly someone had been paying me court with his feet; I had been pulled over the ground to this open place and left all night, tied only by my legs and a long halter at my neck to a thing of wood I could not properly make out. There were besides a host of amulets, little beads and pierced bits of metal knotted into the cords that bound me. And on my breast the leather was ripped open, and the one-eyed snake was daubed there in charcoal.

Then I remembered, and fathomed, too, what they were at. And I recollected also Demizdor.

I was stirring in earnest now, and abruptly a bunch of warriors came around me, and gathered where I could watch them. There were about fifteen of them. They seemed afraid and working to hide it, joking and poking at me with their spear-butts. One spit on me. I had no powers of any kind to answer him; he saw as much and spit again, into my eyes.

The other thing, which had put me here, was like a fever I had had. I could not get it straight in my mind—Kotta's tale, the name of Vazkor, the unleashing of energy. Still, I had come to realize I had slain the chief of the krarl and, from the amulets, that they considered me a magician and strove to protect themselves. No doubt imagining these symbols kept me tame, they began shortly to invent new sports. I was suffering this helplessness on the ground, trying sometimes to lurch aside from the tether and the bindings and the wooden pole, and come at them—though it was useless—when, unexpectedly, the warriors left off their play.

I rolled sideways, and looked. I lay on the hillside above the krarl. I could make out the smoke below from the big cook-fire, now that I had leisure, and the length of the shadows told me it was late in the day. Up along the spine of the hill was coming Seel the seer in his robe of beast-tails and teeth. The wind twitched the tails and clinked the bronze lozenges together. I could not see his face against the vinegar light, but I could guess.

He drew near and stood over me, jabbering softly, and fingering his black-painted jaw.

Certainly he would have avowed that it was spells that had overthrown me in Ettook's tent, those spells which subdued me now; but, like the warriors, he meant to be sure. He leaned down, made some ritualistic pass at my forehead, then darted back, quick as a lizard.

I could do nothing. I was weaker than a sick puppy, and he took note of it.

He clutched the snake symbol on his breast and chattered his fangs at the warriors, telling them to hoist me up and bring me into the krarl again. I suppose they had tethered me for the night on the slope, to keep themselves a safe distance from violent magic.

I was hauled down the hill as they had got me up it. It was no easy journey; the clouds wheeled and the hard ground stabbed, dropped, and slammed the breath from me. Someone had cracked my ribs for me, and presently I managed the girl's trick and fainted. I returned into myself among the crowding tents and the tall stacks of the unlighted fires of Sihharn Night.

They judged me by tribal rule.

In Ettook's stead, Seel presided, and there were very many who spoke against me. In fact, for every enemy I had in the krarl there was found an orator standing in his garments.

As I had always recognized, they had only been waiting for the chance to take me. I had built my own pyre and, for good measure, climbed onto it.

I lay on my back, clenching my teeth and swallowing down my vomit, listening, and catching glimpses of fire and men, with Seel's stink always in my nostrils.

Even Chula slunk by, and whispered to Seel-Na, who in turn whispered to her father. I had been practicing sorcery some while, it seemed, and this was why I had turned Finnuk's daughter from my tent, preferring one of the witch-bred city women. How else indeed could I have overcome the mask-faces in their fort, save by oblique conjurings? The tribes knew well that city raiders were not to be beaten by men, being magicians themselves. Thus even my hero-deed was used against me.

I surmised they would punish me soon and had decided on the way of it, having the clue of the wooden tethering pole. It was a measure of my state that I had no fight left, and scarcely cared what they did. Yet Demizdor had furnished the real horror in my confused thoughts, and their accusations drove me into a turmoil of uncontrollable struggling, at which they were much amused. They would doubtless kill her, too, but kill her by the immemorial practice of men with women, raping the life out of her, and they would hang me upside down from the pole to watch, until my brain burst.

It was already twilight, the sun fallen—I had missed its going, a pity, since it was the last sunfall I should see. Now it was Sihharn Night, when the undead went hunting. The men's side should be mounting the ghost-guard, the watch-fires and torches be lighted, but nothing was done. I wondered that they had not thought it unlucky to leave this business off for mine but, like all their customs, even the darker ones were shallow cups.

I had no gods to pray to. I felt the lack of them then.

I had begun thinking of Tathra, too, my mother—I could not call her otherwise—whose body they would have thrown into the cavity of earth, for there was no bright burial of flame for the women, and that done while I lay on the hill.

Gradually, all of it became a great chaos of lights and sounds to me, my mother's corpse and Demizdor's imagined spread-eagled body, the actual fire gusts and the black sky, the yells and bawlings of the krarl. And into this dream came riding the ghosts of Sihharn Night, because no man had kept watch for them.

Of everything, they were the most clear. Black as the Black Place they came from, mounted on horses black as themselves or white as bone, and their faces silver skulls from which the pale hair still grew. I recall I knew myself dreaming at this point, never having credited this legend of Sihharn's undead, and I jerked myself awake. And saw them still.

The krarl was seeing them also.

The clamor had died on the wind, just the sinking fire spattering now, the striking of shod hooves on the ground as the riders came between the tents, and the faint jingle of bells from their bridles.

Like figures in a tapestry, the braves and their women kept motionless. Only those nearest to where the skull-heads passed drew aside, walking backward as if half asleep. Somewhere, about a mile off over the hill, the dogs of a neighboring camp had set up a howling. It was in another world, that noise.

Near me, Seel breathed raucously through his mouth, and out of his stench came the sharp new stench of his urine,

spilled from him in terror. I could have laughed at that, if I
had had the health for it. I had already grasped who the
riders were, and where they hailed from. Not the pit, but
Eshkir. Their black was tawdry, and the skulls were masks.

The foremost of the horsemen held up his black gauntleted
hand, and halted the column. Then he spoke, in the language
of the tribes but arrogantly, as if it soiled his mouth to use it.

"You have one fettered there, on the ground, the black-
haired. You will give him to us."

It was not a request, nor even a demand. It was an as-
sumption. The krarl merely rustled and quivered, and Seel's
body clattered, his teeth and the teeth of his robe rattling
with his fright.

"You have also a gentlelady of Eshkorek among your
tents. You will bring her. If she has been harmed, your krarl
shall be burned. If she is dead, we shall kill your women and
your children."

The horseman's voice was like dry silver. I wanted to answer him.

Before I could form a sentence or get it to my lips, the
wooden pole was heaved suddenly upright.

Sky ran together with land. I slid the length of the wood
before the thongs bit and held me, and it was as though a
tower crashed downward into my head.

The sky raced, and then the sky was still. I had been
stitched into a sack of pain. When I breathed, a knife between my ribs gored at my life's blood.

"For all his spear-brothers' kind attentions, he will live till
Eshkorek," one said.

"That is his misfortune," another answered, and laughed
gently. "See, Demizdor."

And, against the sky that just then was still, I discovered
the face of a silver deer with eyes of green glass, and behind,
a fall of hair like golden frost.

"Yes," she said, "I see him." Her tone was not as I recollected.

"He shall sing a new song in Eshkorek," the man said.

"He shall die there," she said.

There was blood in my mouth and I could not have spoken, even if I had had words. But I had no words, for they

were speaking in the city tongue, and somehow I could follow but not use it.

Then she leaned near, the deer-faced woman who was no longer quite Demizdor, and she raked my face with the nails of her hand.

"Be happy, oh *king*," she whispered. "You shall have a sweet welcome in Eshkorek Arnor."

Book Two

PART I

Yellow City

1

Demizdor had warrior kin among the Eshkiri; she had never told me of them, and I had never considered it. Her former life had seemed to die from her when she entered mine. That was my blindness, as well as hers, for which both of us would pay, and heavily.

Her mother, the gold-mask's mistress, had also a sister, and the sister two sons, the cousins of Demizdor, like her of the silver rank, and proud and jealous of the much or little they had.

The raid on the Dagkta spring gathering to get slaves had been a wild notion—a bet between princes, for so they did things in the cities, gambling with men's lives and liberty. A force of eighty mask-faces set out on the sport, and, with the cannon, they expected no hindrance, and indeed received none to begin with. Having captured their slaves, they camped at the ruined fortress, but eighteen men rode on ahead to Eshkorek, traveling light, to bring the news home. When the bulk of the force did not follow, presently, some went back to seek the missing princes and their soldiery. Going to the ruin, the searchers quickly found all that I and the Dagkta braves—and after us, the ravens and the foxes—had left of them. Then there was an uproar. It had never before been dreamed that the dregs of the world, the inferior clay of the tribes, should master gold and silver lords and feed them to carrion eaters.

At length they formed a vengeance party, and in the party were the male cousins of Demizdor. That a high-woman of their blood should become the drab of a krarl had them in a hot and cold rage.

It took them most of the summer to achieve their goal. They greatly demeaned themselves to do it, sometimes journeying as ordinary humans among the trader Moi who, blond as they were, had ever been close with them as sheath with sword. Going about in this manner, they eventually imbibed the myth that had sprung up, as tall stories do, from a small grain of truth. The myth said that one warrior alone had taken the fort-camp of the Eshkiri slavers. He slew them all, and left them unburied and took away a city woman as his whore. The warrior of course was black-haired, and without tattoo, unique among the red tribes. I had occasion to recollect, when I learned this, how Moka had babbled to Moi traders of her handsome husband and his new flaxen slave-wife. There were no Eshkiri in the Moi band, but gradually the word ran through the yellow krarls and reached the right ears.

In the end, I was sop enough for their vengeance, since another value had been added to me. Somewhere a red man had spoken of the fight in the ruin, mentioning the bizarre name the city men cried out as they offered themselves to my knife. The Moi had caught this chat, or even the Eshkiri themselves had heard it. They knew the name, of course. It was not bizarre to them. And, in the prosaic daylight, unenamored of their deities as they were, they never reckoned me, as the dead men did, a risen god-magician.

Even before I had learned my origin, they had been piecing it out. They determined the black-haired man was the bastard of Vazkor, a by-blow on some tribal she-goat, wrought in the last months of his life.

They hated Vazkor. I was to discover how faithfully they hated him.

Eshkorek had been the first city to shatter at his fall. He had pulled her after him, for the shadow of his ambition had lain dark on her. His tokens still crammed her, to keep the Eshkiri to remembrance. Even the silver skull-masks had been the sigil once of Vazkor's own guard.

They could not reach the dead; he had cheated them, dying. But they had me, my father by proxy trapped in the hide of a subhuman barbarian.

I can reconstruct Demizdor's part, for she told me after, during the last hour we ever spent together.

While I had attended the Dagkta council, Demizdor had been alone in the krarl. Boredom was her enemy at such times; scorning the women's tasks, yet with none of the books or music or game-pieces of her own people to hand, she would sleep through the day to be done with it, or else take the black horse and go riding. Intent on my own business, I had not thought she might be afraid, alone in the warren that had treated her ill before. Certainly, she never let me see it, or them, I imagine. The braves mocked her on her horse, but she rode better than they. The women muttered and stared, but none dared harm her, now that she was the chief's son's wife. My other two wives, Moka and Asua, had not loved Chula. They waited on her successor like handmaidens, the same way they looked after my gear and war-spoil. Embroidering my shirts and brushing the hair of Demizdor were all one. Yet they would giggle behind their veils at her mannerisms, or gape openmouthed. She was rare and curious, like a brightly colored singing bird I had brought back from a raid.

Two days Demizdor bore this, perforce. The third day she looked for me home. Maybe she had some word that Tathra was in labor; certainly she had heard later that I had gone to Tathra in preference to her. The day passed, the sun went down. She would have heard the death-wail of the women. No doubt she asked Moka, and Moka told her what it was, that Tathra had died. For sure, Demizdor looked for me after that, afraid, perhaps, how I should be. But still I did not return to my tent.

The last word that came concerning me was a babble of Ettook's slaughter and my sorcery, and how Seel had matched his power with mine, and bested me, so that I lay tethered and half-dead myself on the hill. Then she knew herself alone indeed.

As once before, it seemed to her the world had gone mad. She must have doubted her grasp of krarl-talk.

Ready to run to find me, she was ready, too, to run away. She had her horse; she could chance the wild, long way westward. Yet, like many a woman, part of her was nailed on her man's fortunes still. So she hesitated.

Asua was screaming with fright, asking the gods what would become of Tuvek's household. Moka was trying to comfort her to quiet, knowing clamor would draw trouble quicker than silence. But the babies were squealing, and the dogs, catching fear like sickness, set up their own din.

At midnight the men came. They put Moka and Asua on

one side, and there was some altercation about whether my miniature sons and daughters should be slain, seeing the evil was in them from their daddy's loins. However, the braves quickly lost interest in these precautionary measures, being more interested in the war-spoils I had accumulated. Chests were tipped over and ransacked, beer tapped, dogs dragged snapping away and a couple knifed, horses loosed, mounted, and crazily ridden about like a market. With the magician safely subdued, any of his goods were fair game.

Soon, four of them pushed into my hearth tent, and found Demizdor.

The four grinned, and said the things men say at such a moment. One of them was Urm Crook Leg, hobbling on his grudge for me. He unhesitatingly went up to her, for she waited there as if she were frozen. I could have warned him of her tricks, had I been there and his friend. She stabbed Urm in the throat, a clever, swift blow, but she had never killed a man before. She took him by surprise, but herself too. As she stood, letting the weapon go, paralyzed by what she had done, the three others came for her, and she was easy work for them.

Each had her, and would have had her again, for they were lusty that night, but Seel called the warriors to krarl council. Learning of this, they bound her to the tent-pole, and with pegs hammered the rope at her ankles in the earthen floor. They did it with much laughter, for they had enjoyed her company and planned on more of it. Urm they hauled outside and gave a rough woman's burial, since he was lame and girl-slain into the bargain.

Ettook lay in the painted tent, cold as rotten meat. They were saying that when they made the pyre for him—and killed his dogs and horses to go with him—Demizdor should be strangled, and sent to be the chief's pleasurer in the Black Place.

That was the first night.

The next day the seer was busy with Ettook's body, painting it for cremation, and Ettook's bastards, each hopeful and bright-eyed now that I was from the race, were dressing him, and Seel's daughter plaiting his beard.

The warriors meanwhile stood death-guard around the tent, though occasionally some would seek me up the hill, or Dem-

izdor in my tent. The unavoidable intervals between these vis-
its apparently saved my life, and hers.

What went through her head as she lay there in my tent is
all too clear. The men who used her were every one like a ·
facet of myself, and she blamed me—that I had left her to
them, that I had grown from their stock. She wanted to die,
and expected death. She meant to cheat them if she could.
Gradually her mental strivings concentrated only on this, how
she might free her hands and steal the knife of some brave as
he grunted and jerked inside her, or how she must snatch a
blade when they came to take her out.

In the acid sunset of Sihharn she heard the shout as they
pulled me down from the hill on the wooden pole. She was
glad I should suffer, fiercely glad, yet she was chilled as if
with death already.

There was some deal of noise, and no more braves came to
pay her court. The sounds kept up for an hour or more.

Then there was a silence.

She lay in the silence, with the dark plastered over her eyes
so thick that she could not even see her own bruised limbs, or
the dull wink of the iron pegs that held her bindings. Suddenly the tent flap was thrown open.

My wife's heart lurched, and for an instant she was
blinded by an insane weak confusion. When she could see
again, she saw the unbelievable: her own people there in the
doormouth, one of whom removed his silver skull-mask,
showing her the face of her kinsman, Orek.

The skull-masks did not, despite their threat, raze the krarl
or slay its women, or even the several warriors who had
raped Demizdor.

Truth to tell, their party of reprisal had lost its strength
during the months of searching, and was now thirty in number, and they had no cannon and were aware of the neighboring Dagkta campments across the slopes to east and north.
Besides, they had me, the only warrior they actually yearned
to harm, and they had got their lady back. And plainly, to
her, all the faces of the braves who came in her had amalga-
mated into one face, and that one mine. I, the man who had
forced her from her own life into his, and thereby brought
the rest to pass on her.

She had lost no honor with her kin. More, they gave her

back her honor and her pride in minutes. They dressed her in
a yellow robe that the younger cousin, Orek, had carried with
him all the way from the old city. It was rich, of silk, beaded
with crystal. I was to note later that despite the apparently
masculine qualities many city women possessed, they were
generally treated as fragile and precious by their men. Next,
the silver deer-mask was found for her—because it was her
own. (I picture Chula, barely conscious with terror, despoiled
of that last treasure by a skull-headed demon of Sihharn.)

Thus they remade Demizdor into the goddess-girl I had encountered in the ruined fort. Immediately she knew, intui-
tively, that the structure of her self-respect depended on her
hate and loathing for me. Women are wiser in these matters,
or they try to be. A man could not give up his dream so
readily. Yet, having shut such a door with a great and torment-
ed effort, he would entirely forget, and Demizdor could not.

Presently, I was brought—or what was left of me.

They tied me on a horse (I was senseless and did not complain), and soon they were riding west along the sloping land,
slow for her sake, but fast enough that the krarl was far behind by moonrise.

They halted at midnight in order that Demizdor should
rest. She was pale and ill, yet buoyant, feverish with emotion.
Orek held her arm. He was a boy, a year or two younger
than she, and more than half in love with her, and with more
than half a look of her, too, blond and green-eyed, with her
slenderness, and not much of the man in his appearance at
all. The elder brother, Zrenn, was different metal. His hair
was the texture of rats' skins, and dark, a thing not common
among the cities. By contrast his eyes were a porcelain
white-blue that looked as if the sight had been burned from
them by a pale fire.

I woke when the halt was called, and I saw them both,
though not steadily, bending near me, and the silver deer behind. She was the only one of the three confronting me
masked, for she was the only one with something to hide.

It was Zrenn who laughed and murmured that it was my
bad luck I had not died. His mouth smiled, but his eyes ate,
feeding on pain and prophecies of pain.

They were speaking the city tongue and could not guess I
grasped it. Only she spoke krarl-talk, wanting me to be aware

how our lives were altered and our loving done. When she
scratched my face, Zrenn laughed again. I was to come to
know his laugh perfectly.

2

The krarls take forty days or more to achieve that trek
from the mountains to the eastern pasture, or from pasture
back to mountains, stopping as they do each sunfall to camp,
and many days by water or when they fight their wars, and
slow with women on foot, their herds and their bickering.
With the fast horses of Eshkir, tough despite their thin bellies,
and the short camps and few diversions, we were in sight of
the rock walls in thirteen days and climbing them in fifteen,
and came to the outposts of the city in twenty.

Demizdor seemed recovered, though she was not, and rode
consistently as any of the men. For me the journey was less
uneventful. A broken rib had pierced my right lung; I was
choking up blood, and finally they began to believe with
chagrin that their prize would expire before they got him
home. So they took the space to bind my ribs, and fed me, as
they always did, like a sick animal that disgusted them. I
healed quickly enough to be surprising to them, and soon
rode upright, bound in my saddle.

"This is Vazkor's, no doubt of it," Zrenn said. "I have
heard stories that he recovered from a slit throat on a certain
occasion."

A couple of the men declined to accept the tale. They were
all of the silver rank, comrades and not master and hirelings.

Zrenn only glanced at me, and said for my benefit in
slurred krarl speech, "If it heals so well from wounds, it will
be able to endure a good deal of wounding before it dies.
Poor puppy-dog. It would like to bite and cannot find its
teeth."

Indeed, some of my marrow was returning into me. I had

been near gone, and not lamenting, but as my ribs knit and the pain and debility left me, life burned up, and I could have howled like a dog in earnest to get out of the ropes they had locked me into, and caress Zrenn's gullet with my boot. Then I would glimpse Demizdor, and the lead would sink in me again.

She was waiting for a chance to aid me, I thought at first, like a child. At length this puerile deception would not do. I began to see how her pride hung on her disdain. Thus: *Let me come close to her and I should win her once more.* But this would not do either. As the last red-brown autumn days sloughed from the land and my life, I realized she had turned cold bitch on me, and no lover's stroke remained to break her ice.

I was still sick enough that it made me sicker. But we were in the mountains eventually, and I began to have other events to dwell on. For one, my future as scapegoat in the city.

The city, I saw it in its cage of mountains, black on the yellow sky of sunset. And two hours after, having entered its walls, I saw it by the light of torches, yellow on the black sky of night.

I had never encountered a city before. The occasional great tribal gatherings when there were pitched a thousand black and indigo tents, had seemed huge to me. The eastern towns had impressed me as complex. But this thing unnerved me, not only because of its enormity, its grandeur, its leaning weight of centuries, but because of its ruin and wreck. For Eshkorek, pitted with cannon blasts, scorched by fires, decaying, was an ancient yellow skull.

Yet there were lights ablaze in the skull, and sounds of the living.

From the high road that plunged down to it—a road marked by shattered columns, and the surface all broken paving that would have made any horse but an Eshkir stumble—it seemed a phantom city. Whole areas dark, and rising from those dark wounds tiers of starry windows. I remembered how the ruined fortress had stirred the fancy of Death's Court. The city also was like that.

Within the walls there were several broad thoroughfares, torchlit but unoccupied. The flares rebounded from shattered crystal panes and hollow entrances. Rats, perhaps, haunted behind the crumbling facades, but made no noise. Instead, borne on the night wind, a ghostly faint music came in snatches, pure as a bell in the silence. The thoroughfare shortly branched and the Eshkiri turned along the left-hand way. At the end of it, half a mile off along the straight street, a colossal palace tower reared up, its oval windows alive with lamps, the only animate in a whole avenue of dead mansions.

My escort had moved quietly, almost stealthily, ever since coming in the unguarded gates. I wondered what they were nervous of, here, in their own place. Suddenly, about two-thirds of the distance down the avenue, a group of men stepped out of the shadows onto the road. They wore the same shabby patchwork black as my captors, but the bronze masks were shaped like the heads of birds. More important, they were armed for a fight.

"Halt, sirs," one said. "Who is your lord?"

"We serve Kortis, Phoenix, Javhovor."

At this the bronze-masks put up their swords, and murmured. The spokesman asked, "Is it you, Captain Zrenn?"

"It is I. And my brother Orek. All the hunting band, save a few who lost heart before the game was done, and are already home."

Further soldiery was moving out on the street. I could see they had been fair set for an ambush if our party had not proved to their liking.

A quota of these bronze-masks formed in around us, and the horses were trotted up the road and in through the tall gateway before the lighted palace.

It was a giant tower, some seven or eight stories high. In some of its windows colored glass remained, amber, turquoise, ruby, and flares smoked in the lion-yellow walls of it. The music had its source here, too, far up in some hidden chamber.

We crossed the outer court, and rode up shallow steps and in at a portico whose vast doors of iron-work stood wide but presently roared shut behind us.

Here the Eshkiri dismounted, and the bronze soldiery dragged me from the saddle at a word from Zrenn. The horses were led away. We climbed the marble stairway to the floors above. Orek gave his arm to Demizdor on the stair, I noted it as I was absently noting everything, the sumptuous necrosis of the palace, and the city speech, my understanding of which had continued unabated since I woke to hear it on the journey. I was yet enough not myself to let this miracle go unanalyzed. In the same uncanny mood I had experienced before, I felt it as a mark of Power lingering in me, the Power of my father Vazkor in this, his enemies' stronghold.

We arrived in a room as massive as any room would have to be to accommodate five hundred men ranked shoulder to shoulder. Not that five hundred men were currently in it. It was deserted prior to our entry and not much crowded thereafter.

There were pillars down the room, slim as swords they seemed, made of silver, and constructed to resemble trees. The silver branches of these trees fashioned the decoration of the ceiling, and set in them were flowers of faceted glass, wine-red and blue. The floor had a mosaic at its center of wide-winged swans in cobalt, scarlet, and gold. There had been precious stones in the walls but they had mostly been prised out, probably during some past sack of Eshkorek. Tapestries drooped there now, but their goldwork was turning green, and mice had tasted the tassels.

A copper lamp hung from the roof, big as a man, on a chain of bronze. The candles in it burned under jade-green crystal, flecking the gargantuan hall with the lights of a summer forest. There was no hearth, yet an airy warmth rose from the walls and the floor.

While I gazed, a man had come in at a narrow doorway. He wore a long womanish garment of dull yellow, and a golden face.

At once every bronze and silver mask was whipped off. Every person in the hall bowed low, saving myself, but my discourtesy did not abide. A moment later my legs were kicked from under me and I crashed at the gold-mask's feet.

This winded me, and for a while I lost track of the words they were exchanging. Then I heard Zrenn speaking of a black-haired savage who might well be the bastard of Vazkor.

The gold-mask said in a cold impatient voice, "Vazkor was not a man of passions. He desired only to rule, not the bodies of women. His witch-wife was enough for him, and her he took only in order to make sons. I can't believe a story that has Vazkor rutting for lust among the tribal scum."

"But observe, Javhovor," Zrenn said, "he has a look of him,

does he not? We should have shaved his beard; you would have seen the likeness better."

And Zrenn got my hair and pulled my head back to let the gold-mask observe me.

This man was their prince, and they called him Javhovor—High-Lord, a king's title. His mask of gold was something like the bronze masks of the lower soldiers in that it represented a similar curious bird, a phoenix, for so they also titled him: Kortis, Phoenix, Javhovor. His eyes were shielded behind amber glass, but his neck and ringed fingers were knotty and aging. He, too, like the men in the fort, was old enough to recall the features of Vazkor.

And it seemed he did. His hand went up to his masked face, an involuntary gesture, as if he would doff his visor for me, as his captains had done for him. But he checked himself, and under his breath, too low for them and thinking me ignorant of his language, he muttered, "I never dreamed to meet you in this room again, Black Wolf, Black Jackal of Ezlann."

Then I guessed why I had regained their tongue, or imagined I guessed. I looked in his glass eyepieces.

"Did you not?" I said. He cried out aloud at that. I said, "And did you call my father 'jackal' to his face? Or did you rather gnaw the bones from the jackal's table, and run at the jackal's heels like his hound?"

Even Zrenn had taken a step back from me. I got to my feet. Standing, I was a measure taller than Kortis Phoenix Javhovor.

He glared past me and shouted at them, "Did you know he had our speech?"

Zrenn stammered, controlled his shock, and said, "My lord, he never before spoke a word of it. He must have learned from my kinswoman, or the Moi perhaps, who have a smattering of it—"

"I learned from none," I said, watching Kortis. "It is my father in me. It is Vazkor."

For all my bonds and my uncertainties, such a scalding wave of pride swelled me that I feared none of them. It would have been more prudent to fear, to fear and keep silent, but I might have been breathing drug incense. And all the while I felt him there, dark fiery shadow at my side, the emanation of my father. I could remember only my inherited gift of magic power, which must come from him, how I had killed a man with it. I had merely to reach for strength and I should find it. All men, perhaps, must have a deity. Godless so far my entire life, Vazkor became my one true god.

Kortis drew himself up to confront me. His throat rasped like an old man's in a harsh winter.

"Very well. You are the seed of Vazkor. Somehow you have got our speech, which is cunning of you. And your mother, some heifer of the krarls?"

I said negligently, partly to test him and thereby learn more of my heritage, "No tribal woman. A woman from the cities. A woman with white hair and white eyes. The wife of Vazkor."

The music that had been playing all this while somewhere in the palace, some hidden orchestra, just now ceased as if at a signal.

"Then you are Uastis' son," Kortis said, "It is true, she was albino, and her womb was filled by him. Did she escape the fall of the Tower? Was it she taught you our language? Is she living, then, or dead?"

A woman spoke beyond my shoulder. It was like the voice of the one he had named, and the hair rose on my neck. But it was not my lynx-mother, spirited out of the air, it was De-mizdor.

"Javhovor, don't listen to this liar. I never lessoned him in our speech, but sometimes I have used it, and he is sly and quick, this *man*, he has learned from me. The stories too, I told him, of Vazkor and of Uastis. I do not reckon him Vazkor's sowing, despite his looks. He has kept me as his doxy in the stinking tents of the shlevakin, he has defiled me, and I must follow the ways of his degenerate race in order to preserve my life. From this hell my kinsmen rescued me."

I kept my ground, but my bowels twisted at her crying. She was a pace or so behind me, but I could not look about at her unmasked face, her pale fever and her eyes and her hate.

"Javhovor," she said, more softly, breathing fast, "your own kin slew themselves because of this lying dung and his playacting. My lord was one of them. I beg for vengeance." Her quick breathing faltered, and she began to weep.

"There is no need to *beg* for vengeance," Kortis said slowly; he had mastered himself now. "Whoever and whatever he is, he shall suffer." His eyes returned to me. "Do you comprehend?"

"I comprehend that in Eshkorek the women are vipers, and the men dogs walking on their hind limbs."

He struck me with the back of his hand, as if it were an idle blow, simply correction to a stupid slave who knew no better, and his bronze guard took me. Zrenn had them throw me flat a second time and drag me by my ropes to amuse his master and himself.

Outside I was permitted to walk, traveling down the length of the palace now, and below it into dank underground chambers. In one of these, small as the great room above had been large, my bindings were exchanged for fetters, the fetters mated with rings of black metal in the sweating stone.

When my guard had gone and taken the light with them, the rats commenced adventuring in and out, but none came too close, as yet. I did not relish the cell, however, if I should begin to bleed.

The scene in the hall reenacted itself in my skull, the gold-mask's horror, my pride, the demands of Demizdor. It began to seem an hallucination. No shade was any longer at my shoulder to guide me. I had had the power to kill Ettook, but not enough to burst my bonds, it appeared.

I fell into a brief sleep and woke with the rats about my feet like a tide come in. I slashed a length of my chain among the red stars of their eyes and they fled chittering, till I should be quiescent once more.

I thought of Tathra weeping as she strugged to birth Ettook's child, of Demizdor weeping when she believed she had slain me.

I wondered if the sow who bore me had ever shed tears.

3

Three bronze guards came through the passage beyond the cell and opened the metal door. It was their torches and the sound of their boots that had woken me this time; a change from the rats.

In the doorway, Kortis. Somehow I had been expecting a visit from him, and was not enormously amazed. He moved into the cell, and set one of the torches in a rusty bracket, and the guard closed the door, and walked a good way off. It was to be a private audience, it seemed.

The torch splashed sallowly on Kortis' golden face and the gold of his great seal-rings. He said, "After the luxurious night you have no doubt spent here, perhaps your family history has altered somewhat."

"The truth can't be altered," I said. "but I expected nothing more of your hospitality. There are rats in all the rooms. Some squeak, and some wear gold on their faces."

On this occasion he did not strike me.

"Your father," he said, "would have answered with more care."

"My father would have seen you dead."

"Yes. That is true enough," he remarked quietly. He turned a little looking off into his past. "In the days of the glory at White Desert, when the Alliance held, I was the nephew of Eshkorek's Javhovor, and I was not content. One sundown when I had gone hawking in the waste, my party met a company from Ezlann, and with it, Vazkor. They had come for the spring horse-catching, for the finest mounts were the mad ones of Eshkorek. He was only a young man, not much older than you, my savage; but he had a tongue like the adder's bite, and his eyes made you believe him wise. I have heard it said he had slave blood, something of the Dark People in him, which may well be so. I have heard also he

126

was a sorcerer, and that I have never doubted. That night's camp we shared on the desert's fringe, and he made a plan with me, piece by piece, like the fitting of a puzzle. Though it was some years later that the goddess opportunely struck down my uncle, and Vazkor set me in the royal chair of Eshkorek." He glanced back at me. He seemed bound to tell me those things, and weary of them and weary of telling them, for I could see he had spoken of them many times inside his own head. "When Vazkor's power was on the wane, when he had overreached himself, I threw in my lot with the five cities of the Alliance. I don't think he felt a particular hate for me; he was incapable of hate as he was incapable of pleasure. No man mattered enough to him that he should hate him, and no woman either. Apart from one, maybe. Uastis. I never set eyes on her, the risen goddess of Ezlann, but I believe her power matched his, and if she lived after him, then no doubt she, too, betrayed him, as I did."

He went to the torch and took it again, then came close to me, staring up into my face, seeming to nerve himself to do it, and his eyes behind the amber glass were fixed and wide.

"Son of Vazkor," he said, "if you have his sorcery in you, you had better use it. Eshkorek is split in factions, and I am no longer the only man bowed to as Javhovor. Yet we are united in one thing. To kill you by inches will be a rare dish for those of us who have known only the grim aftermath of Vazkor's battles."

His voice, dead calm and empty as a dry well, made me fear the prospect suddenly as I had avoided fearing it before. Where there was this blankness, there seemed no hope of a weakening, and none of any sort of clemency. I would rather have Demizdor's lashing, that even then I think I knew was only love wrung in another shape. I swallowed, for there was a hemlock taste in my throat.

I said, "Suppose, then, they do not believe I am Vazkor's?"

"You shall be tested," a new voice answered me.

I turned my head and saw Zrenn. Softer than a cat he had come creeping in. He no longer wore the black garments and silver skull, but ocher picked out with silver ornaments, delicate as a girl's and a silver fox-mask.

Kortis turned also.

"Well, what news?"

Zrenn bowed. There was a yellow topaz in the fox's brow, catching the torchlight.

"The messenger went out, my Javhovor, and returned. Nemarl, also Erran, agree to meet us, as you stipulated, but first they have sent a man to view our prisoner. Their caution does them credit, my lord, don't you agree?"

Kortis said, "Is the man here? Then let him come in. Why wait on ceremony?"

Zrenn gestured into the corridor. One of the guards called to another, and there came again the tramp of feet and pitch of torches. Soon the emissary entered. His clothes were more ragged even than the scabby splendor of the Phoenix and his captains, and his mask was of a gray cloth. Some lower citizen, an unfortunate appropriated for this work by the rival princes, he was expendable and entirely aware of the fact.

He immediately fell on his knees before Kortis, fumbling off his mask. His teeth were grayer than the cloth, his face nearly as gray.

"I entreat the immunity of a messenger, great lord, Kortis Javhovor. Don't harm me, only an old man who is nothing, nothing—"

Zrenn slapped him lightly across the head.

"Shut your foul gob, decrepit. Identify the warrior, as you were told to by your gentle masters. My lord Kortis is sick already of your noise."

At this, the emissary looked up at me.

His red-rimmed eyes bulged as if they would burst the sockets. From being on his knees to Kortis, he now plunged face downward before me, whimpering.

Zrenn kicked him.

"Vazkor, it is Vazkor," the old man shrilled. He edged crawling along the floor, over the rat droppings, and clasped my manacled feet. "Mercy, Overlord." he whined to me, peering up as if into a strong irresistible glare.

Zrenn broke into his soft and sinuous laughter.

"Proof indeed," he said, and laughed again.

"How does the old man know him?" Kortis inquired. You could tell nothing from his tone.

"He is a tame creature of Prince Erran's. The prince says the old man was among the infantry that marched on Purple Valley, under Vazkor. He got some wound that saw him home before the offensive broke."

"Ask him if this is true."

"My lord." Zrenn strolled over to the old man and toed him away from me as if clearing garbage. "Do you hear the Javhovor? Did you fight under Vazkor?"

The emissary stumbled upright. He mumbled an affirmative. His eyes pleaded with me not to visit my wrath on him. The bronze guard clanked through the narrow door at some fresh signal of Zrenn's, and pulled the gray messenger away.

For all the visitations of my father's memory, this had shaken me. It might have been his ghost reproaching me for my fear, my lack of ability; for whatever power had been in me, I seemed to have exhausted it.

"Where is the meeting place, and when?" Kortis said.

"The Temple—Prince Nemarl's joke, I venture to suggest. Midday."

"How many of their swords in attendance?"

"Nemarl says five captains, one hundred bronzes. I think Erran will bring more."

"See we are equal to them, and preferably superior."

"My lord." Zrenn went to the door, hesitated, and said, "Javhovor, my kinswoman asks that she may accompany you."

"Demizdor shall remain here," Kortis answered.

"That will grieve her, my lord. She's hungry to see the savage writhe."

"No, Zrenn," Kortis said, "it is you who are hungry for that. Demizdor hungers for other things. I will have no ladies at such a meeting. Vengeance is a slender thing to make a truce from. Tell her to stay in her apartments." He turned to follow Zrenn out, nodding at me, courteously. "Bear with the dark a little longer, son of Vazkor. Soon you shall have light in plenty."

Certainly, there was light, a bright, still day at the brink of the young winter, sky like hammered platinum. A scatter of leaves blew in the streets from trees in overgrown gardens, charred cinnabar papers at the base of the looming deadness of Eshkorek.

Light in the Temple, too. A goddess temple, rededicated, as I had been told, to Uastis (mother-mine) in the days of her power, since decimated, roof fallen, walls breached and left gaping—a colossal, empty, echoing forum, filled only at its eastern end. Nemarl's joke. Yes, surely. To decide my punishment under the shadow of she who had been my father's wife.

For the great goddess statue was still standing. A giantess of yellow stone stained by ancient fires, a skirt of bronze and gold and necklets of emerald and jade, with ruby nipples in her breasts. She stood too high to be looted, like a small mountain. You would need heroes to scale that scarp and wrench out the gems. She seemed as tall as the sky. She would have seemed taller if she had retained her head. But the same shot that brought down the ceiling had severed the skull of the Eshkirian Uastis. In those days they had cared enough for religion to sweep up the pieces like broken eggs, but you might note the cracks in the mosaic floor where her marble brains had been dashed out.

So much for Kortis' promise of light, and for Nemarl's joke.

There was another joke, Zrenn's.

They came in my cell, unchained me and led me above. In a little mildewed bathing chamber, they stripped my krarl garments and offered me the bath, gracious as for a prince. I mistrusted the barber with the razor, but he only shaved me carefully, and did not cut my throat, as I half imagined he would. This done, I was clad in black velvet breeches and tunic, royal finery, even boots of leather with buckles of gold. Bronze-masked men, with grinning eyes behind the glass eyepieces, brought me a chain of golden links, an armlet of jade thick as two fingers, a black ring.

I knew very well what they were at; I could hardly miss it. They were dressing me as Vazkor had dressed, perhaps in the very clothes that had covered his body—though I doubted it. I had surmised already from their talk and whisperings that his corpse was never found beneath the fallen Tower. Only certain soldiers of his who had unintelligently surrendered to the besiegers, had left the six cities a legacy of their black gear and silver skull-masks with which to frighten the tribes.

If it was Zrenn's joke, it was not a jest for me. No longer chained but clothed as a prince, I felt my courage come back to me, strong enough to make me wince at the fear I had felt before. If they were to kill me, they would do it. They should not at least be titillated by my cowardice into the bargain.

In the yard before Kortis' palace was a black gelding

trapped with purple, green, and gold. When I mounted up, their Javhovor and his soldiers came down the steps. Zrenn ran forward to me, swept off his mask, and bowed extravagantly.

"Greeting, Vazkor, Overlord of White Desert, Chosen of the Goddess!"

He was like a boy going on his first hunt, so joyous was he at the prospect of grief and torture to come.

I was ready when he looked up smiling, and spit in his face.

This he did not like. His smile twisted, and he wiped his smooth cheek with one hand, searching for his sword with the other. He had got too close. It was easy for me to catch him lightly in the chest with my new boot, and topple him backward. He went sprawling. No one ran to help him, but there was all about the rasp of metal abandoning scabbard.

Then Kortis said, like a man quieting rowdy children, "No, sirs. Leave him be. Zrenn, if you have made a Vazkor of him, then you must honor him as a Vazkor. If you cut him into joints now, how will you console my fellow princes?"

Zrenn had regained his feet. He showed his white, hating teeth at me, and donned his pretty fox-mask, and called to his horse.

I saw that many of the silver men had kept on the livery of Vazkor's guard for this drama, the skull-heads and the black. A man of these moved up on either side, his drawn sword across the saddle bow, pointing at me. Others rode in behind. The strong, cold sunlight did not spare the mangy garments, all that remained of antique splendor. The braid of my harness was half-eaten away.

Kortis Javhovor wheeled his gray about and trotted ahead of us, five of his captains and the bronze soldiery following. My own part of the procession began to trot after. I glanced back. Thirty behind me, parody of Vazkor's men. No chance to make a break and no weapon in my belt. On foot, runners keeping pace with the horses. Each resembled each, ugly, muddy-dark of flesh with blue shaved pates, maskless. I recalled seeing their brothers in the fortress on the rock: city slaves, and born to the destiny, slave right through, the soul bred out of them.

Rather be free and die and than live and live death.

Of the legendary quantities of enslaved tribal warriors, culled on raids, I had seen none.

The white midday sun balanced above the Temple when we reached it, and somewhere a bird was cawing harshly from a roof or autumn tree; I remember that for it was the only one I ever heard in Eshkorek.

We passed into the Temple, and there were mounted men already arrived, and waiting.

Kortis' band halted; across the way the first band stared from their masks, six of which were of the gold. The ragged furs were much in evidence there, and under them dark gray and saffron. It was another kind of gold phoenix-mask their leader wore, but still a golden phoenix. He raised his arm listlessly and Kortis replied, each like a doll on a string, with no verbal greeting exchanged.

The second phoenix called, "It seems Lord Erran declines to meet you, my lord. Afraid of the risen one, I suspect."

Thus I knew him to be Nemarl. I was wondering what plans he had devised for me, what plans Kortis had devised, how long they would make my dying last—all this in a kind of dire, calm, inner debate, numb as if every one of my nerves were gone—when a third group of riders came stealing out of the shade at the statue's back.

Ten faces of yellow metal here, and the foremost not the phoenix but a golden leopard, and his tunic sewn with plaques of gold, gone bald in spots.

"Not afraid of ghosts, my lords," he said, "cautious of men. I see Ezlann has come to Eshkorek. That is how Vazkor looked in the days of his magnificence, eh, Kortis? It must make you feel young again to have him so youthful."

"No, Prince Erran," Kortis said, "it doubles my years. But he is very like Vazkor."

"And I hear that he himself claims it as his heritage." Erran turned to me. Confronted only by masks now, the scene was becoming like some awesome dream. "What shall we do with him, then? Make him our king?"

Nemarl said heavily, "We have a score to settle with Vazkor. The crimes of the father have descended to the son. This one shall pay the debt. It is on this understanding that we meet. To savor justice too long delayed."

It occurred to me Zrenn himself had joked when he spoke of Nemarl's joking. Nemarl was not a man for jokes. He was perhaps forty years of age; he, too, would recollect my father.

The soldiers about me began abruptly to ride forward, and my horse trotted obediently with them.

We were at the center of the space now.

I thought, *If I had a sword, a knife even, I could cut free of them.*

There was part of a column left there, in the paving, like a splinter of bone left in a wound.

Zrenn came around my horse. He bowed, more of a safe distance from me than the last time.

"Dismount, Overlord," he said.

Could I swing at him again? Get the short sword from his belt?

I knew I would not do it. I knew that no man could be quick enough, that they would have me down, disarm me, carefully not kill me. I would not give them that honey to sweeten their wine. I would not struggle with the fate they laid on me.

Someone bound me to the pillar stump.

With a deft stroke, Zrenn tore the velvet tunic across my breast. His eyes were slitted behind the mask. I could hear him breathing, quick as a dancer. This was the drink he had thirsted for.

He glanced around at the company, the princes and their men. He said, "There's some story, is there not, that Vazkor could heal from any hurt. We shall see—"and a tiny slender knife flicked out in his narrow hand.

The first out was like a silver razor or the sting of ice. He laughed and danced back at me, and the iron licked me again. I felt the blood flow. It was not particularly real. I said quietly, just loud enough for him to hear me, "You will never get a son this way, little man, spilling it in your drawers."

That drove him mad, as I had meant it to, for in fact his pleasure was not quite of that order. He slashed me across the face and I felt my skin fold off from the bone. I had hoped he would open the neck vein, which would be quicker for me, but he missed it, from fury or cleverness. I was trying to plot the stages of my execution as they were, in order to outwit them, and I think I was part out of my head, for never before, and only one time since, have I been so negative, so dull on the outskirts of my death.

Abruptly Erran shouted, "Enough! Kortis, whistle off your hound; he's stealing the meat."

One of my eyes had gone blind with the running blood. One-eyed, I saw the statue of the goddess looked to be tottering. The solitary bird cawed, inside my brain now.

Erran had walked up to me to inspect Zrenn's handiwork.

"There are elegant sculptings. If he heals from them, I shall truly consider the dead has risen from his tomb." He spoke indifferently. Presently he added, "Well, Kortis. He is your captive. What now?"

"My messenger has already told you, my lords," Kortis said. "If I am to make a show of him for you, you must pay me. And, like any thrifty merchant, I should prefer a portion of my fee in advance."

"Odd to hear the great Phoenix bargain," Erran said.

Nemarl said, "For a little sport, you can't ask a high price."

"A moment ago, you called it justice, my lord," Kortis murmured. "But, no, I ask little. A friend's measure of the yield of your southern fields, Nemarl. You recollect, I think, my plantings perished in the harsh weather, together with the slaves who might have saved them. From you, Erran, I ask less. You never knew Vazkor, your hate is necessarily more abstract. Give me the three foals your mares bore last spring."

"By the yellow whore"—Erran jerked his thumb at the headless giant-woman—"I will give you one. And it is too much."

"Two at least I will have," Kortis said calmly.

Nemarl turned away, as if disgusted by their wrangling like tribal wives over a bronze pot. To this the lords of the cities had been reduced. I learned on the pillar, my ears buzzing and my blood soaking in the fine tunic they had given me, listening as they haggled away their honor and my life.

Presently the chaffering stopped. They had agreed my worth and I had not listened to it.

They were mounting up, not bothering to take me with them, talking, as they did it, of some ceremony of justice here tomorrow, when they had seen how Zrenn's carving had progressed, how much of Vazkor there might be in me. Erran rode back to me.

I looked with my single eye at him, the other sealed fast.

"You speak the city tongue," he said, "so the old Phoenix tells me. Speak then."

I said, slowly, in order I should get it right, "May you eat dung and pass blood, and may the ravens squabble for your liver."

"You will regret your good wishes, tomorrow," he answered pleasantly, and spurred his horse away.

It appeared I was to be excellently guarded. About the open forum some twenty of Kortis' bronze soldiers were lingering, and the dark slave-men building fires and raising awnings for them against the chill, in the angles of the ruined walls. Three silver captains of Kortis' band were dicing near the statue in a shelter already prepared, and well heated by a brazier. It seemed no golden-masks—commanders or kin were left to Kortis Phoenix since his men fell on their swords in the pavilion on the fortress rock. Maybe he had special cause to hate me for that.

The sun's brilliance was already darkening, seeping away into a twilight afternoon, taking my perceptions with it. Blue clouds bulged in the western sky. The wind passed like a comb along the streets of the city.

Perhaps I could die in the night, if it obliged me by growing cold enough.

The rats in my cell would be sorry I had not been returned to them. I could feel their teeth gnawing, even so, in the slashes on my chest and belly and the great chasm in my face, the rat teeth of pain.

Kotta, the blind woman, had called me handsome.

It would take a blind woman to think me handsome now.

4

I woke suddenly, hanging in my bonds like a carcass, and felt the strangeness that was in the night, or in me.

It was cold, but not bitter, the sky above the open Temple roof more white than black with all its stars and the low hunter's bow of the moon. The shades and lights lay straight across the paved floor in stripes, with only the few dull gems of the dying fires to break them. Not a sound in the world, even the wind sleeping. The soldiers were sleeping, too, or mesmerized at their watch-posts, if any had been set.

My face tingled, and itched like new beard pushing through. I worked my jaw, and felt the dried cake of blood crack, but there was no pain, no stiffening in the raw flesh.

And I thought at last of the snake bite, the tattooing needles, the warrior wounds that healed clean and left no scar.

No time for more. There was a soft, insistent surging of vague movement all around me, deceptively fluid and gentle—then the clatter of the brazier going over, the red coals spilled, and from the shelter of the three silver captains, one silver masked man staggering out with another on his back, like some play of drunks or children. But the silver-mask fell heavily, and the man astride lifted his arm and plunged it down with the almost noiseless thunk a blade makes penetrating human fiber. Presently he excavated the knife, wiped it on the corpse, and stood. As all around Prince Erran's men were standing up from the dead guard Kortis Phoenix had left me. They had stolen in, soft as snow, and done their work like a kiss.

I saw I was to become another man's property. Like any valuable buck ram, I had been captured, bought, sold, and finally thieved.

Erran drank wine, green wine in a golden cup. He said, "I do not pretend I am not a man, you see. I eat, I drink, I urinate, I defecate, I sleep, and on some day shall die. If my ancestors were gods, the strain has failed and *I* am not a god. Kortis and Nemarl and two score thousand may pretend otherwise, but I am not one of them. Which is why I have subtracted you from their guardianship. Why waste you on godly vengeance when you might be put to use?"

He had taken off his leopard's face to drink, for the city masks had no aperture at the mouth. He was a young man with blond clever looks and little amused eyes.

"Well, you may answer, my Vazkor. Tell me. Would you not be better pleased to live than to die? You shall be a kindly treated slave, don't fear it. Your blood is half good at least. My rival princes would chop off your limbs; I would rather put them to work. Instead of castrating you, I will send you the comeliest of my bronze and satin mask women, and you shall get me fine, strong slave-sons on them. You shall have a pleasant and not overarduous existence in my service."

I was no longer bound. Watching him, I put my hand to my face, and felt again the whole healed skin.

"Yes," he said, "there is always that. I am hoping you will pass on that gift with your seed, as the Black Wolf of Ezlann did with his when he fashioned you. I have been wondering. If Kortis' dog had lopped off a hand, or dug out an eye for his sport, what then? Should you have regrown the member as you have regrown flesh without scar?" He came and looked more nearly at me. "Yes, it is remarkable. Just a coloration, pale now as if your lady had petulantly slapped you there. It will be gone by sunrise, I would judge. The wounds on your body, of course, have vanished completely."

He was close enough; I could have strangled him. He seemed to become aware of this, and walked away, grinning at me. He poured green wine into a second cup, not gold like the first, but polished wood, good enough for a slave.

"Will you drink?"

"Not with you."

"Ah, but we have had all that. My hounds never bite me more than once. I was considering you might break horses for me, but I can always send you to tend the hot pipes in the cellar."

He upended the wooden cup, and let the green wine spill on the flags of his palace floor. Certain city customs he adhered to; drink poured for an underling was no longer fit for a prince.

"You have regained foolishness with health," he said, not angry, merely bored by my reluctance to serve him.

He pressed an iron knob in the wall. The knob was shaped like a dragon's head, another marvel. This building was less carious than Kortis' stronghold; the sack and the war fires had spared it. He had more people, too; the mansions that towered away down the sloping streets behind had had an appearance of habitation, lights and dim murmurings, talk and music and the distant clamor of a smithy rising up on the pre-morning air, together with various smokes.

"There is another small reason why I have brought you here," Erran said, "beyond your usefulness, beyond the mild pleasure of outwitting Kortis and the rest who obey the ancient codes like fools. This other reason I shall show you."

On this cue, the tapestries folded aside. A man held wide the carved door, and Demizdor came into the room.

I had not expected her presence here. I had no reason to.

She had had space to steel herself for this confrontation. She walked to Erran, bowed to him, and stood, slim and proud and immobile, the immemorial stance of Demizdor, the pose in which I had so often seen her. She did not hide her face in the deer-mask—etiquette did not permit it, presumably, before a gold lord—but she kept that face like white enamel. She wore a dress with tight sleeves and a nipped-in waist, dyed Erran's dark ocher, which was an ugly, barren shade on her.

I surprised myself then. I found that no longer did I feel anything unique or disturbing for this woman. My liking had healed like the scarless wounds. She had been too much trouble for too little recompense, and she had spit venom on my name one time too many. Yet it was not quite that. My lovesickness was dead enough that I could even pity her, for, without the love, I saw to the roots of her now, where the maggots were biting at her heart.

Erran was scrutinizing me with interest.

"This lady," he said, "sought me yesterday. Her beauty is unrivaled in Eshkorek, and her person currently unengaged.

She has promised she will remain with me if I will spare your life."

I had already fathomed enough of him to know it was not the acquisition of Demizdor that had tempted him to my rescue, but a desire for power over his fellows. A fledgling of my father's ilk, maybe, he wanted me for his pawn. And now he did not parade Demizdor as an acquisition, but to see how much of a hold he might gain on her by owning me, how much of a hold on me by possessing her.

"That was generous of the lady," I said. "No doubt she has mentioned how I raped and degraded her among the tents of the shlevakin."

"No doubt she has. Do you think she asked me to spare your life in order to bring you ease? She wishes you to live that you may endure slavery. She desires that you grovel in the bowels of Eshkorek twenty years or more. When your spirit is smashed she will draw her breath in peace. So she asserts." His voice and his smile indicated that he, too, assessed her motives differently.

There was a certain way he looked at her, a certain inflection when he spoke of her, that told me he had had her. It did not even rasp on me. I thought, *You have bought a dry bed, Eshkir prince. She will not be for you as she was for me.*

Her enamel face was aloof, cool as morning.

Erran said, "Demizdor, my sweeting, I must disappoint you, just a very little. I am planning to breed mighty boys from this one. He shall rest soft for today and tonight, for he has had two hard nights of it." At that she came alive, turning to him wildly, but he clapped his hands and a bronze-mask came in. "Take my guest to his apartment," Erran said. "See he has what he wants, except, of course, a silver woman, or the key to the doors."

"My lord," Demizdor cried. Her color was up and her coldness all gone. "Am I to see this vileness every day about your palace?"

"Do not be importunate," he answered. "Perhaps he will not take to luxury, your royal tribal barbarian. Then I shall have no choice but to send him below. You can always hope for that."

He waved me toward the bronze-mask.

Having no option, I obeyed him and followed his soldier-servant into the frescoed passageway. As we went, I heard him say to her, in that winsome, smiling tone of his, "Come, Demizdor, it is nothing. Imagine your gown was muddied and now it has been cleansed. Do you see this pendant of gold? It was my grandmother's, but you shall have it. Look at the gold, and forget him, pretty Demizdor. You have not necessarily been foolish, coming to the house of the leopard."

The dawn was burning up behind an apricot window when the door of my new prison was shut on me.

It was the best lodging I had had for some time.

Amber walls and amber drapes, interrupted by two great windows, each of a hundred pieces of thick-colored syrupy crystal set in a frame of heavy leading, the eastern one of which now threw a fantastic shattered patchwork of flame and shadow onto the marble flags. Having pointlessly tried the door, I investigated these windows on a sort of ironic reflex, but was not surprised to see that the city streets lay far below. Even if I could have breeched glass and frame, the leap would have cost me a whole spine.

Against the south wall lay a sleeping couch, wide enough for two, or three had you the mind for it, with thick pelts spread for comfort. Several narrow tables and benches littered the body of the room. The floor was warm from the slave-manned hot pipes, a delicate reminder, perhaps, of my punishment if I thwarted my owner. A bathing cell led off the larger chamber. It had a bizarre marble latrine that might be flushed by a bronze faucet, and brazen lions' heads spit water into the bath.

I had not been long in the apartment before two men with brown cloth faces entered through the recalcitrant door.

One was a barber with razors and a pot of scented grease. He bowed to me, making me curious as to what rank Tuvek the slave might have been promoted, then set about shaving me, dexterous as Kortis' man had been the day before. The other cloth-mask laid out a fresh set of clothes and city linen.

When they were gone, having acquired a taste for the Eshkirian bath, and with nothing more pressing to attend to, I took one and presently dressed. I kept the black garments I had got from Zrenn's prank, all but the tunic that he had sliced to ribbons. The color of the new gear was Erran's, an extra branding I could have done without. Yet he had left me the chain of gold links and the arm-ring of jade; only the black ring was gone, sent back to Kortis as proof of my capture, probably.

As I was belting on the tunic, the door opened again and in stepped a satin-masked girl with a tray of food. She set this on a table, and fled.

It was bronze wear on the tray. My master had ostentatiously promoted me, no doubt of it. On the bronze, an average meal of bread and meat and autumn fruit, good enough, but not suited to the surroundings. This was not his condescension, but the poverty of the city showing itself like the cracks in the plaster and the mouse-holes under the drapes. Only the wine was princely, as clear as the crystal that contained it.

All this while I had been amused, irritated, impatient, and at a loss. I was Erran's pet, his fierce beast with a dubious pedigree. I could see no method of escape, but I had vowed to observe and to prepare against the hour when some chance would come. It did not occur to me that, I, too, should be observed, or that any immediate trap would be laid for me.

However, the wine had medicine in it, and soon after I had drunk it, the floor tilted and the light of the window went out.

I recovered my senses when the five physicians were still present.

The chamber was scattered with their anomalous and eccentric instruments. They themselves were of the bronze order, and wore Erran's dark ocher. They were muttering over their philosophies like five elderly hens, one of whom has laid a square egg.

The dazzle in the apricot window was still golden. At first this puzzled me. Then I realized it was the opposite casement, and that the dawn was long past and the day had descended to sunset as I lay drugged on my couch, naked as a babe under their dissections.

I felt no apathy or weakness now, rather a towering mad rage.

I came off the couch in one great jump, and the five yellow hens retreated before me, clucking.

"Sir, sir, be calm," one cried. "We are Lord Erran's ministers. We have done you no harm. Merely examined your body in order to ascertain the source of its wondrous healing—"

They had left, alas, no handy surgeon's knife for me to grasp.

I shouted; "Well, then, what you have discovered? Am I a sorcerer? Or a god, maybe?" I was thinking that if I panicked them, they would fly out of the door, leaving it wide for me to follow. Then I, presumably clad only in my skin, would make for freedom, unhampered by guard or sentry. At length, however, I regained some of my wits, abandoned the scheme, and sat down on the couch, at which the physicians gathered their paraphernalia and crept to the door. This, after they had tapped on it, was opened and the gentlemen departed.

Then the lethargy came, turgid as the sludge of some river.

I lay back on the couch and the sunset died gloriously in the window glass. I was a fool. A dog, kept in an opulent kennel. And this reality mated with a heritage eternally lost, and an abnormality that made me cringe when I remembered it. For I was sobering now, in the way every drunkard must, recalling my abilities with fear and amazement. My whole life I had accepted the unacceptable. But the chase had caught me up. It seemed to me at that moment that I might as well serve Erran, for all the use I had or ever could make of myself.

There came eventually another, more gentle whisper of the curtain at the door. I did not raise my head to see who had added themselves this time to the concourse in and out.

"Whoever you are," I said, "the pet slave is in a killing mood. You had better take your leave."

A couple of soft little cries went up like two pigeons disturbed on a roof. At that I looked.

They were two girls, ambered in the last of the afterglow, their faces bared, pretty as flowers, their bodies almost bare under thin dresses of what seemed pleated cobweb. They were not really afraid of me, for they knew men, or thought they did, and had been sent to pleasure one. But, finding me naked and angry, they had acted, as any schooled whore will do.

I would have liked to turn them out, for I had had a surfeit of Erran's gifts and subtleties, and I had mused also on his plan to breed me like the bull. Yet I felt at once the sort of dreary urgent concupiscence that sometimes comes with fever.

Seeing me aroused—I had no means to conceal it—they glided at once to the couch. One kissed my mouth, the second caressed my body; then the second fastened on my mouth, and the first lay in my arms. It was like supping from two cups that changed their perfume and their sweetness at every sip, as each mingled with the other.

I appeased my hunger and my wrath with a murmuring, four-limbed, twenty-fingered, double-mouthed goddess of smoky desire, while the window reddened and dissolved in night.

My duet of lovers left me at sunrise. Later, the barber came back with his pots and blades. I looked at the razors, set out and gleaming, and I knew I should not be robbing him of them. The fight was done and no blows struck. The panther was safely locked again in his tasteful cage—if he had ever been out of it.

Erran visited me an hour before noon.

He glanced about, unmasked, smiling as ever, and indicated my untouched breakfast.

"No appetite, Vazkor? I'm sorry to note that."

I said, "The last meal I ate here had a curious effect on my digestion. I fell asleep and dreamed that five senile old men were probing my body with their unwashed fingers. And when I inquired what they were at, these same perfidious old men declared that you, my lord, had sent them."

Erran's smile broadened.

"You are learning to be elegant," he said. "How entertaining. To make a neat sentence one must control one's anger. I see you have done so. However, I assure you the food hereafter will be pure."

"I can forego eating with no trouble," I said. "I have always needed little. A legacy of my sorcerer father, perhaps."

"Perhaps. Certainly you are not quite human, my Vazkor. Though human enough, I surmise, to enjoy the other fare. Did the girls entertain you?"

"Ask them. No doubt they also had your leave to study me."

"That test was rather one for you to set yourself. I want your answer, you see. Do you wish to live well with me, or ill? Agree to my terms, and you can stride about my holding like a free man, though with a bronze or two to guard your person from the other princes of Eshkorek, and also, I must admit, to dissuade you, should you unwisely suffer an urge to leave my court. There will be food and fine drink, women in plenty, boys if you've a notion for them. You shall break horses for me, the fiery stallions of the Eshkorek valleys. Not mean work for a strong tribal brave. Your rank will be of the bronze, but you shall sit in my hall for your meat. If you are obedient, you may rise to the silver."

"You do not need a breaker of horses," I said.

He looked at me.

"What, then, do I need?"

"A pawn for whatever power-game you are mindful to play." I let him savor that, then I said, "So, my lord. I am your pawn."

His shrewd blond weasel's eyes ran over me.

"Your surrender is more swift than I had hoped for. I thought after all you would require some lessoning."

"I have no better existence to look forward to than this you offer. The day I find one, you shall know of it."

"Oh, yes, my warrior. I shall know, and never think I shan't." He walked to the door, turned, and beckoned me to follow. "You can come and go as you want," he said, "now that you are in my service."

When I went up to him, he showed me a silver ring and the slot in the door that it fitted (this being the sort of key they used most often in the cities), then put the ring into my hand.

Accordingly, the son of Vazkor and of the goddess-woman Uastis became the horse-breaker of Erran, leopard prince of the yellow city.

As I had told him, I guessed eventually I should be more than that. I should be his pawn in his game of Castles. Maybe I had some inchoate purpose, some forethought that when he began to use me, I should, in being used, use him, and once ambition and power were close enough, I would slough my mentor and carve for myself. Maybe.

But in truth, I think I was only like the warrior in the antique story the Moi tell, who straying in the cave of the dragon, and finding it too large to slay, lies down before it on the pile of gold, and swears fealty till the moon goes out.

5

The city months were longer than those of the tribal calendar, and possessed of more elegant names. In the early days of the season they called White Mistress, the first of the low mountain snows covered Eshkorek, turning the fulvous city and yellow terrain to leaden white.

All that winter I was a bronze-mask, Erran's bond soldier and horseman. I perceived that if I had chosen to serve one of the three princes, Erran should have been my choice. For, by the standards of the city, he was rich in many things: slaves, grainfields, horses, and also herds, driven to pasture on the lower slopes all summer, and directed home in autumn. Even their winter feed he had provided for, along with food for his strongholds in Eshkorek. It was not astounding that angry though the princes were at the capture of their prize, myself, they held their wrath in check. More often than not they would need to deal with the leopard during the cold months. Though there were constant clashes between the soldiery of this or that lord, and no man went abroad by night without a goodly company and some measure of sharp steel, Nemarl and Kortis never spoke rough to Erran.

The ancient order was on the wane, this much was sure. Kortis and Nemarl clung to their traditions, wore their phoenix-faces, spoke of lost greatness, and ate behind screens; Erran the Leopard spoke of the present, which mare was to bear the stallion, which field must lie fallow, which soldier should advance his rank, and every dusk his captains feasted and drank wine in the wide palace hall, among the crimson candles and the half-nude serving wenches.

Most days I would be in the horse-pack. There was a bronze-mask equerry, an alien from So-Ess—part of the five-city army that attacked Eshkorek, he had been snared in the fighting, but he was well used to bondage now, and took a

145

pride in Erran's fine stables. This fellow taught me more about horses in a month than I had reckoned to learn, having been on and off them since I could walk. He was known as Blue-Sleeve. Erran, having him wear the blue color of So-Ess, had spiced the dubious privilege with an appropriate title. Blue-Sleeve appeared to accept this pleasantry, indeed, he gave no other name to those who asked.

The horse-park also provided Erran and his court with game and hunting. It had been some long-dead noble's retreat at the edge of Eshkorek. Erran got it by a trick, and held it currently by weight of numbers. Most of the mansions in this far-flung quarter had missed the cannon blasts and the ensuing sacks, when firstly Purple Valley and next the Alliance of White Desert raped the city, before drawing off to quarrel among themselves.

When I was not with the horses, there were games of dice and chance, or the more cunning variety that entailed checkered boards and pieces of onyx, ivory, and green jade. Books, too, were to be had, bound in fine leather for the lower orders, though the golds stuck their masks into volumes of yellow metal, crusted with gems.

My first book, I thought, might be some trouble to me. I had learned only the crude tribal script, but with my occult gift for the city tongue, I gambled I should master their writing, too. Yet I put it off, only fingering the books, till I saw a man smiling (he was masked, you learned to tell a facial action by the movement of the eyes), and I lifted up the book and opened it, and found I could read, clear as day, what was put down there. I turned about with it, and read out to the sneering bronze a line or two, as it took my fancy. Only later, I wondered. It seemed to me these things were too marvelous. But, having no control over them, I adapted myself once more to my abilities, putting questions and doubts aside, as I had with my new life.

I learned to play music, too, at Eshkorek, and discovered I had some ear for it. Their songs were strange, the melody could go where you did not look for it, yet somehow the effect was pleasing. The girl who taught me this skill taught me other things also. Sometimes, looking at me under her lids, she would fashion chords on the silver-stringed neck of some instrument, winding up the bone pegs, then striking her narrow fingers over the sound box as a cat scratches at a ray of sunlight, to produce a high-pitched, delicate, silver trembling note that was like the music she herself would make in bed. I had much choice in girls that winter, but her I liked very well. Her name meant Sparrow, and she had a little mauve mark on her left breast, like a butterfly.

Other than girls, I had few companions, and no individual to trust.

Erran's gold and silver men gazed askance at the cuckoo in their nest. One second they would mean to treat me as an inferior, a slave like the Dark People, to be despised, that they might kick end to end of the palace and not be called to account for. Next moment they would recolleet I had Erran's protection, his special favor. I was in his store cupboard for future need, and therefore I must not be hurt.

Despite this stamp of immunity, I had myself tutored in Eshkorian swordplay, and found the lessons useful, since once in a while a gang of soldiers would seek me out for discord. These were always bronzes, my supposed class equals, who resented the promotion to their midst of a bastard tribesman—none I think believed I was Uastis' progeny, though many agreed I might have begun in the loins of Vazkor. There would be caterwaulings, spittings, and presently a merry dance, during which they would learn that, whatever else they do mistakenly, the tribes breed man hard. At length, all of us bloody, and I alone upright, a scatter of silver captains, having observed the fray, would clap me on the back and boot their officers in the breeches, and I should be thankful for the poision-taster at dinner that evening. I managed, after the first, to derive entertainment from these scenes and from the silvers' condescension. *You are the man's dog, thought I, so be his dog. Bark, snarl, and bite, then wag your tail when the lords pat you. The bones are juicy, are they not? And inside your doggy hide you are still a man, and the son of a greater man than all this pack of curs together.*

Erran set a guard around me, day and night. Not only the four bronzes who rode with me about the city or the cloth-masks who tested my liquor and meat— none of whom died; their presence was enough to deter the bane—but in addition certain others, infrequently seen yet ever-present, that I had guessed to be Erran's spies.

One day, when I was riding to the horse-park with my four guards and some fifteen others, down a narrow street generally acknowledged Erran's territory, an arrow with a silver flight shot from the sky. I had not fought krarl wars without some sagacity coming of it; I was from my horse as soon as my ears picked up the whine of the shaft. As well. The thing parted my hair; another second and it would have combed my brains.

Two heartbeats later a swarm of men dashed over the walls.

There is no nicer place for an ambush than a ruined snowy street.

I had been permitted a sword, of Erran's bounty, and cut around with it to reasonable effect. Then I saw our trouble. The attackers were mostly silver men, and although plainly an enemy, there was a stigma to the bronzes involved in mowing down a superior class. Generally, only captain fought captain, mere soldier fought mere soldier. Although Erran must have tried to hammer the dogma out of them, yet he still expected bronze to kowtow to silver and to gold in his own palace, and so undermined the teaching at its source. True, the rallied, and true their swords slit up the guts of many a silver-mask, yet their hearts were not in it, and I could foresee a black future as the ambushers were easily twice our number.

Then from over the same walls the ambushers had scaled, came bounding city slaves, the Dark Men with their indigo-stubbled pates and their wood-knob faces, like animated ugly effigies set going by some demented magician. Without a battle cry or a death moan they plunged into the silver-masks' swords and finished them. The fight concluded, the slaves slunk away.

That night I approached Erran and asked for a guard of Dark Slaves. He told me I had always had one, and who else did I suppose the reinforcements were?

The futile attack, I heard meanwhile, had been set by Orek, Kortis' man, the kinsman and worshiper of Demizdor. Erran launched no reprisal. I lived, Kortis had lost men he could ill afford, and no doubt Orek would be made to regret his impulse.

Three city months passed, near four of the tribal calendar. Deep in the upper valleys, far east of Eshkorek, the krarls would be waiting out the snows in their tents. That other world, with which I had done forever, seemed like a story I had read in one of the Eshkorian books. Only in my dreams did I go back there, fight again in their battles, and live again by their codes. I dreamed of slaying Ettook, not as I had, with a power that came only once like lightning, but with my hands or my knife. Over and over I would wring his fatty neck or drive my blade in his belly; over and over he would rise, laughing blood, and I must grapple him again. There was another nightmare also, one I would start up from in a sweat. In this I saw Tathra, all black, in her dark robe and shireen and her black hair that never, even to the last day of her life, showed any gray. She was standing above a well when behind her, stark white against her blackness and the gray gloaming of the dream would come a woman like a ghoul, white robed, white haired, and with a white cloth over her face. For a long time, or so it would seem, this woman would remain motionless at my mother's back, and Tathra would not see her. Then, quite slowly, the white woman would draw down the veil from her face, and she would have no face at all, but a silver skull, and that not even of a woman, but of a great cat, a lynx. And at that moment I would understand that Tathra did not stand above a well, but above a grave.

The strength of dreams is very strange. Explain away these symbols as trite and childish as I might, I could not get free of them, and every twenty days or so I would frighten the girls who shared my couch by shouting and striking out as if an army were upon me.

At length there was a night that the dream came in the old way and I began to shake and shudder in my sleep, when suddenly everything was changed. The veil fell from the white woman's face, and revealed only the blurred, weather-chipped features of a statue under it, mossy and harmless, while my mother Tathra bent to the well, and when she straightened, she was beautiful, as in my boyhood.

That was the exorcism of this dream. I never had it after. The priest who saved me from it was none other than my music girl, the Sparrow. She told me in the morning I had been crying out in the dark, and she leaned to my ear, and whispered to me all was well, without waking me. It was a trick she had learned long before to calm the nightmares of a sister when they slept together in one poor little bed in the lower quarter of Eshkorek.

Despite Erran's proposals, as far as I know no girl conceived by me in his palace, nor by any other man, for that matter; I never saw a lifted girdle in all my days there, though plenty of lifted skirts to account for it, and there were few children. I suspect the city women grew barren, their wombs shriveled like the brains of their men, by legends and excessive glorious poverty.

The snow broke and the winds came. They roared like ghostly cannon through the city.

The fierce horses liked to race the wind. You could see them do it any day, when they were out on the flats of the park. Tathra had told me in my infancy that to her own tribe the wind god was a black horse; sometimes he would sweep down the slopes and get the mares in foal. It seemed all the Eshkir horses were children of the wind god, and roused at his passing to pursue and follow him.

The So-Essian equerry, Blue-Sleeve, said we should be going on the spring horse-catching through the northern mountain valleys once mild weather had laid hold. He leaned on a thin black cedar tree and whistled after the horses as they ran madly up and down the landscape of brown-bleeding thaw snow, the speed and the gusts fraying out their manes and tails.

Over to our left, the cluster of grooms disbanded and pointed along an avenue of rotting green statuary; Erran was coming on a crimson trapped horse, about thirty of his silvers around him, and a group of golds. There were women, too, their veils and wrappings billowing in the wind.

Every man on the flats doffed his mask save for those already unmasked, as I was. I scarcely ever bothered with my metal skin—some artisan's shaping of a falcon's head—but wore it fastened on my shoulder as others did when going bare-faced.

Even some of the horses ceased running, as if they sensed the lord was near, and froze, intently staring sideways through the smoky afternoon.

Erran rode out onto the flats, his company trotting behind, and reined up, looking about with his golden leopard-head.

"Blue-Sleeve," he called to the equerry.

Blue-Sleeve hurried to Erran. He bowed, and stood answering questions with nods and brief humble sentences. Like all Erran's dogs, he was well trained.

I glanced at the silver people, in particular the women. I had not seen many females of that class. Generally they did not eat at the evening meal with the captains. Not a face was on show. Even the round breasts and arms so frequently offered to view in the palace were muffled from the cold. Then I saw the deer-mask of Demizdor.

I had not laid eyes on her for fifty or sixty days, and on the last occasion I had glimpsed her, it was from a distance. She was walking to and fro on a high gallery in her yellow gown, but becoming aware of me, she had quickened her step and gone away.

Today she wore a black fur hood, and though her face was silver still, her dress was fringed with gold and her velvet sleeves ringed with it. However, she was not with Erran but with a stocky golden bear. He fondled her wrist in its velvet gauntlet, but she was staring straight at me.

Erran called a second time, my name, or the name I had been given here.

"Vazkor."

I went to him, more leisurely than the equerry. I put my hand on his horse's neck; it knew me, I had had a part of its training a month before.

"My lord."

A few of the ladies murmured that I had not bowed to him (I never did), and I heard some man say, "This is the proud tribal dog of the mixed blood."

"I have been telling Blue-Sleeve," Erran said, "that we should like his best riders to put the horses through their paces for us. He has recommended you, Vazkor, above all the rest. There is none to match you, he says."

"Ah, yes, my lord," I said, "that is no doubt because of my tribal pride and my mixed blood."

The man whose sentence I had borrowed swore. I nodded to him politely and went away to do my tricks for Erran's brainless court.

There were three others picked beside me. It was the equerry's compliment to us, rather than an effort to please Erran. Still, it rankled, and for the thousandth time I must recite to myself the old spell: *Act his dog, for you are not his dog; it is worth the play for the bone.* I had not yet learned the lesson that when you are forever telling yourself that such and such is worth the price, then the price is too high and has been paid too often.

The grooms led the animals over. We mounted up and had them do the usual things that show a horse's mettle, and please any gentlemen and ladies who happen to be watching: standing jumps, and jumping over obstacles of various heights, and a mock fight, horse with horse and rider with rider. This bout, having been choosen for it, I won. I was not sorry to knock my opponent out of his saddle; he was an imbecile I had had dealings with before.

Presently, when it was all done and we were walking the horses to cool them, three golds came up to me with their silver women, and one of these princes was the bear who escorted Demizdor. Partly I had forgotten her in the hard exercise, and that she had changed hands.

The golden bear put his palm on my elbow and another finger under my chin to halt me, for all the world as if I were some serving girl he fancied. I stopped and looked at him, and felt stupidly like a boy who had been touched up by one of his father's guests and must keep quiet about it when he would prefer to answer with his fist.

"Excellent. I applaud your skill," Demizdor's new master said. "Do you lie with the mares to make them so cooperative?"

I pulled my wits together, smiled courteously, and asked him with deferential interest, "Do you recommend it, sir? Is it good?"

His friends laughed. I was a dog who could crack jokes as well as ride horses. The golden bear, however, was not finished.

"Well," he said, "we've seen the fancy dancing, but not how you break a horse to your lord's service. That I should like to witness indeed." Whereat he turned about and shouted to Erran, "My lord Leopard, have I your permission to get this breaker of yours to tame a beast of mine?"

Erran had been talking with Blue-Sleeve; he left off and crossed to join us. Behind the eye-holes of his mask his eyes were bright with piercing interest, and, more than any other thing, Erran's eyes told me I should beware.

"Tame a horse of yours, my lord? I believed your beasts were tame already."

"Every one, save for the red stallion."

"The red? But you won him at four-headed dice a month back."

"So I did, my lord. And he has been a curse to me."

"Surely you exaggerate;" Erran said smoothly, enjoying the dialogue with unmistakable razored anticipation. "That gentle stallion is softer than your lady there, damask Demizdor."

If he had meant to warn me—to this hour, I am not certain—he could have done it no more plainly.

"Yet, my lord Leopard, I beg your permission," the bear said.

"Well, then, if you are reduced to beggary, sir, you had better have it. You will not object to exercising this gentleman's animal, will you, Vazkor?"

"Ask me again, my lord," I said, "when I have done so."

The bear had slapped one of his silver men on the shoulder, and the man had gone off down the avenue of statues. After half a minute, a closed-in horse box of black metal was brought at an even pace up the avenue and onto the flats.

The box was a sort of prison-on-wheels, a city object I had never taken to. Now I and the whole company could hear there was some need of it.

Something inside the box was kicking and lashing and bellowing to get out.

Erran's eyes currently conveyed entire surprise and mystification.

"Why, my *lord*," he said to the gold bear, "can your passive beast have grown into a demon overnight? I think we had better withdraw before the creature is let loose. My Vazkor, do you judge you can handle this horse?"

I looked the bear in the face, and said, "I should say this horse had been handled somewhat already."

Surely a babe yet warm from the crib could have guessed the facts. If they could not doctor my food, they could doctor the food of their horses. From the noise of it, my lord Prince Bear had stoked his animal with the seeds of death for both the steed and whoever should happen in its path.

I had never been so angry since I had been a boy in Ettook's krarl. Anger that he should waste a fine beast for his wretched villainy, anger that I must risk my life to make theater for them, and a darker, sicker anger for the woman I knew had been behind his scheming.

I stood there on the flats while the lords and ladies of the leopard's court drew off to safe harbors, and the mad horse screamed and lunged in his jail. Even the grooms ran, leaving just one poor cloth-rank boy with a bare face like gray suet, who slipped the bolt on the box door and pelted for safety.

This time I thought, *If I survive this show, it shall be the last. By the sow-harlot-bitch-whore goddess who grunted me forth from her belly, this hound has offered his last trick.*

Then he was out, and I stopped thinking neatly in words.

He was not like a horse. If I had been remembering the legends of the wind god of Tathra's tribe, this was surely he, not black but red, not wind but whirlwind.

He shot from confinement like ball from cannon, smoking foam, and came right at me with his eyes on fire.

I had reckoned on that. My legs and entrails said, *Fly him.* But instead I ran to him as he to me, and leaped for his great blazing horse's head.

I got his breast, hard as rock, in my side; the impact almost winded me, save I had been ready. I swung over his neck and landed on his back like a gasping fish slung down on some heaving ship's deck, and grabbed the foam-sticky mane.

He squealed, from pain or panic or his madness, and reared up, kicking the sky. He was slick with sweat. I clung as I could, and slipped and clung again.

I had believed I could only hope to hang on him like a mountain cat, till he died of the poison or dislodged me and tore out my vitals with his teeth. Suddenly something else swarmed through me. It was like the bite of strong liquor, like lust even. It was the notion I could mend him.

There had been one earlier day, long past, when I had kneeled over two does by a winter pool, and I had known it was life I took, the possession of another. And now, hugging the plunging stallion, washed by his pain, snowed by his bloody foam, I felt his life and his right. Both to die for the whim of a pusillanimous fool, or both to live?

What happened after that was swift but very certain. It was like the wave that suffused me, the light that burst me when I slew Ettook. Yet it was different. It was like a dam holding back the sea, and the dam breaks and the sea pours through, but there is no substance to the sea, no heaving force, no tumult, only a faint shining on the back of the eyes, and a stillness after.

The horse was still, also. He stood there, breathing and shaking his head softly, as if embarrassed by his wildness before. He picked up his hooves as though to examine them or the sensation of their being on solid ground.

He had voided the muck and they had given him all along the flats; the dung was greenish and had an acid smell. Maybe it was after all that this voiding had cured him, not any mage-craft of mine.

I was shaking as if I needed food or a woman. Then the shaking went off and I looked around about me.

Erran's courtiers were at a loss, Some had been cheering me, I vaguely recalled, for my berserk dash at the stallion's head, but this was beyond their scope.

The golden bear had wandered a little to the front of them, trying to puzzle it out, doubtless.

I slid off the stallion and shouted for one of the gawking grooms to come and cover him up, for his sweat was still steaming in the icy wind.

I walked straight to Demizdor's gold bear. I was no longer angry or bemused. I was precise, knowing what came next.

I did not carry a sword out in the park, just a knife for cutting rope or hard earth from the horses' hooves. I stuck the knife to its hilt in the bear's belly, and watched him wriggle and stagger and try to pull it free, and finally roll down in the broken snow, and die.

In the cities, a bronze-mask does not kill one of his lord's gold men.

That is the way of it, with no going around.

I suppose I had turned crazy, having endured the cage when I should have refused it, now refusing when I should have endured. Like many a man before me, I acted at the wrong moment and in the wrong way, because I ought to have acted sooner and had not.

My wrath was finished. I was only adamant, aware I had lost everything, life, too, most likely, and had no more to cast away.

I was taken back to Erran's palace and flung down head

first into my room of apricot windows. Any weapon here was removed, the ring-key appropriated; I was locked in.

Presently Erran visited me with three silver captains.

"I am disappointed in you," he said. "You are a fool."

I said, "I have upset your plans because you made me a toy for idiots. You should have judged me better. You are the fool, my lord."

"We shall see," he said.

He walked about before me, relaxed and easy, as if he need watch for nothing. Obviously, it would not serve me to kill him; there were too many who could step into his boots.

He picked up one of the books that lay on the table. He said, "You have acquired quite a taste for city things—literature, music, love . . . . Some while ago, when I got you from Kortis' servile clutches, I think I told you how your healing process fascinated and intrigued me. Because you have transgressed, because you must be punished for it, I have decided to learn thereby the answer to my question. You can be of no other use to me."

Despite myself, my mouth went dry. I would need to be a fool in truth not to see what was coming. He said, quietly and without undue coldness, and with none of Zrenn's excitement, "I shall begin by cutting off your right hand, my Vazkor. I shall then be able to discover for myself, as indeed will you, to what extent your body is able to reproduce its tissues. Later, I will put out your eyes, extract your tongue, and sever your windpipe. If you survive so much, my physicians shall remove your inner parts. You may, naturally, die of shock before we can proceed so far. If you live and are able to repair—which is a debatable and curious thought—it may be that I shall reinstate you as my underling. It would be shortsighted not to retain such a prize—an entirely invulnerable champion."

A terror like black worms oozed up my throat, but I would not let him see it take hold of me. I said, "When you are on your deathbed, Erran, pray that you never meet me in the place you are going to."

He made a gesture that cried, *Ah, the savage is back in him. What is this nonsense of meetings and afterlife?* Aloud, he said only, "We begin at dawn tomorrow. For tonight you shall be brought food and liquor, women, if you want. Enjoy your senses while you have them."

The sunset dulled to magenta behind the thick panes of the western window, yet speared in bright orange flashes through eyelets of broken crystal.

This strange and contrasted patterning was a result of the handiwork I had been putting in on the window with a bench, a table, the bronze-ware cups and jug. To no avail. The leading held, the glass sugared into fragments, none of them large enough to furnish a weapon.

Long before the sun went down, constructing its ominous sorcery of color with the casement, I had consigned myself to an assortment of grim alternatives. That I should come on some fighting means unexpectedly during this last night, or that tomorrow I could ask for the barber to shave me before Erran's guard arrived, forcibly borrow his razors and do some business with them. Other wild thoughts ran about my skull. I might tempt in the sentries who had been set outside my door; they were bronzes, partial to wine . . . a sword snatched, a break made—I should be trapped and slain, no other thing seemed possible, but not chopped up for death like a piece of butcher's meat that still lived, and some should go with me. Then, too, I think I dreamed I might escape them, knowing I dreamed it.

The window became somber and the wind came through where I had damaged it.

An hour after sundown, the door was opened. A silver captain and ten bronze guards entered to supervise the setting of my dinner by two cloth-masks. With perverse generosity, Erran had sent me excellent fare. When the men had gone, I ate some of it, thinking to fatten myself for bravado, but the taste was dust and ashes, and the meal soon abandoned.

Beyond my prison, I could hear music playing in the city. There was always some melody or song abroad in Eshkorek by night.

I smashed my fist against the leaded frame of the window, because this was no time for songs.

It was later that the door opened again.

It opened only a crack. Through the crack stole a single figure, the ultimate horrible jest. For Erran had sent me my last woman.

The candles were smoky; I could not make her out at first. Slender, muffled in a flimsy shabby veiling, the hint of light catching a bronze mask—I had been going to be rough, but checked myself.

"Sparrow," I said, "of all of them, he should not have sent you to me."

Yet she was too tall for Sparrow. Suddenly the veil slipped from her hair and the candles blazed in it. She put up her hand to draw off the mask, and she wore one long scarlet glove of blood from fingers to elbow.

My guest was Demizdor, and in her grasp the red-wet gleaming of a knife.

6

Her face was white. She said, as if it explained everything, "I have killed your guard. There was only one."

I must have started toward her, for she held out the bloody knife to me, the grip to my hand.

"What can this be?" I said. "Has Erran sent you here so I can slice your neck as my final worldly joy?"

"Erran? Erran did not send me."

"Why come, then, lady? Are you so hungry for earth in your mouth?"

Stonily she said, "You may kill me. But then you will never escape them."

I took her wrist and plucked the blade from her fingers. I said, "That I am to die is your doing. You primed your golden bear to his sport."

"Yes," she said.

"Then you are happy. Why talk of escaping? Why kill the guard?"

Her eyes were fixed on me, blank as two green pebbles in her colorless face.

As if I had not spoken she said, "Erran stationed only one bronze at the door. Since you have none but enemies here, Tuvek, the prince never imagined any would send you aid.

Only among the pleasure-women do you have friends, and they would never dare to help you. Except for one. I summoned your music girl and took a loan of her garment and her mask. She shall say someone stole them from her if any question her, but I don't imagine that they will. The route I shall take you is known to very few of the gold and silver rank; the bronzes know nothing of it. When I come to this door, I told the guard that Erran had sent me for your night. When he turned to unlock, I stabbed him. I did it clumsily, but he is dead. I took the ring-key. Another will come this way in an hour, at midnight, when they change the watch. We must be swift."

"You go too swift for me already," I said. "I am done with you, and you with me, girl. I'll put no trust in anything of yours."

She smiled at that, sneeringly.

"Are you a savage still, Tuvek? Will you throw away your solitary chance because *I* bring it?"

"Why bring it, then?" I said.

"Why," she repeated. Something twisted behind her empty eyes and her mouth twisted with it. "Because I can't be rid of you. Because you have got my soul with child, and even the child is you, and I can never bear it or be free of you." And she caught my arms and sunk her nails in them and stared into my face.

I said no word to her, having no word to say. What had been in me for her was long silent. Her passion and her anguish confounded me; they were unchanged or had swelled the greater, under the mask of disdain and hate.

"You want me away then," I said. "Very well. I am ready."

She let go of me, and turned her head to hide what no longer needed to be hidden, since I had seen it all.

The guard lay at the threshold in his blood. He was the second man she had killed because of me. I took his weapon belt and his mask and donned them, and put on my own cloak and drew up the wolfskin hood to cover my too-recognizable hair. She told me that the way we were to travel was a chilly one, and any seeing us would not marvel that I went hooded. She told me, too, to wrap my uneaten dinner in a packet and store it in my shirt. She said I would be needing food on my journey.

I followed her out into the passage, and along that into one of unpainted stone, dark-lit by far-spaced torches. And all the while I was considering that another turn might bring me onto someone's sword, that this was a fresh game of the court. Yet I knew, beneath my disquiet, that she had been true to me at last, my city wife, that it was as she had said.

At length we came out on an open rampart of the palace, and I got there my concluding sight of Eshkorek, its craters of blackness and its starry-lighted towers. But then there was a stairway, and we had passed under the angle of it and down, and Eshkorek was gone.

We descended into the cellars, the depths of Erran's palace.

Twice we met gangs of the Dark Men. The first toiled at a huge arrangement of vats and cisterns, in the dull red luster of the torches; the second group marched out of one dim vista into another, passing us in the gloom as if we were invisible. Only once did we come on bronzes, overseers probably of the slaves. They sat grumbling and dicing by a brazier, nudged each other when they saw us, but offered no challenge. When we had left them behind, I asked Demizdor why this was. She said the underpassages were common night roads to the bed-chambers of the princes above.

Apart from these, and similar questionings and replies, we exchanged no conversation.

I did not know where she was guiding me, but surmised it must be onto some unfrequented path from Erran's territory, maybe even from the city itself.

We entered a passage with no exit, and I guessed the trick of it before she set her schooled palm on the place in the wall that swung it wide. Beyond lay blackness and a smell of gray bones.

"I don't see in the pitch-dark, my lady," I said.

"It is only a short distance without light," she said, "but you must take my hand."

So, hand in hand, we stepped into the solid night and the wall folded shut behind.

That hand was very small and cold in mine; it was the white one without the blood, a slim, sad hungry hand that clung to me against its will. It made me recall, that hand; it brought back shreds of what had been before. It woke up my pity, thinking of her pain.

Then the black began to dilute, and she drew herself away from me.

We had come under a street, and the paving had burst overhead, opening the passage-roof in places, just enough to wash the dusk with starshine.

Everything seemed fossilized here, not even a rat to scuttle.

Shortly the gaps closed above us, and tunnels ran off to the sides, and the sourceless luminescence of a sea-cave lighted everything.

There were faint markings on the stone sides of the passages; I suppose she told the way from them.

In the end, she led me through another magician's wall into a vast underground hall of broken pillars, and here was a black horse tethered, harnessed, and with a pack at his saddle.

Her resourcefulness brought me to a standstill. I could see she had been planning quickly and thoroughly; her mind surely had begun to work on it the second my blade went in her lover's gut.

"The horse is sound," she said. "I brought him here by another way at sunset, and he carries a little food and water and some other items for your journey. I could not get you much or my endeavors would have been noticed. There are flints and a parcel of resin torches that you will need later." She spoke calmly, as if she were a stranger I had asked for directions on my road. She pointed across the space, beyond the horse, and said to me, "The opening by the leaning pillar. Go down it, turning neither left nor right. Presently you will notice a mark like a serpent on the left-hand wall. Put your palm over his head and he will open the stone for you. Have you noted what I have said, for I accompany you no farther?"

"I shall remember," I said. "Where then?"

"The tunnel runs straight," she said, "through the belly of the mountains southeast of Eshkorek. I don't know where it ends, but it will be far from here. Nine or ten days to ride it."

"And you?" I said. "You will tell Erran where I have gone?"

"I shall not tell him."

"He will suspect your complicity and he will make you tell him."

"He will not. But he may detect for himself. The princes

are aware of this tunnel, though few of them wish to enter it. It is a thing They designed, who came before us, our ancestors from whom we are degenerated."

She paused there, no longer fierce or pleading, only remote, as if her spirit had been emptied from her, and her eyes seemed blind. I thought of the nights and noons when we had coupled, when my world had been only Demizdor, and that she had said to me, "One day you will regret me." Now there was only this beautiful, unknown, unloved stranger, murderess and savior in a single day.

I said, "Maybe you would be safer if you rode with me."

She said, "Don't offer me dross. I shall be safe enough here; these are my people."

And then she talked, quietly and succinctly, of the hours before her kin took her from the krarl, how she had thought me dying or dead, how the braves had raped her and tied her and returned to rape her, how she had lain awaiting death herself, the anguish and the shame and the rage and the fear of it—everything she told me, till she was a lesson I had by heart.

To lose love and find how you have lost it, neither to blame, like sightless children groping in shadow; there is an edge to that like the knife itself.

"Demizdor," I said, "come with me. We may be friends at least."

"Oh, but I do not want your friendship. It is your love I want, and yet, I don't want it. Go, or I shall curse you. It will be a curse that sticks, for women's curses are more cruel than yours."

I saw it was past reasoning. I turned and untethered the black horse and mounted up.

When I had trotted him across the stone hall, she called my name, my tribal name, as she had used it earlier.

So I looked back. The tribes say it is unlucky to do so. There was a story Tathra had whispered to me, about a warrior who was enticed into the Black Place by a woman's spell and half regained his liberty, but the witch uttered his name, and he glanced over his shoulder, and she drew him back by the fox-fire in her eyes.

There was no fire in the eyes of Demizdor. I could barely make her out for the gloom, only the pale face, the one pale hand.

"You are my life," she said.

And she stepped away into the dark and vanished like smoke.

I did not call after her. I foresaw she would not answer me. I rode into the tunnel's mouth and did not look back again.

PART II

The Wolf Hunt

1

Eleven nights, ten days I traveled that thoroughfare. Judging by the additional passages I had observed leading to the hall of broken pillars, many of the great houses of Eshkorek had secret access to the under-city, and thereby to the ancient tunnel. Kortis' palace indisputably contained one of these entries. How else should Demizdor have known the place or the trick wall-openings unless she had been familiar with them from elsewhere? Besides, others took the route later, and not via Erran's cellars.

Having discovered the serpent marker on the stone and activated it, I entered a narrow, low-ceilinged run, speckled with the light of green and gray fungus, and with a foul, damp dungeon odor. This section took an hour's careful riding, occasionally bent double to avoid the roof. Then the way spread out again into some hall or cave, and grew black enough that I could not see a knife's length before me. I halted, struck a flint, unparceled one of the torches, and set light to it.

The resin flared up, but presently the flame sank a little, for the air was turgid and enclosed. High overhead, where torchlight could not reach, bats stirred, if bats they were; I never viewed them to be certain.

The floor was level and gave the horse no trouble, though we went slowly across the huge cavern, hidden at its perimeter and still shadowy before.

Then the burning resin flashed on something up ahead, and flashed again. A moment more and, lifting the torch to the length of my arm, I perceived a thing that made me swear aloud by gods I never knew I owned. It was not a cave wall but a wall of dressed stone, and in it an open arch taller than any tall tower of Eshkorek Arnor, and wide as seven streets. The lintel of the arch was a slab of red marble that glowed far overhead like a ruby in the semidark; the uprights were a

164

pair of columns of polished black granite, both close bound from base to summit by the twinings of a serpent of pure gold, whose massive jaw-wide head and heart-shaped hood in either case formed the capital. From foot to cap, each column stood at least a hundred feet; the height of the blood-glowing lintel was nearer a hundred and twenty. And in the marble there, carved letters filled in with gold, which named this colossal entrance by the most scornful of paradoxes:

SARVRA LFORN

Worm's Way

I sat my horse, torch in fist, staring. The thing confronting me was like some wondrous laughing malice, still fresh, though made in the youth of the world, a joke and a magnificence to outlast earth.

I remembered how she had told me They had built it, whoever *they* might be—the race from which her people had "degenerated," the supernatural god-folk, who had no need to eat or squat and who, presumably, had possessed riches without limit and slaves without number. And somehow it stole over me, the thought that I, like the princes of Eshkorek, did not wish to traverse this ancient way, this Sarvra Lforn. But I had no choice, being a fugitive, with perhaps even now the hunt up for me, and betrayal or cunning showing them my path.

I guided the horse forward. It tossed its head as if it wanted to progress no more than I.

The enormous hollow of the arch caught up the sound of hooves, the sputter of the resin, even, it seemed, my own breathing, like the giant soundbox of some instrument.

And then I came into the tunnel.

The quality of the atmosphere was altered at once. The torch sparked up, for, from vast heights and channels, fresh air filtered down. There was a dry, half-spicy smell that clung there, fragrant, pleasing, terrible, as if, just half an hour before, incense had burned and music played on this road none had traveled, surely, for a hundred years or longer.

Meanwhile, the torch was smiting like a sword on a thousand shades of brilliant color, on gems, on precious metal.

Dust had dimmed only a fraction, not enough. Decay had brushed with its rotten fingers not nearly all it should. It was an enchanted sweet, stuck in the throat of time.

The torch showed merely fragments, like bits of some broken mosaic I must fit together, and as I pieced it out, I was glad in my belly I should not see all at one moment, in a solitary glance.

Columns lined the broad concourse, slender carmine stalks with flower heads, lotuses and orchids of gold that met a roof like black looking-glass. Lamps hung there, fringed with webs now; once they had burned.

A marble paving ran beside the road. The walls of the tunnel rose beyond, tawny Eshkorek stone, yet smoothed to ice, and plastered, painted, fashioned into pictures. At first I thought they lived, those figures drawn there, they were that faithful to the life, and the scenes behind them seemed to stretch away into the walls themselves, where they could not go, but somehow did.

They were curious, the frescoes. Men flew through the sky in them, sometimes winged, more often wingless, always soaring, above wide plains and jagged peaks, the bow of the new moon or the red eye of a sinking sun beneath them. Lovers lay clasped in heatless conflagrations, or rode the backs of fish, or dallied with snakes, panthers, and lions. All these picture-people were sorcerers. They could tame the wind or send it, call beasts, call fire, calm ocean. . . . And one more thing I noted in them, other than their powers and their handsomeness—a few were very dark, dark as my father must have been, and as I was; but most were pale, paler than Demizdor's race even, not blond with eyes of jade or blue corunda, but white as alabaster with eyes of white flame.

White as Uastis, my albino mother.

White as a picked bone.

The construction of the tunnel was such that you could ride it at a gallop, meeting no obstacle. However, mistrusting the perfection of the paving—the roof which might have fallen farther ahead, some nebulous danger I had no name for (and wished to leave unnamed)—I kept the horse to a brisk parade trot. He was a strong, alert beast; we got several miles in this fashion.

Then the torch began to bow and smolder, and a weariness came over me like the weariness of the flame.

Up in the world it was near dawn, I supposed. I wondered if hounds were already stirring on my trail, or if they were yet in confusion at my escape. But, whatever their plans or mine, the need for sleep made me leaden. I was aware that I had been making on this long, without rest, not at the thought of pursuit, but because I did not relish halting here, let alone lying unconscious in this exotic desert.

At that moment the panting torch revealed an unexpected thing in the wall to my right—an oval of featureless darkness.

Curious, and not at ease, I swung about to look, and made out a recessed entrance that appeared to lead into some inner chamber.

I was intrigued, put aside my child's fears of lurks and haunts—to which this place, against my rationale but most definitely, made me prey—and rode between columns, up the marble pavement, and into the recess.

Inner chamber it was indeed, an apartment designed as a lodging, obviously for the god people who journeyed the tunnel.

At least the curtain that hung inside the entrance was perishable. It shivered to dusty particles as I brushed it, giving me the sense that I had wrongfully disturbed something I should not have presumed to touch.

The dying glare of the resin swept once over the big room, catching, as before, a variety of objects and glitters and, to the left of me, a man-high stand of solid silver with candles on iron spikes. It was only an arm's stretch to let the last of my torch kiss their wax awake. In seconds a warm pallor enfolded the entrance, and showed me similar stands about the room. It was oddly and unpleasantly irresistible to me to dismount, take up one of the burning candles, and walk around the chamber with it, giving light wherever it would prosper. Perhaps it was some spell of theirs, the old ones, wanting me to see the grandeur that was their monument. I remember I thought myself a fool after, for my actions and apprehensions in the tunnel.

It was a beautiful room; I had anticipated nothing else. The ceiling was green onyx carved into a forest-roof of leaves and vines where the light played glorious havoc with form and shadow. The rugs and draperies had turned as fine as spider-spun; you laid hand or foot on them and they were no more. Otherwise, the furnishings endured: the love couches in the shapes of mated ivory swans and ebony cats, the vases of chalcedony. I came on a huge silver dish of fruit, pristine as if newly plucked; then, putting in my hand, drew out an apple of chilly wine-red crystal, an amber peach, and grapes, each fashioned from black tourmaline with leaves of jade— the toys of men and women who regarded fruit as ornament, having no need to fill their bellies.

It seemed the legends were true. There was something else. A sumptuous bathing apartment opened behind a door of gold. I found it abruptly and went in to see. The sunken bath was full of moss and the golden dolphin taps no longer dispersed water. There was another lack. Accustomed to Eshkorek, I searched about. At length I grinned stupidly, for I was afraid—of the story, the reality, of a difference so absolute. There was no latrine.

It was like a crude joke. It was like a blow in the face.

Any man who crossed their exquisite tunnel must leave his dung like a rat. It was later I discovered the narrow, dust-choked privies they had had built that their human slaves might not soil the thoroughfare. There is a certain black shame to see one's irremediable self through such eyes.

Finally I tethered and fed the horse; Demizdor had thought of all such necessities. I lay down to sleep. Not on one of their love couches, unconcealed and brazen as nothing else of theirs needed to be, but on the webby floor, wrapped in my cloak.

It was a sudden sleep that took me, and deep, though not agreeable. For with slumber, the wall paintings came alive. . . .

A woman stood over me. She was winged with light and garbed in it; her face was like a star. She stirred me with her foot. I could not rise or move my limbs.

"Vazkor, man, magician, warrior, Black Wolf," she said. "War-lord, king, fool, dead, maker of a son. Vazkor son of Vazkor. Who is your mother?"

In my dream I assumed she was a ghost, and my hair shifted on my neck, as if ants walked there.

Later I was crawling in an intricate maze of white marble, trying to reach a plate of fruit laid out for me at its center.

The god-race had shut me in the maze for their amusement, to see how intelligent the inferior human might be. I could hear them laugh and lay bets on me. When I took a wrong turning, a woman's voice would cry sharply, "No, Vazkor, Not *that* way." (In Eshkorek I had seen the gold- and silver-masks indulge in a similar pastime, setting a mouse in a miniature labyrinth, and watching it scurry hither and thither after the food. If it found the dish, they would pet it and reward it. Some of the creatures perished of hunger before they solved the puzzle.)

Once in the dream I was flying. The upper air was blue with dusk and I threw a black shadow over the plain below. Before me a woman darted like a white pigeon. I caught her by the hair, and it was Demizdor, and there was a dagger in her hand. I said to her, "We are the sun of our achievements, nothing more and nothing less." And she said to me, "Vazkor, you are a *human man.*" And she struck the dagger to its hilt into my brain.

There was no pain, only a blazing and a blindness; then a sense of icy water, and in the water a million knives.

I started up, soaked in my own cold sweat.

I thought, *Is it to be thus, then, I must be a battling ground for them, my father and my mother? He got her with me, and she worked some curse on him and he died, and they will reenact it forever?*

I lay sleepless then awhile, too worn out to rise and make on. When I slept again, there were other dreams. I was to grow accustomed to them on that journey.

The beauty of the tunnel became monotonous; it never altered.

Generally after many hour's riding, I would seek the elaborate rest-chambers for my slumber. Each time I must steel myself against the dreams. It was as if the ghosts gathered to mock me then. At last, even that niggling horror lost its edge. I woke unharmed, and awake; no phantom challenged me. My own mind was my enemy and my obscure heritage, nothing else.

Sometimes the apartments in the tunnel achieved peaks of fantasy. There was a particular stopping place all shades of red, ceiling of strawberry glass, furniture dyed with vermilion-red copper lamps, even a dish of polished garnets cut to resemble plums—somehow, I never thought of stealing them. There were other rooms like this, all green, all black—many were a treasure trove for thieves, yet they had never been plundered.

Then, too, there were curiously poignant surprises. The small silver harp left lying on a couch, as if put down only an instant ago, and in an instant more, she—it had been meant for a girl—would be back to take it up again. Or the board game like Castles, yet unlike, with pieces of gold and enamel standing on their squares, the play unfinished now till eternity.

By the eighth day the dreams had begun to ebb; rather I had a waking dream, which concerned my earlier life and the men and women who peopled it.

This was like a pursuit that had caught up to me now that I was alone and had the leisure to remember. Human action seems dogged by guilt, frustration, and melancholia. There is always something to think back to, and say, *I would I had not; or, I would that I had.*

Of other pursuit I had some warning on the tenth night.

I was reckoning in nights and days, though I had no evidence of them, keeping to an earlier assessment of the passing of hours. The tribes reckon by the sun and moon, the position of stars and shadows; the cities have other ways, great mechanisms of iron, pendulum clocks, and clepsydra. So, I had learned two methods: the old instinct inbred in me from the krarl, the means of measuring from Eshkorek. In the tunnel anything to hand became a measure for time: the length a candle took to burn, or a torch; the hours of the stomach, hunger and thirst; and sleep. When I emerged aboveground, I was not far out either, in my judgment. . . .

That tenth "night," having dismounted to water the horse from the shallow vessel Demizdor had provided, I heard a sound behind me, miles away back along the length of the thoroughfare. It was the faintest drumming, scarcely more than a vibration, faultlessly transmitted through the rocky roadway, the walls, the polished roof: hooves, and hooves coming on at a gallop.

My own horse was untired; he had had an easy ride of it this far. I let him finish his drink, then mounted up and set him trotting. Presently, when he felt his legs, I lightly slapped his side, no more powerful urging being needed for an Eshkorian beast, and he shot forward as if glad to be going.

I had to trust my luck, then, if luck I had, that no sudden subsidence or barrier would present itself. Till now the path had been mostly straight and always open, a fact the men behind me seemed to take for granted, coming at the pace they did. At all events, with them a day behind or less, I needed wings.

The dreams and retrospections sloughed from me.

The journey had shrunk to more natural if no less ominous proportions, and I should, in any case, have no margin for sleep the next "night"—this much was obvious.

For the hunt was up.

2

My horse was sound as a bell. He bore me through the tenth night spear-swift; the tenth day, after resting him and myself two hours, he took up our flight again as if it were a personal thing with him that I should get away. Indeed, on the eleventh night, my last in the tunnel, when I was scorch-eyed and light-headed from missing sleep, I began to think my city wife, child of magician stock, had placed a magic on him to keep him fleet.

My last torch had burned out somewhere in the previous "day," and I had appropriated a gold lamp from one of the rest-chambers, and lighted that. I had not wanted to use Their equipment, but had no choice.

About what I assumed to be midnight, I dismounted, knelt, and laid my ear to the paving. There was no vibration of hooves; no doubt the hunters took their ease at nights. I slept three hours, having observed the usual precaution of setting the iron water flask against my side; you need to be near dead not to turn in your sleep after an hour or so, and the hard object woke me each time, and each time got a round cursing, but without it I should not have woken till the hounds had me by the throat.

Waking, and hearing no noise still, I walked the horse for a couple of hours before remounting, to save him. I should not be done with him, even at the tunnel's end.

If the tunnel ended. Maybe it was witch-work and had no end.

Then the lamp fluttered and went sick green and was suddenly extinguished.

The air was bad; it had a sour smell. The horse jerked his head, snorting, and my throat closed. I thought, *Now I stifle in the dark, fine end to my escape.* But I was not in the dark after all. As my eyes adjusted after the lamp, I could make out a jumble of rock ahead, and through that a shaft of gray that marked, however faintly, the outer world.

We went cautiously over the debris—it looked to me as if there had been some tremor of the earth that had cracked the rock and brought down the roof in one huge slab. It was the only blow that had befallen the architecture of the tunnel. There had been a broad stairway there before the quake, and probably another imposing arch-mouth to make men shrink. Nothing now but rubble, and an exit between broken blocks.

But no matter—soon I was breathing the world's air, and the smell of that air was sweet as flowers. The horse shook his mane, and kicked the earth with his feet.

The tunnel emerged on the floor of a stony valley with, away at its sides, shallow sloping hills, black-green in the moment before dawn. The opening faced to the south—leftward the sun was rising a blue veil of mist, one of those suns of earliest spring that seem to have no substance and no depth, yet flay the land with light.

That sun. It was like the air, better than any sun that ever rose. I could have yelled for pure gladness at being above-ground.

I looked back; the mountains were fading off north and west, many miles behind me now, their lower parts missing in the haze, their tops transparently glowing with the dawn, like islands in the sky.

I mounted and the horse sprang off, galloping southeast.

I had only two notions on the matter of direction. First, that the pursuers might guess I would strike back east and north, west even, to get on the old tribal routes, and lose myself among my adoptive people. Second, that my shortest road to the sea lay southeast. The sea was a phenomenon I had never clapped eyes on for myself, yet it seemed, from the tales, a destination ultimate and uncompromising. The ocean's edge, the brink of the land; the lip of Chaos. Who would reason the hunted wolf would run that way?

The fresh air had me drunk with optimism. My food was three days gone; I picked up stones from the way, and used my belt as a sling to get a hare for my dinner, a trick I had learned as a boy. Now that I was free of the tunnel, and the ground rising, I kept a check on what came behind me. Seeing no sign of followers through the daylight, I made a fire that night in a hollow of the low hills where young oak trees grew, and broiled the hare's flesh, while the horse cheerfully cropped spring grass. There was even a pool to drink from among the trees. These normal things were bounty after the ungiving majesty of the under-mountain road.

I made on before sunup. Having gained time, I had no mind to lose it again.

It was hilly country for the most part, though off to the east lay a flat, smoky plain, mirrored by countless dim green waters, so that it seemed at times portions of the bright sky had fallen there among its spreading osiers; the edge of some marshland I was glad to have bypassed.

The second night, there was a cave. I slept too comfortably and lost some hours riding.

That day the land peaked up, rough grassy country and thin woodland, spruce, oak saplings, pine and ivy-clad rock-thrusts, and here and there a great white mound of limestone, old quarries mined no longer and sprinkled yellow with premature wildflowers.

Having got high enough, I watched some minutes among the trees, scanning through the cloud- and sun-play over the terrain below and behind. It was raining northward, obscuring the insubstantial mountains. Presently, between the rain and the light, I made out a formation of dark specks. The hunt.

They were less than a day away from me already, and had gauged my direction. Perhaps they had seen me on the skyline ahead, or picked up the marks of hooves in the softer clays of the marsh-skirting slopes.

I remembered, with a sour irony, how I had tracked the Eshkir slavers through the mountains the spring before, guided by their horses and their negligence.

I had rationed the hare, now ate none of it and rode on, dismounting at moonrise to rest the horse from me, but continuing on my feet and leading him. I had exercised care since I spotted the hunting party, keeping to cover, or skulking along under the tops of the hill crests.

With the hunt this close, I needed stratagem rather than pace.

I eventually foresaw I should have to relinquish my horse.

It is the oldest trick of the quarry to dismount, and thrash his beast on ahead to mislead those who come after, yet it is not a step to be taken lightly. Once the horse is gone, he is gone for good, and then you are on foot, half as slow and half as vulnerable again as you were before. However, you cannot instruct your horse not to release his dung, not to make dents with his feet in mud, and, unless you want him wind-broken and dead, you can only force him to race for just so long, and no longer.

The hunt had a guide, a clever one; I had reasoned this out. He could follow the horse tracks perfectly. The fifth dawn had come, and I saw riders gathered behind and below me in a narrow green trough under the hills. There were only nine or ten of them, and one—the guide—kneeled on the ground among some rocks, examining the place where I had allowed myself an hour's sleep. That decided me. They were gaining rapidly, the guide was astute, they anticipated I should ride till I dropped from my saddle with bone-weariness. Thus, I must let the horse run on alone, and hope to make fools of them.

I walked the horse till noon. The grassy hills had ragged tops of chalky stone; between, the way was level enough to give him some decent running. One of the Whip winds was blowing up from the north; at least he would not be plunging into it. I let him eat as we went, removed the bit and bridle, and loaded the saddle-pouches with clods and rocks to minimize the difference the depth of his tracks would show the guide, once I was off. I slung my water-flask about my neck, and set the horse easterly. I trusted he would not bolt onto the treacherous marshy plain, but keep to the edge of it.

There was plenty of speed in him still, and the Eshkiri horses like to run.

I stung him with my belt to make him go. It seemed a rough and thankless parting to offer a good mount, but there was no help for it. He shot forward, the grass spraying from his hooves, and shortly vanished over the green ridges under the blowing black and white sky.

The ground was hard enough here, I hoped, to bequeath no track of my own. I turned due south, carrying the bit and bridle perforce, so as to leave no clue, and broke into the rhythmic, mile-eating man-trot the boys learn in the krarl. If your legs and your lungs are whole, you can keep this up for quite a while and make excellent time.

Then all my planning want for nothing.

The wind cracked the sky open. A white lightning flash, and rain slanted on the gale like a gray sheet. Three flashes more and I was engulfed in a curtain of water.

What would happen now was this: The rain would wash out the beguiling traces of the decoy horse; it would additionally form mud which, if the deluge ceased as abruptly as it had commenced, would dry the perfect imprint of my own footfalls. Meanwhile, blundering blindly through the wet. I would distribute as many obliging tokens of my passage as there were unseen bushes to trample through and branches to snap. There was also one other pleasing thing. Some horses will not run in a storm. Maybe my Eshkorian steed would balk, freeze, or bolt back the way I had sent him, empty-saddled, into my pursuers' midst.

I stood in the lightning-splintered rain, cursing myself to further thought. It seemed to me I should proceed no farther than to the nearest hiding place, and thereby create as few tracking signals as I could. The horse, if it continued going despite my doubts, would mark indications of its flight the guide might yet discover. And, whatever happened, they would not imagine me crouched at the wayside. They would believe I had pressed on.

Accordingly I made up the adjacent slope to the little natural tower of limestone at its summit, Here, between two porous spurs, is the black glue of the mud, I resigned myself to waiting out the storm.

It was to be a long, long wait.

The storm battered on the hills, sometimes stampeding off

a way, then returning. The rain and wind did not abate. Four hours must have passed, and with grim humor I began to keep a look out for the hunt. I had by then started belaboring myself; I should have foretold the foul weather, the warnings of it had been there to see, I should have retained the horse, I should have run on south, trusting the rain to hold and confuse my track. In short, I should have done everything I had not.

Presently five riders dashed across the slope below, heading southeast.

Obviously the party had split, no longer sure of my direction.

They were all Kortis' men. Even through the rain, I had made out their black, their silver skull-faces with black glass eyes. Only the captains of Kortis Phoenix Javhovor wore the uniform of my father's guard. Still set on retribution?

I wondered how far they would get before they came up with my horse, or else turned back for cover. I wondered, too, where the other four or five had taken themselves and if any of Erran's soldiery were with them. Though my usefulness for Erran was over and he had no particular interest in vengeance, there were still his scientific philospher's experiments with my flesh. Maybe he had offered some reward for me, and Kortis' impoverished captains were riding for it. Nemarl might have sent men, too. Yet there were only ten I had noted. Not many for the pelt of the Black Wolf, son of the Black Wolf of Ezlann. Perhaps there were other parties abroad I had not yet seen.

This conjecture made me sullen, at myself, my situation, my lack of advantage.

Suddenly three more riders came through the rain, this time moving slowly. As they drew level with my concealment, the first dismounted, kneeled in the mud, and cast about. The horse of this, the guide, was smaller and stockier, and he was unmasked. A Dark Slave. The two captains, hooded against the weather, showed me their black silver skull-heads; then one reached idly to brush the rain away from a clump of grasses growing in the hillside. It was a fatuous womanish gesture, his wrist slender in its gauntlet, and so I knew him; Demizdor's kinsman, Orek.

"Well," the other called to the slave, "what do you make of it?"

The slave mumbled something in a stilted version of the city tongue.

The captain said, "We have lost him, Orek, unless our luck turns."

Orek flung around in his saddle furiously.

"No, by my soul, We shall find him. Ah! Why did Lord Kortis give us no bronzes?"

"He thought it wasted effort. He would not set soldiery to catching Erran's wolfhound."

Orek struck his thigh with his fist, that mannerism especial to girls and girlish men hoping to ape virility.

"Erran shall not get him back when we have him, no, by the golden whore." Then his voice broke like a boy's, as if he wept. That surprised me. I thought, *Does even Orek weep because he is angry?* Before I could reason it out, he slashed his horse viciously with the silver-headed crop, and it floundered forward and away into the rain, after the rest.

Next moment the Absurd took a hand.

The remaining silver captain dismounted and began to lead his horse up the slope toward my limestone shelter, calling to the slave over his shoulder, "I've had enough bathing, fellow. I am for waiting here till the storm's done. Ride and tell Zrenn where I am. Tell him they'll be riding blind till midnight. We'll find no tracks till this downpour's spent."

The guide got back on his horse, and rode off northward to where, presumably, the remaining group of men were searching. The captain continued walking up the hill toward me.

I had had plenty of roosting in the wet, and plenty of being hunted, too.

I quickly unsheathed the bronze-mask's sword I had stolen, waited till the silver man came around the first spur, then stood up and cut him clean through, breast to back.

His glazing stare of surprise was evident, even through mask and smoked glass eye-pieces. I pulled off the mask and the rain danced on his eyeballs.

The horse, used to storm and ungentle behavior, stood patiently, observing me with indifference. I looked at the wet black clothes of the dead man, his mask, his horse, and I thought, *Why not?*

One quarter of an hour later, a silver captain rode down the slope, masked, gloved, hooded, leaving a half-dressed corpse wedged in the chalky mud of the hilltop.

The captain had not gone far when two others rode up from the north, hailing him with cries and news.

"Zrenn has made south, with Nemarl's seven and the slave. He thinks Vazkor has gone that way, and Zrenn means to circle around and trap him between two bands."

"Does he?" said the silver captain.

The two riders trotted over to him and cowered in the rain. If they had known how near dry dust they were, they would have savored every drop. The silver captain leaned to the nearest and knifed him between the ribs. As this one toppled, his neighbor, with an oath, snatched at his sword. Not quickly enough. The captain's own sword, already bloody, went through his neck, ending oath, intention, and life.

This silver captain, clearly a renegade and madman, thereafter turned his horse and galloped southeast, letting the rain clean his weapons as he went.

We see what we have always seen. It if seems, it is.

The renegade mad captain—I—soon came on three more silvers. The storm was slackening at last, in sinking buffets. The rain eased and left a sky purpling with dusk, with one brass hammerhead standing where the sun should have gone down. Beneath a rocky overhang, three men wrung out their cloaks and reviled nature, and spoke of Zrenn and Nemarl's seven captains and the lack of bronze soldiery, and, noticing me, hailed me, and soon lay in the grass, one without his head.

From being quarry, I had turned hunter, and it pleased me.

These men who had jeered as they watched me writhe in Eshkorek now ended their quest on my blades. I should not, had they caught me, have ended so daintily. I did not mind leaving the clues of their corpses for guide and pack. Coming on their dead, the living must have imagined witchcraft was afoot in those southeastern hills.

I was learning, too, from their snippets of dialogue before I killed them, the strength of their forces and their method of campaign.

All told, there were eighteen silvers, seven of them Nemarl's men, scouring the land for me. It appeared an odd number. If they were intent on having me, why send this few; if I was worth little, why bother with me at all? It seemed a personal feud, as before. I considered that Demizdor could have rallied her kin kinfolk on my trail, her bitter love curdling into hate again. That would certainly account for the small number of Kortis' men, and for the sparsity, yet determination, of Nemarl's band, for no doubt there were several in the city who were sweet on my blond wife and ready to run her errands.

As for their plan—some rode ahead, less, now that I had had dealings with them; some rode around, circling for me. The storm had disorganized the hunt, and the wolf had fallen on the pack from behind.

The night dawned black, rain-washed of its stars.

The marsh had slid from sight to the east; the hills were leveling into rolling uplands of gray chalky turf and clawing trees.

My body felt hollow from wanting sleep, but I had a powerful urge to keep going, and to say I had got no keen joy from killing my enemies would be to lie. In fact I was looking forward to next meeting them with a distinct thirst for blood, a raiding warrior again, with a store of fury to spare. I had been slave and coward and sophisticate too long in Eshkorek, and the gilt was wearing thin.

Eventually, I saw a red glow on the black ahead of me.

In an ancient quarry about eight feet below, a fire burned, and around it sat seven men. Two were unmasked skull-heads, the other five wore the ragged gray and saffron livery I recalled as being Nemarl's. The slave guide was also with them, roasting over the flames on a skewer a couple of ill-skinned rabbits.

I was curious to learn how they would eat these, the households of the two Javhovors, unlike Erran's, keeping as they did to the pretense of secret stomachs. But I never did learn, for one of the skull captains turned to me, took in my gear and horse, and said, "Well Skor, we have abandoned the search for tonight. Did you come across Zrenn and Orek and the rest out there, chasing their tails in the dark?"

So it was the cousins of Demizdor who were yet absent, together with two of Nemarl's men. All others I had accounted for, bar these in the quarry.

"No," I said. I was smiling in the mask, biting on the feel of violence to come. Seven men for killing. I never thought I should not do it. Even if they wounded me, I would heal. They were babes left in the grass of the lion's run.

"No? That's a short sentence for Skor," a man remarked. "What, no grumbles about the storm and the ride, and a wolf hunt with no wolf to be found?"

"Oh, there's a wolf," I said.

And I rode the horse straight over the edge and across the fire at him, striking him down as I passed, wheeling, and leaning to slaughter three more before they realized properly what devil was loose among them.

The Dark Slave had tumbled aside. I took up his skewer, the roasting rabbits still fixed on it and got another unmasked skull-head through the brains with it as he came for me.

Then someone had stumbled the horse, which crashed over, and I with it. A man of Nemarl's leaped on me; I twitched aside, and his blade, missing the heart, pinned my right shoulder to the earth. I wrenched up the length of it with a howl of agony and rage, and smashed my fist into his jaw, and as his head snapped back, I stabbed him left-handed in the throat.

He fell on me, stone dead. I got up from under him and worked the sword out of my flesh. Only the slave and I remained. The last skull-head was scrambling from the quarry, yelling for Zrenn (or maybe for his mother; it was hard to be sure). I wished for an arrow or spear to bring him down, but had none, and a knife would not travel far enough.

But I did not require an arrow. Now, when I barely needed it, I grew aware of the armament I had in me, as I had in Ettook's painted tent.

Yet it was not the same. On that occasion the energy had used me to escape into the world. Currently it seemed I could control the thing, saddle and ride it, and dismount when I was done. I pulled off the silver skull-mask, dropped and kicked it aside.

Become easy, I scarcely felt it leave me, that sorcerer's power, by the door of the eyes.

A thin white skim of light over the quarry. The yelling man floundering there let go his hold and flung wide his arms as if to fly, and dropped back among the scattered embers of the fire, and was silent.

I felt dizzy, but not weak; I had contained the power, utilized it, and put it to rest. This exhilarated me. I turned about and found the Dark Slave still standing near me.

His ugly face showed no fear, enjoyment, or chagrin at the death I had inflicted on his masters. But he got down, without a word onto his belly, and pressed his face in the mud and ash before me. Then rising, still speechless, he sought the murdering skewer, the end of which was affixed in the forehead of a man, plucked off a part-roast rabbit, and loped away with it into the pit of the night.

I had been worshiped as a god, and I had been ignored as valueless.

Two strong liquors to mingle in one cup.

My shoulder was spurting blood. I assumed it would heal quickly and paid no heed to it. Indeed, I was very arrogant about the matter. After this I remember little for several days.

My game with the power of white light had cost me something after all. My wound was slow to close and bled much. Weary as I was, I must have staggered for miles, forgetting the horses or that four hunters remained to seek my trail.

Somehow I eluded pursuit, or else my drunkard's insane wanderings took me out of the path of it.

I went mainly east, I think. At one point I rambled over a thread of river by a bridge of stone older than the old trees that grew there.

I lost about four days in this obtuse state, and finally came to myself lying by some pool where I had crawled to drink like a sick bear. My wound was healed, and my thickheaded stupidity with it. The air smelled new to me, an open, singular smell, and the pool was salty.

I muttered to myself that never again must I kill by use of a white energy harvested from the brain. But I sounded like a lunatic mumbling there. I could hardly believe any of it, and a sense of reality returned to me only in stages.

3

That evening I met a black witch with a red cat, walking on a headland above the sea.

I had reached the sea unexpectedly, but the sea is unexpected in any event to one who has never known it. You think it land at first, or sky, and penultimately mist. Then you realize a vast azure mass of water lies like a dragon in the sun's last rays, breathing and shifting on the beaches.

Like a sort of madness itself it seemed to complement my own bewildered wandering. When I saw the girl, she, too, was like an oblique figment or expression of my mental process.

A striking wrench, black as a coal, with a black satin mane, born demonstrably of the black marsh tribes, except that when you came near, you saw she had some mixed blood, for out of that delicate ebony face (the black women do not wear the shireen) stared a pair of wild eyes, the pale blue-gray of the sea behind her.

She had on a dark shift, plain krarl women's garb, and a bracelet of greenish smooth stones, and gold studs in her ears. Around her neck was what I took for an orange-red fur hood, but it was a foxy cat, with a fierce glare.

Both their heads went up when they saw me and both their eyes flashed so that I smiled at it.

"Well," she said, "I have summoned you, and you have come. Are you specter or man or conjuring?"

"Man," I said. "Shall I prove it to you?"

Then she smiled also, a different, woman's smile, and turned her face. Her profile was chiseled, aquiline and almost flat, like a carving, save for her full mouth, the lower lip indented like a plum, but the color of mulberries.

"You are too tall," she said, "and too white, but you are handsome for all that. Maybe I will lie with you, but not yet."

"Lady," I said, "you should not play games alone with a man, and no one within call to help you."

"Oh, I am not alone. I can draw spirits to help me at a need. I am a witch, I am Uasti."

That name checked me for sure, though I had been pleasantly considering other things, for generally, when a woman talks in this way, "maybe" means "certainly" and "not yet" means "why are you so slow?"

"Uasti?" I stupidly repeated. Although she spoke it differently, less soft and fewer letters, it was the name of the Ezlann cat-goddess, my bitch mother's name.

"Thus I am known," the black girl said. "I am witch and healer, and women who learn cure-craft from the priests of my people are called Uasti. It has always been the custom. My cat, too, is the mark of my calling."

"Uasti is a city name," I said, stupid still, "and the cat the symbol of a dead goddess there."

"Perhaps. In our tongue are many old words, borrowed from the Ancient Golden Books of the priests, or so they say. Uasti is one, meaning healing and wisdom, and its symbol is the cat, for who does not know that the cat is wise? Are you not, beloved?" she added to the fierce red creature about her neck, which responded with an alarming howl that might indicate a variety of attributes, wisdom being the least of them.

"However," my witch added, "I have a secret name that you may use. That is: Hwenit."

Then it came to me, and for the first, that she spoke a language I had never heard in my life—yet I recognized and could speak it with her.

At that I stopped dead in my tracks.

I had uncannily mastered city speech, laying the ability, with childish complaisance, at my father's door. This, however, I could find no excuse for. I marveled at it and it shivered my neck. Each fresh revelation of Power—the killing light, my healing skin, this gift of tongues—had staggered me, but not sufficiently. This made me half crazy, afraid of what was in me. It appeared I had been growing since infancy into some fabulous denizen of a myth.

"Hwenit," I shouted, "you are a witch and can bring demons. Bring one, or I shall have you here and now."

Her pale gaze turned to knives and she showed her teeth.

"Don't think I cannot," she cried, "but the cat will gouge out your eyes before I need to work magic."

"Show me this sorcery," I said, lunging at her. "I am a sorcerer, too. Subdue me."

She eluded me, and the red cat raked my forearm with its daggered paw. Somehow, I knew I could make the scratches heal faster than any wound, small or deep, had healed on me before. I held out my arm to Hwenit-Uasti, where she could observe the blood. I did not watch the scratches close, only her face.

Presently she said in a small, thin voice, "I have seen a priest do this, once, when he had been in the place of the Book. I cannot do this thing. If you are a healer, you will not hurt me."

"Don't be positive, morsel of witch."

"I wish I had not summoned you now," she said, fidgety as an autum wasp. "You are too big and too clever. I should have left well alone."

"So you should. Why do it? And do you suppose such a powerful magician as I have turned out to be has no free will, but must appear at a snap of your black-jade fingers?"

"Well," she said slyly, recovering herself somewhat. "You are here."

Then she turned and ran away, looking back once to see if I followed, and hesitating when she saw I had not.

"Come," she cried. "Make the Summer Dance with me. Come, Mordrak; catch me and I will let you in my door," and she ran along the edge of the headland through the brown dusk, the cat around her neck howling like a furious ghost.

Her village lay half a mile off, in a thatch of flinty meadow on the bony cliff-top, which crumbled down to a beach of mingled pebble and ocean-folded sand. Other cliffs of the range jerked from the coast to left and right of it. Tall grasses rattled in the wind, and the sea groaned as the tide pulled it from the shore, then dragged it back, an ever-unwilling slave.

The village was small, about twenty or twenty-five huts of mud-brick. Jet-black goats maundered or skipped through fenced enclosures beyond. Red fires were burning up in the salty evening air, Clearly, Hwenit-Uasti's krarl was no longer

nomadic, as the tribes usually were—red, yellow, or black—
and I wondered what choice invisible pickings had encour-
aged them to put down roots in such a spot. Maybe they
relished fried fish?

She had let me come up to her when home was in sight,
but I had not actually been chasing her, only letting her lead
me, guessing she was going to her krarl-hearth. My brief flare
of sexual appetite had long since abated. I had been starving
for food quite a while, neither had I slept soft, or had shelter
for many days. I had forgotten the four hunters and the mas-
sacre I had scattered over the hills inland. Even my sorcerous
powers seemed abruptly banal and unimportant. As for the
girl, I could believe almost anything just then, and possibly
she *had* summoned me by witching. After all, she said, I was
there.

I had heard tales of the black folk. The red tribes reckoned them simple; they were not. They must at some date
have come from hotter lands, to judge by their skin, but that
was long ago. If they knew of it, they gave the knowledge no
utterance. As for their healers and their worship of gold
books of old lore, there had been tribal stories of this, too, all
nonsense, as anything chattered by the ill-informed must be.

Some of the women were outside their huts, cooking the
evening meal. Slender and dark as night, they did not fall to
gawking as Hwenit conducted me into the village. A group of
men at the village's lower end had been erecting two more
hut-houses, and had broken off, as the light went, to discuss
the work. To these Hwenit called, in an imperious voice,
"Where is my father?"

The men looked up, nodded politely to me as if they had
seen me many times, and the nearest answered, "He has gone
walking, with Qwef."

At that Hwenit-Uasti shook her hair, as if the name or the
fact irritated her.

"Follow," she directed me in her empress tone, and stalked
on, nearly bowling over a small black handsome child, who
courteously, and prudently no doubt, gave her right of way.

Hwenit-Uasti's hut was the last one, set a little apart from
the others, having a fine doorway of dressed stone painted
pink and yellow, and a lighted lamp of red clay and a
string of tiny black rodent skulls depending together from the
lintel. A strange tree grew beside the hut, a surprising dwarf

fir, which the lamplight showed to be a powdery blue in color.
It was of the sort the antique kings, perhaps, nurtured in their
gardens; I had never seen its like before.

"Because I am Uasti, I have a well-made house, and a blue
tree to mark it out," said Hwenit. The faces of the men and
women in the village had been enigmatic and not unfriendly,
yet I had sensed a faint air of affectionate indulgence directed
toward their healer. Were the doorway and the tree toys for
a talented and precocious child? "The women will bring me
food," said she, "and some for you, since they see I have a
guest. Enter, but touch none of the herbs or instruments of
my trade."

Ducking under the hut door, I yawned. I pondered whether
she feared it would be clumsiness, my igorance, or my magic
powers would cause some damage.

Inside it was dim and warm from an iron brazier already
fired. The bent boughs and stem of the blue fir impressed inward through the mud wall; a witch's clutter was everywhere.
Thick rugs lay over the floor. I sat there, and soon stretched
out, lazy as a dog in the sun. A drowsy inclination came over
me again to draw her down at my side, but I never stirred. I
could hear the rumble of the sea turning in its chains, and
smell the smoke of the sultry flames and the smoky scent of a
woman's body, and I needed no other charm to wile me
asleep. She would be safe enough with me that night. Possibly
too safe for her liking.

4

I woke when the sun, lifting above sea and cliff, had begun
to stream in through the hut doorway. This pale midmorning
light was like a beacon of danger to me. I came alert, raw to
the memory of the hunt, the killing, the four who lived to
dog me, sure they were on my track and close behind.

I rose at once, and clattered my head against a mummified lizard suspended from the low ceiling.

A copper pot was silkily bubbling on the brazier, giving off an aromatic herbal steam. Hwenit and her cat were gone. Outside, gulls were crying and the goats *maa*ing faintly, but no other sounds.

Then a woman came in with the sun at the door, bearing a reed-woven mat, and on it a dish and a cup. She had come silently, but they were a silent people—comely, too, from the look of it. The stranger smiled and set the mat and the food before me on the rug.

"I am Hadlin," she informed me, "By what name may I call you?"

The thought of the hunt on me, I answered, "Your witch calls me Mordrak."

"Then so will I, if it will be agreeable," said Hadlin, kind, sensible, and very sweet, as if she guessed me in some trouble.

The name Mordrak did well enough certainly. Its roots were in the black tribe's word for ivory or white bone, but its construction suggested also their obsolete title for a warrior—the black people eschewed fighting, and I would come to learn they never slew even an animal save in self-defense. Their clothes were woven of reed flax and bartered wool, they ate no meat, not even the fish obligingly to hand in the ocean. The food in the dish was, I found after, a steak of beans and chestnuts, baked over the fire, tasty in its own way but curious at first. The drink was goat milk, though, at various seasons, they brewed and drank honey mead.

I sat down again to eat, thanking the woman called Hadlin. She turned to leave and murmured as she went, "Peyuan will seek you in a little while."

"Who is Peyuan?"

"Peyuan is our chief, the father of Uasti. He wishes to know only if he may help you."

"That is generous of your chief, but I must be on my way. He will help me best by letting me go swiftly."

"Oh, but you may go at any hour you wish. There is no constraint."

I did not intend to be ungracious to this pretty woman with the gentle manner, (I had changed somewhat already from my warrior attitudes, despite the cognomen Hwenit had given me). Nor did I want bickering with their chief. I said I would wait and see him, though the nerves in my spine told me I should not linger here.

He was not long in coming, just long enough for me to eat—they were masters at such intuitive niceties.

"I am Peyuan," he said, prefacing himself with no honorific.

I stood up, careful this time of the dried lizard, but he indicated I should sit, and sat himself.

Peyuan was between forty-five and fifty, his long hair graying, his hard body going to flint rather than flaccidity as he gained years, like a slim, aging tree. He had leaned on a spear, symbol more than weapon, and he laid it between us on the rugs, the staff pointing west in a sign of peace.

"My Hwenit brought you," he said. "She imagines she magicked you from the ground. She has such fancies, but she is a shrewd healer for all that. She fancies, too, that you also have some magic power, but I shall not ask you this, for it is your burden, not mine. I will only inquire, since you are a wanderer, if we may be of service to you on your road?"

"My chief," I said, "I am grateful for the help I have already received. I will say this, I am being hunted, and must make on before the hunt comes here and does harm to your krarl as well as to myself."

"No harm will come to us," he said calmly. "Will you tell me why they hunt you?"

"An ancient feud. Vengeance. They have a score to settle with my father, and the penalty has devolved on me."

He looked down at the spear between us, then up into my face. His dark eyes—it was Hwenit's mother who had had the blue ones—probed me with a solemn concentration, not discourteous but profound.

"I will recount something strange to you," Peyuan said. "Reply or not, as you choose. You are strong and hard, you have been a fighter, yet you bear no scar. Something in you, the set of your eyes, reminds me of another I once saw, some twenty years ago. A woman. Let me describe this woman. White skin without a blemish, hair like ice."

"And her face," I said, before I could stop myself.

He said, "I never saw her face. She wore the shireen. Only her eyes, which were pale and very bright, still-water eyes. Yet, though I never saw her unmasked, she was lovely. This you could perceive in her every movement, the turn of her head, her limbs, her body. She would have owned great beauty."

"You had her, then," I said.

"No, we did not lie together," he answered quietly. "It seems strange to me now that, at the time, I never thought of her in that way, never desired her."

"She was my mother," I said, dry-throated. "She bore me and left me. I never knew her, but I have heard from some who did. She betrayed and killed my father, that I am sure of."

"Did she?" he asked. "That's very odd. She never seemed to me a woman who would kill for spite. It is long since. Perhaps I remember poorly. She came among us like a lost child. We were journeying then; I recall we believed a big cat, a lynx, followed us across the marshes, but it was she. One night she stole the offering we left for our gods. Yet when we found her and took her in, she was withdrawn and compliant. The woman said she wept as we walked. Then she would talk to herself, names and phrases in other tongues. But this ended. If she was distracted, it was the mania some god had sent her. Also, I recollected after, it was said that she had spoken a language very like that which our priests revealed to us, before the krarls were scattered—the language of the Golden Books. That was uncanny, for we were on our summer wayfaring then, making for the sea, and a tower where one of these Books lay hidden. In those days, my krarl came every year to the spot—it lies not far north of this village an hour's journey or less. Qwenex was the chief. He brought out the Book when we had gathered at the tower, and showed us. She, too, the white one, put her hand on the gold. Later, after the Summer Dance, when the Circle of Remembrance had been formed, she came and broke the Circle, thinking we were tranced, or dead perhaps. Thus she learned that the pages of the Book are blank, that only through empathy and dream can we reach back to the suffering and the terror, those cruel lessons to be garnered there, along with the lesson of Power. This she did not understand. Neither our Circle, nor our motives."

I said, "She stole from you, and, as your guest, interrupted your sacred rite. This sounds like her. Did she do you any good?"

He smiled at me.

"Must you be done good in order that you love?"

"Love," I said. "If you loved her, you loved Mistress Death."

"My life, at least, she saved," he said.

Indeed, he spoke of her as if he loved her, but without regret. I thought of the blue-eyed white woman he had lain with to father Hwenit, and wondered if he had found a ghost of my goddess-dam in her. As for me, I was caught in the tale like the fish in the net. She seemed to have been everywhere before me, Uastis, my ice-witch mother.

Because of this, I sat still as a stone with ears before Peyuan, the chief of the black krarl village, and let him tell me the story of her coming there, and her going away. How at the onset she had appeared in their midst like a demented orphan, lacking home or people, how she had passed from them like the Priestess of the Mystery, into water or air.

The Book was precious to his tribe, and he did not say much of it. It had contained the contrition of gods at their fall, a race of unparalleled magnificence, magicians without equal, ruling the lands like emperors; dying like ants when the hill is crushed. The black krarls, by their rite, strove to glean some glimmering of the old race and its powers, the arts of healing and of mental control, rejecting only the hubris and the cruelty that had evolved from them. Even the Circle the krarl formed about the Book had significance— Time, the never-begun and never-ending wheel, the link of all men to all that had been, all that was to come.

When the white witch broke the Circle, Peyuan saw her, the way you could see such things, he said, though the soul was gone to ride the winds. He became certain afterward that Morda (that was the name the krarl gave her, sufficiently similar to mine, so that I winced at it) had been a survivor of this lost Magicican Race, her abilities destroyed or mislaid. And this heritage of glory and fear drew her, repelled her, drove her to strange deeds and sorrows.

When the Circle disbanded, Peyuan and two others, Fethlin and Wexl, were also drawn, or driven, peculiarly, to follow her. They had no reason for this action. It was like the urge to shift ground with the seasons, the nomad's instinct, yet it was stranger. They knew it came from their gods, or from Morda's gods, and there was no resisting it. Nor did it exactly trouble them to do it. They had a saying: *At some hour, every man must sacrifice.* Their hour had arrived and they were ready. It was she, Peyuan remembered, who had been uneasy, almost frantic when she glimpsed them, crying out they must go back, go away, that she would not be responsible for their lives, which they would lose if they remained. But she could not shake them off, and in the end she was silent, hanging her head, as if in despair or shame, letting them accompany her.

Southward from the tower lay a bay and white ruins, the decayed cities of the Lost Race of the Book. It was to these ruins she had gone, and into those ruins she went, they going behind her.

She was plainly searching, this woman—exhaustedly, proudly, and wildly searching for some clue, some hope, or maybe merely for death.

"Sometimes," said Peyuan, "she was like an animal, swift and alert, trembling with a sight of things men never see. Sometimes she would walk like a little girl, like a daughter who is seven years old and asks to be carried because she is so tired; and it would need all my strength not to pick her up in my arms. Then you would see abruptly the witch-power, the royalness. She would move like a white spear through the shadows, and there would be gold binding her hair and golden scales her body, though she wore the krarl woman's dress and no ornament of any kind."

Yet she did not find what she sought, though he told me a tale of perils, a tremor of the earth, and finally a dragon, from which, he said, she had saved him by bravery, sorcery, and an acquaintance with the gods. True, the beast had smitten his first, a blow of blows. Yet when it had been slain, he had started up alive, apparently to this incorrigible witch's delighted surprise. She had touched his shoulder, as if to be sure he were real. Seeing the joy in her eyes, and sensing it in her touch as she appraised him sound, he hugged her close.

"She had a fragance to her," he said, "a green pure fragrance like spring leaves or the smell of the morning on the hills. It was not a perfume, some cosmetic from a jar. It was the actual scent of her flesh. Holding her, I felt only love, not desire or heat. She was like a girl I had known the whole of my life, someone who had never failed me, who had always been gentle, someone who had enriched my days. And now," Peyuan added, "seeing you will not otherwise believe in the dragon, let me show you proof."

He turned himself that his back should be to me, and lifted up his long, graying hair. On his neck and up along the lower ridge of his skull was a cindery toothed scar, broad as two fingers of my hand. The sort of wound a curved blade would make, or an enormous claw.

The sort of wound, too, from which a man should not recover.

"I never guessed I wore this," he said. "It was my wife who found it, the white girl I wed, Hwenit's mother. She asked had I got it in some battle. Thus, on my marriage night, I discovered that I had come as near death as a man may that half year before, out there on the black beach, my scalp opened by the lizard's paw. It was she, Morda—by some exercise of her lost Power, by her passion and desperation that I live—who had turned death aside from me, and healed me and made me whole. But clearly she never knew fully what she had done."

Then he glanced about, and observed I had swallowed his words like a dish of salt, unwilling and choking on it, but to the last grain. And what now should I do with this woman, half malefic, half tender? No, his account concerned a moment of her existence; her aspect had been benevolent to Peyuan and he had loved her. If this were true with him, she had been other things to other men. My father had not profited by her, or considered her benign.

"What comes next?" I asked Peyuan. "A god, maybe, on silver wings, to bear your lady into the sky?"

"No," he said, "it is less gaudy that that. The dragon dead, we slept past sunrise on the shore. There had been a watch, and I near asleep at my part of it, and she told me she would stand in my stead. But when we woke—Fethlin, Wexl, and I—the sun an hour risen, and she was gone. Only her footsteps, which led down into the sea, showed the path she had taken."

"Into the sea? She made some big fish his breakfast, then? More likely she stepped through the shallow water, and came ashore again at some other bay."

Peyuan nodded.

"Yes. But there were lights seen in the sky, the night of the lizard, and other nights. Like great stars falling to earth and departing again."

"Thus. She is a goddddess. It is a pity she didn't want her son. He might have had some rare times with her in her palace of jade and crystal up in the air."

He regarded me gravely, and he said, "Now I see one scar, after all."

"You have the scars," I said. "not I. One on your skull, one on your memory."

"I am rebuked, and justly. I did not mean to anger the guest of my krarl."

I was at once uncomfortable for having spoken roughly; he had been courteous enough to me, if too quick for my liking.

"No, it is I who am to blame, my chief," I said. "Let us forget the woman." Then, for courtesy's sake only—I had begun to remember the hunt again at my back, and the need to be off—I added, "But tell me why your people settled here, for you were travelers formerly?"

"Oh, that is a small thing. I met the woman I spoke of, a fair-haired girl of the yellow Moi tribes, one day when we had gone to barter with them. I was younger then, and I won her liking and wed her. On the marriage night she found the scar for me, the lizard's token. She journeyed that year with us to the sea. She had never looked on the ocean before. It drew her, as some it draws, like a charm or spell. When the time came for going inland, at the year's turning, she was sorry, though she tried to make light of it. I had already taken her from her own folk, now I did not wish to take from her the sea. Besides, she was already quickened with our daughter. And I had been considering, too, I will admit, that my life had almost ended once in the dark sea bay, when the dragon struck me down; it seemed in some manner fitting that I live out my restoration near that place. So we chose this spot, on the route of the old Summer Dance. The land was not bad, and would grow vegetables; there were wild fruit trees and grazing for the goats—I had but five then. The ancient cities lie almost a night's journey away to the south; we do not like to dwell too near them. Having said I would remain, become herdsman and gardener of the soil, two others elected to remain with me. Not my earlier companions. Wexl had married and gone elsewhere. Fethlin, too, was gone northward to seek the wandering priests, or the priest-hermits who live in the mountains there. Some say there are priests of the Book, healers and nomads, who live beyond these mountains and beyond other mountains also, unaccountable distances north and west. Maybe Fethlin sought even this far, for he was unquiet after Morda left us, saying his own gods had laid it on him to guard her, that he had failed, and that the work was forever unfinished.

"Still, the men who remained with me were vigorous, and helped me with the labor, their women and their sons and daughters, too, clearing the ground and planting. With our portion of the herd we did well, for goats are earnest in love. Their numbers soon doubled, and doubled again. Later, other men and their tents joined us, and the village was built. To-day there are seven fields beyond the great pasture, fields of beans and grain, and a wood farther on of berries and apples. It is easy to barter for seed from the wandering tribes, who have little use for it. As for the fruit trees, some kindly wind must have foretold our coming. Then, too, we have learned to make boats. The ocean is massed with sea wrack, which we gather, a weed that is useful to us in many ways, not least to eat."

My mind had begun to run on the subject of their boats but I said, "And your woman, Hwenit's mother?"

"She died," he said simply. "She was in the autumn woods, gathering windfalls, when she put her hand on a little snake. Hadlin was with her; she said there was no pain. My wife seemed not to notice she had been bitten, laughing it off, and in the middle of the laugh, she shut her eyes and sank down, and when Hadlin went to her, she was dead. Hwenit was not a year old on that day; it is an odd thing, for Hwenit has grown to be clever in cure-craft, with snakebite particularly."

His calm disturbed me. His woman died, he loved her but did not mourn, dismissing grief as superfluous. Perhaps it had been different at the hour, but I did not believe so.

He glanced at me and appeared to note my thoughts. He went on, "Hwenit was twelve the summer the krarl of Qwenex returned to the tower with a priest in their midst, journeying to the Golden Book. Always my krarl would meet with Qwenex's people, and when he set eyes on my girl, the priest came straight to her. He asked questions. He said she had the healer's gift and must be trained. He stayed here three seasons, the priest. He seemed no different from any of

our people, save that he could set a bone, and the bone
would heal straight and swift, or mix herbs for a sick child
and the child would grow well again, and it seemed as much
from the touch of his hands as from the draft. And these arts
he taught Hwenit, and she became Uasti. I recall he showed
her, too, the Mysteries of the Book, which the priests will not
always show a woman, the things very few master—the
wound that closes at the word of the priest, the power to
raise the body from the earth as if it were winged. These
magics were not in my daughter, though she was envious of
them. Some nights she crouches by her fire and summons
demons, and they never come, for which I am very gateful."

"Are you now, my father?" said a crisp voice from the
doorway. "And here you sit with the very demon I *did* summon."

It was Hwenit in person, who came in to tend extravagantly the copper pot on the brazier, that all this while had
placidly seen to itself.

5

"I will require the warriors to leave my hearth," said
Hwenit-Uasti. "There is a baby with a fever I must have here
to care for."

"My thanks for the night's lodging," I said, "and the
demon must, in any case, be on his road again."

"Oh, but you must not!" cried Hwenit, leaving off splash-
ing and stirring the mixture to pounce around on me. Today
she did not wear her cat but a necklet of white bones and
amber beads.

"My daughter," said Peyuan, "our guest has spent too
much time already listening to the chief's prattle. He is in
haste." He touched my arm as we rose. "I have gone over in
my mind what you have said to me. I will suggest to you that
we should visit Qwef, who has a seaworthy boat."

At this, Hwenit flung the iron spoon into the copper pot.

"Qwef!" she yapped. "Qwef! Qwef! Is this the only name I am to hear?"

"We shall presently be gone and you shall hear it no more," said Peyuan.

"I will not have you go!" Hwenit shouted after me. "Go, and I curse you."

"Curse on, maiden," I said. "I will bear it as best I may." And I ducked out quickly to avoid the wet spoon she threw after me.

It was a serene day, between the winds of early spring. Daylight showed the krall village engaged in quiet activity. Trees and garden patches grew at the backs of many huts; a well had been dug in the shadow of a sea-blown acacia, and two women were standing in its lacy, winter-bared shade, drawing water.

Hwenit-Uasti's cat lay sunning itself along the painted lintel, and spit at me for old time's sake.

I said to Peyuan that his daughter had taken exception to the name of Qwef before. Had he done her some wrong?

"Yes," said Peyuan, "a single wrong. He has not offered to court her. For that reason she conjures demons to flirt with, to make the young man mend his ways, and instead of a demon, you appear, and she will use you as readily if you let her."

The village, the ocean's murmur below, less complaining than in the night, the enterprising trees and tranquil people, had got me to the stage again of not actually believing myself in danger. Had I really killed a gold-mask in Eshkorek? Had I really escaped Erran's palace by way of the great tunnel of the magician men, the same magicians, I hazarded, who left Golden Books in towers? And had I, Black Wolf, son of a black wolf, been hunted to the sea's blue-as-the-eyes-of-Hwenit edge?

But Peyuan, good and excellent man that he was, had adopted my plight like his own. He pointed out to sea, into the mauve haze that rimmed the water's horizon.

"There is an island, some miles from shore. Only in the clearest of seasons do you see the shape of it. Indeed, none of this krall knew of it till the young men went adventuring in their boats. The weather is even-tempered today. If Qwef will guide you over, you can be there before nightfall. There is also space in his boat for food and a krarl tent to shelter you. Those who hunt you will not imagine you in a place they cannot see. If and when the hunt has passed, you shall have word, and return."

I had considered begging a boat from them; this was better than I had hoped for. I said, "Why do you bother yourself with me, Peyuan-Chief? Is it for your goddess's sake, the white lady who vanished into sea or sky?"

He made no reply, and just then a woman came between the huts toward Hwenit's dwelling, carrying an animate bundle in her arms. The mother's expression was not wild; a shireen would have been tearing her hair and screaming, for the baby coughed and crowed and looked wretched. For some reason the comparison made me think of my own children in the Dagkta krarl, my little sons and daughters I had barely glanced at twice, and of the child I had wanted by Demizdor and now should never get.

Peyuan stopped the woman at the door. He took the infant gently from her, she making no protest. Then he came and put the baby in my hands.

I had no answer to this, and I wondered what he supposed himself doing. The poor thing struggled feebly; I must hold it or it would fall.

Seeing no alternative, I ducked back in at the door, to give the child to Hwenit.

Bent, red-lit above the seething copper, seething also with her discontent, the girl straightened with a sharp word, but changed when she saw what I carried into one mute, sinuous, and protective gesture of acceptance. This, more than anything, moved me.

I placed the child in her waiting arms, and was about to go out again, when she cried aloud in a terrible tone, "What have you done?"

The baby, too, commenced bawling, loud, raucous, and vehement, from a pair of brazen bellows secreted in its tiny chest.

I whipped around, and Hwenit held it up, kicking and howling in its wrath. Her dark face had a shrunken look. She asked me, "What did you do?"

"I did nothing. Your father gave the child to me, and I gave him to you."

"You have healed him. He was very sick. It would have

taken me three days, and then he might have been damaged in his bones. Let me see your hands."

Nonplussed as she was, thinking her distracted or mistaken, I showed her.

Hwenit peered and stared as if at some fresh ailment.

The baby roared like a terrible little machine.

"You are a magician," Hwenit said. "You are a healer." Jealously she whispered, "You are more powerful than the priest who taught me."

Qwef's boat, a skiff, had a place for a single pair of oars, a primitive sailless craft, but the first water vessel I had ever seen. It took the sea with a rolling yet dependable motion, breasting over the waves that from the shore had seemed azure, and now revealed themselves as brownish-gray with caverns of marble greenness beneath.

Qwef managed the oars, at which I later took a turn, having been instructed, This was an easy enough task once I had the knack of it, and truth to tell, I was glad of something to do. The sight of so much liquid earthquake all about unnerved me.

My mind was racing, too, out of rhythm with everything. I had been thankful to be off, as if I could leave bewilderment and unease behind me on shore. But like the changeable sea, the quality of the inner debate had altered, become ambient. Splinters of white foam—something of a wind had got up, after all, when we were about a mile out—broke from the wave crests. Flashes of scenes and events dashed off the surface of my thought like the foam, and under these, the hollow green sea caverns of a menacing disquiet.

Nor did it help that my black witch had come with us.

She sat sulkily among the pile of tent, tackle, and provisions, with which Peyuan and his people had packed the skiff amidships, and to which she had added a copper cook pan, rugs, and other minutiae of living, while her demoniac cat—stuffed into the large wicker cage like some unlikely bird, that it should not escape in terror and fall into the sea—set up a persistent, resentful, and panic-stricken wailing. Hwenit said she had visited the island before in the boats of the men to gather certain herbs that grew there. Probably this was true enough, though the reason for her traveling now was plainly in order to impress upon Qwef that she companioned me.

Qwef was a good-looking youth, somewhat younger than she, with the same carved aquilinity of feature that seemed common to the whole tribe. He spoke to her politely, as to me, and said she was welcome to share the journey, though he was constrained at her presence, and she did her best to set him boiling, darting him mad blue looks, telling him how poorly he handled his own boat, turning his every observation into a jest or nonsense. It was a trick a few krarl women had tried on me when I was around sixteen, as he was, and got the flat of my hand as a reward.

At a point when we were exchanging the oars, she began to fiddle with her cat's cage, saying she would let the beast out. I told her the cat would then surely drown, and the boat would be upset, and Hwenit remarked in a honey moan how intelligent I was, and that she would obey me in all things. This trick misfired for, catching each other's eyes and aware of what she was at, both Qwef and I burst out laughing.

As the wind continued, she screeched that I should subdue it with my magician's powers, and I informed her that I would put her to sleep with an oar if we had any more chat from her.

In any case, the wind did no more than rock the boat and shear the caps from the waves. We sighted the island at length, and soon ground on its seaweed beach.

Qwef and I pulled the craft above the tide-line, into the lee of long rocks, white-faced with the droppings of birds, and vivid green elsewhere from sea lichens. The wind flapped like idle wings among the tops of the great bare trees with mossy trunks that edged the beach fifty yards away.

Gray gulls mewed, causing the red cat to growl in its cage.

"The wind will drop by daybreak," Qwef said. "I will return to the mainland then." He stood looking at Hwenit, as she walked ahead toward the trees, and if ever I saw a man engaged by a woman, it was he.

I said, "She will have you if you ask her."

"Maybe," he said, "but I cannot ask her."

"Why, man, do you take her gibes for earnest?"

"No," he said, quiet as the sea had suddenly grown. "Certainly my father sees no wrong in it—it is not our way to make iron rules, like chains, and hang them on men and women. And yet, to me it seems—unlawful."

I did not understand him, and told him so. The girl was

willing—urgent, even—Qwef's father gave him blessing, and was Peyuan ungenerous?

"But that is my problem," he said, laughing a little. "My father and Peyuan are one man. He wed Hadlin after his white girl's death, to obtain a mother for Hwenit, mostly, though he grew to love Hadlin after. And Hadlin bore me. I am Peyuan's son. Hwenit and I are brother and sister."

Everywhere laws are different. Among the Dagkta, a man who lies with his sister is flogged and the girl branded between her breasts. Most communities frown on incest. In some, death is the wage it earns, and though the black folk were openhearted toward the fact of love, wherever it took root, I saw in Qwef's eyes, side by side with his desire, a cold revulsion. To lie with the fruit of the seed that also fruited you; limb by limb with that which one's father's limbs had fashioned. The answering coldness stirred in my own groin at the dream of it. The oldest cringing in the world.

Behind us all, a dull maroon sunset began to sink upon the invisible mainland.

PART III

The Island

1

I lay in the tent on the island. I dreamed this:

I was flying. As in the tunnel, I imagined myself black-winged. The beat of wings lifted me from one shore to another. I came back to the mainland, moving high over the ocean, seeing its blackness break below me into white gold on the headlands, finding the white skeleton of a city in a bay.

This was the curiosity of the dream:

Equipped with the wings of power, I knew myself yet for what I was born to. A tribal savage dressed for the summer wars, and on my body the scars of those wars, the scars I had never kept. It was as if I had been thrust back into a mold that had been expected to form me, rather than the actual clay of which I was made. And I thought in the dream, *This is how she reckoned I should grow, the bitch who bore me. A human warrior of the krarls, with no birthright but battle and battle-death. Or worse, wolf's death at the hands of the city men who hunted me.*

The grim glowing ruin stretched up, and seemed to try to pull me into it, but I beat away, grinning, for even in the dream I was too strong to succumb to its rotten tugging.

And then I saw her, hanging in the sky like a flake of the moon. A woman, her face masked by a black shireen, her body by a black krarl shift, but her white arms spread, and her white, white, bone-white hair blowing all around her like a flame composed of smoke. Recognition was immediate. It was my loving mother.

I shouted at her.

"Your son, Ettook's warrior! Do you like what you have made of me? I have killed forty men, and I have four wives and thirteen sons, and three days from now I will die with an out-tribe spear between my ribs. I might have been a prince in Eshkorek Arnor, or in Ezlann. I might have been a king

201

with a great army at my back, beautiful women to please me, and Power to make all men do as I wished. Do you like what you have made?"

It was crystal clear to me, what he had meant for me, my father, Vazkor, what she had robbed me of. I drew from my belt my hunting knife and threw it at her heart.

She hung in the air, and said to me, cold as silver ice, "This has no ability to kill me."

But she was wrong. Sorceress though she was, the knife pierced her breast, and she fell away down the night with a cry, and died into the darkness.

I woke from this dream with a purpose as transparent as glass before me, cool, in possession of my waking senses, and bitter calm.

Qwef was sleeping his serene young man's sleep not far from me, loose-limbed as a lean black dog. Hwenit had bedded deeper in the tent, invisible behind a drapery she had flamboyantly erected to exclude us.

I got up silently and stole out into the island night.

The moon was down, the wind had dropped.

We had raised the tent in the shelter of the bare trees, near a little spring of sweet water. Several paces farther on the rocky hump of the island started curving up like the shell of a tortoise, a bald carapace of rain-and-wind-polished slate. The island was small, not quite a mile from end to end.

I halted at the foot of the incline; it seemed a private spot.

I had only the tribal ways to fall back on, I had seen no religion or reverence in Eshkorek, save for the spitting of men at the name of Uastis. I cleared a space in the rough weeds, and piled up a mound of stones, leaving it hollow at the center. Into the hollow I pushed dry stems and stuck a flint to kindle them. The fire flared, quick and too hungry, an ephemeral blue. I took my knife—it had drunk her blood in my dream—and stuck it in my arm, and let my own blood sprinkle the blaze. I cut off a piece of my hair and gave him that, too.

I thought I knew what he wanted, my father. I recalled how I had woken once before, dreaming of his death and said, "I will kill her." Now all the uncertainties, the powers of healing and slaying and all the rest, came together in one ferocious urge I recognized as another's. The gifts were his, the wish was his, the deed was his. Vazkor, unquiet in his death; my unquiet life showed me the manner of it.

I said aloud, soft into the crackle of the brittle, already dying flames, "I swear it, Vazkor, on the fire and on my blood. Vazkor, my father, she has cheated both you and me, and she shall pay the price of it. I will strive to find her. When I do, I will kill her. You have revealed it to me. Now I know. Be still, Vazkor my father, wolf-king, Javhovor, only leave it with me."

It seemed to me then, the brief ignition faded in the stones, a shadow oozed from the fire and rested flickeringly against the slate wall. The fire's shadow, a sort of shadowfire itself, resembling the dark reflection of a brightness and a strength burned out what was lingering, with a faint dull luster, in me.

"Believe it," I said to the shadow.

At that the flame dropped to nothing. I was left with the empty sea-rocked night, and my iron future.

Near dawn, Hwenit stole through the weeds and discovered me sitting there against the slate.

"Why are you here, Mordrak? Are you sick?"

"How can a demon be sick? I'm unused to your tender care. Go back, girl. The sun's not up yet."

She slipped close and put her fingers on my neck in a touch that made me shiver.

"You do not understand your powers," she said.

"That's true enough. Yet I think now I begin to comprehend the seed that planted them."

"I mean," she said, "you have no way to master your powers. They master you. You heal without being aware of it. Perhaps you kill as rashly."

I looked at her. The sky had paled enough to show me her face, which might have been the face of another girl, steady, clever, and compassionate. I saw then what her priest-tutor had seen, the day he singled her out for healer and witch.

"If I am rash, who will set me on the right path?"

"I," she said, "if you permit."

"I permit," I said. "How do I recompense you?"

"Lie with me," she said.

"In order that you may make your brother burn? In order that you may pretend I am he? Oh, no, blue-eyed witch. I am not for that game."

"Trust me," she whispered, bending near. "It is you, I crave. Though you are white, you are handsome and lusty."

"I have been sung that song before, and by women who believed it. As for you, little witch, you are half white yourself, under your black silk skin."

"Lie with me," she moaned, melting my ear with her tongue.

But I pushed her off, maddening though it was for me to do it.

She stamped her foot, and ran away deeper into the wood, and presently I made out a reddish cat's tail going after her through the tall grasses.

When I returned to the black tent at sunup, Qwef was already gone. My teacher-temptress and I remained alone.

There followed two or three peculiar days, during which I found out for sure that Hwenit-Uasti was two persons, as her two namings implied.

Uasti, witch and healer, a woman indubitably honored and respected among her people, wise though young, patient and of infinite sympathy, materialized between the hours of sunrise and sunset. This being instructed me in the shade-walks of my own brain. Her fabulous knowledge, garnered from generation upon generation of priests—those poet-physicians and sorcerer-philosophers of the black tribes—was delivered to me simply and directly. I have met few others since who could compare with, or better, this mentor, a girl more youthful than I, slight as a sapling and mercurial to a fault. I think, too, that she was the superior teacher because she had not the mastery of these "arts" herself, while being fully cognizant of them. She gave me, at any rate, the key to doors, both to unlock and to seal them. A paradoxical key, simple but perverse. You must get it right before you tried the turn, or bring the house down. As to method and logic, to explain that would be to sit ranting in a jar for seven years, as the Moi say. You cannot truly define power, or why power will come. A child will learn to walk, but you must persuade him not to put his hands in the fire.

That, then, was my psychic guide, Uasti, the composed and the humane.

The other Uasti usually usurped her when school was done, first sparking up in her oceanic eyes when the fire was banked in preparation for the evening meal. This, in fact, was not Uasti but Hwenit the witch, the one I had met to begin with.

She was all the other was not, skittish, heady, sharp as cat's claws, and bent on seduction. A sore trial to me was Hwenit. I felt like a man being coaxed to steal his brother's riches, and the brother off at the wars—yet Qwef was her kin, not mine. I resolved I would not be party to her snares and plots.

We had been on the island two days, and that day's sun a pale memory of rose across the sea, and the woods powdered with dusk. Hwenit lighted the fire and set out the food, and scolded her red cat, which would not eat its portion of nutmeats, since it had killed a bird in the high grass that afternoon, and was entirely satisfied with this gory fare. The scolding concluded, Hwenit turned to me.

"Tonight I shall gather sea wrack from the beach. Shall you go with me, Mordrak?"

Confusing one Hwenit with the other—Uasti—for a moment, I complied. Shortly, supper finished, I followed her among the rocks and tide-glazed sands. She picked at the red-purple weed and cut it with my knife, then the green-brown and the black. The light was gone. She judged the varieties by starshine, and placed them in a reed-woven basket.

"Once all weed was black," said Hwenit. "Then one man killed another and his blood fell in the sea, at which some weed became red. But the green weed grew when the Green Maidens, who live on the sea's floor, swam up and lay with men. It is not weed, but green hair left for a token of love between water and land."

Catching the drift now, I said it was a nice story, and started to go back up the beach. But Hwenit, the little fox, unlaced her shift and ran into the sea, and returned like a Green Maiden herself, save she was black not green, scented with ocean, with water-jeweled breasts and chains of silver on her thighs. And that was that.

After, she was silent as a rock, as if she must atone for her pleasure with melancholy as some do. It was not her first time by any means. The black folk had no rigid moral laws, being too moral and too lawful, to construct them.

We went to the tent and she hid herself behind her drapery, and then I heard her crying.

All this I could have predicted. Her thoughts ran on Qwef. Presently she called out to me like a child, "What shall I do? What shall I do?"

There is no reasoning with a girl in this mood. I got up, took down the silly drapery and put my arms around Hwenit, surprising myself somewhat at my own gentleness with her. Demizdor had weaned me to different ways, I supposed. It would have taken a woman who did not consider herself a milch-cow to show me that women are not cattle.

Next, Hwenit hissed, "Mordrak, you are a magician. Make him belong to me. You will be kind, for I have helped you toward your sorcerer's power. Use it, and help *me*."

"I won't help you to that. Besides, my gift is scarce out of its cradle, as well you know."

"For this it is strong enough. Oh, Mordrak, I am nothing without him. I shall die of it."

I laughed, and assured her she would not.

She wept, and assured me that she would.

When she was quieter, she said. "It began between us, between Qwef and me, small as the first thread on the loom. Each day wove a little more. Now the garment is finished."

I said, "You are his sister, Hwenit. This is why he will not."

"Oh, the fool," she said. "It would only make us closer. It is *why* we are bound. Flesh speaking to flesh, because the flesh is one."

"Be thankful, girl, you are not a Dagkta woman. They would whip you for dreaming of it."

"The red people are cruel and blind. Why should it be a whipping matter?"

"If for no other reason, because the children of two so near in blood will be sickly."

"Are the beasts sickly? The animals of the hills and the fish of the sea, and the birds of the air? And often they mate, parent with young, and the infants of one womb together."

"Well," I said, "but we are men."

"And the poorer for it. I never yet saw a man outrun a beast, outswim a fish, outfly a bird. If they fall ill, which is rarely, they need no healer to tell them what herbs they should eat in order to be well. They take no slaves and make no wars."

I said, "There are plenty who would court you in your krarl. Leave Qwef be, and choose another."

"I have tried. Two years I have tried. You see the result of it."

"Think," I said, "what it would mean to lie with him."

"Trust me, I do, and frequently. Brother is a word; sister is a word. Do you feel a *word*? Do you suffer a *word*? Love you suffer, and desire and pain." She put me from her with cold small hands, and oddly, I saw she was Uasti again, the calm, elder Uasti, deep as a dark well, and sad to the profundity of her depths. "Go sleep, warrior. Leave me my dreams at least, for which your Dagkta curs shall not beat me."

I left her, but later I heard her rise and go out.

In the morning, I walked up onto the slate parasol of the island, and came on the black clinkers of a fire she had built there, and the tracks of her feet going around and around in the ashes of it. Some circle spell she had made to glamour Qwef.

2

That day, the third, was still and windless, the trees carved on the sky, and the sea tumbling on the beach in slow rushes, without hunger.

Noon came with a white sun; it was chill after the warm foretaste of spring we had been having. The quiet grew disturbing and I fancied foul weather was blowing up somewhere, gale or rain coming back to scourge the island, and wondered how high the tide would run in a storm and if I had best shift the tent.

There was apprehension in me, too, something I tried to shake off. I found myself going over again the details of that dream I had had, the dream of wings and vengeance that had made me swear my oath to the shade, or rather the memory, of my father. In the dream I had listed, in warrior fashion and very thoroughly, my deeds and possessions, even to the quantity of my wives and sons, even to the tribal expression of having slain forty men, which forty stood for uncountable and unlimited numbers. I had also prophesied my own death: an out-tribe spear between my ribs—three days from that night. Today.

This delicacy crawled about in my belly, till I cursed myself, all the more since having noted Hwenit's burned out witch-fire. For it had come to me, bit by bit, that if the island was hidden in haze and night, one bright bonfire atop it might yet serve as a signal for any eyes on the shore.

Hwenit had kept away from me all day, collecting her eternal bundles of herbs, ferns, weeds, thistles, thorns, and osiers, which she set to dry on little wicker frames about the tent. Her red cat stalked minute animal life through the grasses.

I had gathered earlier that a man would row over for them on the morrow, and to bring news to me, providing no danger from the hunt had shown itself on the mainland. I made a resolution that I would go back with him, whatever had or had not happened. To be stuck forever on a mile of wooded rock afloat in water was not to my taste.

In the middle of the afternoon, a scarf of wind blew up and a light drizzle dappled the island. Presently, the sky opened its doors.

The cat flew in the tent, disliking the sudden bath it had got. Soon Hwenit came running, her shawl over her head, and huddled in beside the cat.

I began thinking of the last cloudburst I had crouched through, in the lee of those limestone spurs, that day the wolf hunt caught up to me.

This rain was like an omen added to my former misgivings.

"Hwenit," I said, "I am going down to the beach. Stay here."

She gazed up through her hair at me.

"What do you look for?" she asked.

"My back is crawling. I feel the hunt is coming here, after all."

"The city men?" Her eyes widened. Abruptly she whispered, "I lighted a fire on the rock!"

"Maybe someone saw, maybe not. I'll watch for a while. In this rain any boat would have rough work coming in."

"Mordrak," she cried to me, "I could think only of him—of Qwef—it was to bind him I made the fire. Oh, I am a fool, and have endangered you."

"No matter," I said. "Probably it is some old woman of a fear got into me for no reason."

But as I went between the trees, I recalled she had not liked me much the night before, and though I did not believe she intended to betray me, perhaps an angry mischief in the dark hidden part of her mind, "Light a big fire, and there is a means to thrash this pompous oaf." For I had been pompous, and an oaf, for all I imagined myself so forbearing with her. Ride a girl, then tell her who else she might or must not ride with. Fine morality.

The tide was coming in, brown and pocked with rain. Through deluge and spray, I could pinpoint nothing moving on the water.

I waited among the sea wrack, on the slick sand where last night Hwenit and I had coupled. I waited there some minutes before I heard her scream in the wood.

I did what the half-wit would do. What they reckoned on. I turned and plunged back into the trees toward the tent. And right into a man with white-blue eyes and wet rat's-skin hair, who stepped from the mossy trunks into my path, holding Hwenit and a blade at her throat, and laughing softly, interestedly, the old laugh I remembered well.

They had come ashore at the far end of the island, the other side of the trees. The current was less favorable there, but they had managed it, or, to be accurate, their slave had managed it. This was the Dark Man, the guide who had tracked me from the tunnel and obeised himself before me when I slew the silver-mask with white killing Power. Presumably the guide had returned to his masters next . . . telling them what? Little, I guessed, for the Dark Slaves in Eshkorek had seemed to speak only in answer to direct and unequivocal questioning, never volunteering information on their own.

Apart from the Dark Slave, their navigator, there were two men. The other pair of the four must have grown bored with the chase and abandoned it. These however, had their own personal reasons for keeping after me.

Zrenn stood, playing with Hwenit's hair and stroking her throat with the flat of his knife, looking at me for my reactions, his porcelain eyes alert. He had taken off his mask, I think that I should have known him the more swiftly.

It was the fragile Orek who had come up at my back to put his own knife against my ribs.

I had been wrong. Not a spear but a knife. In a moment I should feel the iron enter my lung. His slender hand trembled with anger or gladness.

The slave was by a tree, and noncommittal.

Hwenit's face was narrowed hard. After that one cry, she had ensorceled herself to black adamantine.

"It is a delight for old friends to meet once more," Zrenn said. "It has been our hope that we might see you again, my Vazkor, before you depart this life. Not that your going shall be hasty. Erran, the leopard-chief, is not isolated in his artistic plan for a death. Slow and painful, my Vazkor. A limb, less— an organ, a finger at a time. I see you are healed of the cruel cuts I gave you in Eshkorek. We shall have to mince you very small to be certain you remain beneath the earth, shall we not? And between whiles, we will play with this midnight doll you have thoughtfully provided us."

It seemed to me I could turn easily and disarm the willowy youth behind me. Meantime, Zrenn would slash Hwenit's throat. This fathomed, I kept still. My grave was near as Orek's hand, and I had foretold my grave. Yet it appeared ludicrous. As Zrenn reminded me, I healed of wounds. Could I recover from a death stroke, as Erran had more than half believed?

"Did you find the love-tokens I left you?" I said to Zrenn, gently as he. "All about the hills? The silver-masks peacefully sleeping in their blood?"

"The jackal, slinking up on the baby's cot. Oh, yes. Like your noble father, Vazkor's son. You did it winningly."

I sensed the blade at my back come a hair breadth nearer.

"You have too many deaths to pay for," Orek rasped in his broken boy's voice.

"He shall pay with many deaths," Zrenn said, smiling.

It is not simple to kill with Power, once you understand the trick of it. You bring extinction by summoning it from yourself, and it touches you also, like a burning, bloody wing. That is why sickness follows. And when the price is high, you do not spend indiscriminately. This held me, even now, in this second of stupid extremity, poised between a girl's neck and a boy's knife.

The savage, who knew only how to wield bludgeon and ax, must learn more subtle weapons.

I indicated the slave. I said, "Did he tell you how I killed the last man, the man in the camp?"

Zrenn prepared to dally a long while, followed my procrastination almost with approval.

"His face was congested. I presume you choked him with your strong warrior's paws."

"Not so. Ask him now, your slave, how Vazkor's son slew the silver-mask."

Zrenn, yet smiling, jerked his head to the slave.

"Inform me, clod."

The slave said in a flat, though thickly accented and unhandy voice, "Black lord stare, and white light come and fair lord fall and die."

Zrenn's mouth slackened. He frowned.

"What do you mean, you dreg, *white light?*"

"White light from eyes of black lord. White light strike fair lord. Fair lord fall. Fair lord die. Light go out. Black lord god."

The slave's tone was extraordinary. He might have been talking of the weather. I recalled how he prostrated himself in the mud before me, then walked away into the night. It seemed he and his stony people had grown accustomed to recognition and universality of demons in some remote and dismal past.

I was trying to assess what ability lay in me that I dared use. You will see this plight in the brilliant marksman who manages his marvels by instinct. Force him to study his art, to explain how he focuses magically on his target, and he will grow mannered and unsure and presently miss his mark altogether.

Abruptly Hwenit spoke. Striving to alter her predicament, I had forgotten her as a live being. Forgetting, too, that though I comprehended city speech, she did not, and the whole dialogue thus far had been gibberish to her.

"Mordrak," she said, "don't bargain for me. This is my fault. Let him kill me if he wishes, but get free."

At this Zrenn shook her. He asked me, "What does the black wench say? Does she say she loves me, Vazkor?"

I said, to get more time (when would I have had sufficient?), "She wonders how you came here."

"Oh, the slave sniffed out the little cavern where her clan keep their disreputable boats. He speaks their tongue, but they lied to him in the village about you, Vazkor. They told us you had gone by them on the trek north. If it had not been for the slave's sharp eyes and mine, seeing that pin-head of beacon fire last night, we should never have dreamed where you might be. When I am done with you, my brother and I shall revisit this bitch's tribe, and roast them in their huts."

Just then I saw a bright orange marker in the grass—the tail tip of Hwenit's red cat. Next moment, yowling, the cat sprang up Zrenn's booted leg and bit him in the thigh and sprang away. Zrenn yelled and half whirled about, slashing with his knife after the cat, which had already been too quick for him and was gone. Instantly Hwenit darted from his grasp, but, unlike the cat, not quick enough.

Zrenn moved fast as a lash and caught her by her hair as she was running from him, and reeled her about. His face was crazy with a white fury of pain, irritation, and maleficence, and full in this dangerous face Hwenit spit, and with a single movement of his arm, unpremeditated, directed by spite alone, Zrenn hammered his knife into her side.

Then came stasis, Zrenn letting slip between his fingers, like the motivating strings of a puppet, the black stands of Hwenit's hair. As she gradually loosened and slid toward the ground, his expression altered to total disbelief. He had played the wrong game piece, and too soon.

I discovered myself already spinning around, crashing my fist hard into Orek's arm so his blade went flying, smashing the other fist into his belly. He folded soundlessly away into the weeds, neat as a lady's fan.

When I looked back, Zrenn had recovered himself.

He waited for me, part crouching, his red knife flickering, eyes bright. But I was done fighting. I did not glance at the shape of the woman; my guts were knotted up, but I kept her lessoning.

"Zrenn," I said.

"Fight me, warrior."

His eyes, white-hot, the blue sucked away by the heat, danced at me. Then the dance went out of them. Confronting mine, they fixed like enamel in the kiln. It took three breaths to mesmerize him, this lord of the silver, even for one new to the practice. He looked as small to me as a gnat. It was no difficulty for me to take control of him.

"Zrenn," I said, "come closer."

"No," he muttered, but he came.

I took the knife from his fingers and he could not prevent it. His face worked and struggled all about his calcined eyes, to tell me I must not hurt him. To no avail.

I held his rat's-skin hair, and cut his throat. He gargled in blood; it reminded me of his laughter. It is a vile death, but brief.

After that, I went off a way into the wood, and threw up, as if I had never killed a man before. I mused drearily, as I leaned shuddering on a tree, that I might as well have used the killing Power in me for all the good I had got from restraint.

When I returned, everything was very still. Some time ago the rain had stopped, and I saw the red cat was picking a path inch by inch, through the bladed grass toward Hwenit's body, stiff itself as a moving corpse. I watched this sight a minute, but a stirring nearby put me in mind that there was unfinished business.

Orek stared up at me, lying on his back. His mask had fallen off, or he had pulled it off. His face, like that ghost of another face, and the eyes the green eyes of that face, made my gorge rise again. No, whatever else, I could not kill this distorted image of Demizdor.

"Zrenn is dead," I said to him.

His eyelids fluttered, and his lips. He was not less proud, but less royal than she had been.

"Did you love her?" he croaked at me. He could mean one only. He said, "I will tell you before you butcher me, I will tell you why I came to hunt you down like the stinking diseased dog that you are. Shall you listen, dog? Or will you silence me before I can tell?"

"I don't want your life," I said.

"Don't you? Nor do I, filthy, mangy dog. Listen. She was better than any, fairer than any woman in Eshkorek. And you lay on her, on her white body. Shall I say what became of Demizdor? Shall you like to hear?"

"Erran," I said, halting. My heart beat in great slow thunders, like the surf hitting the beach below.

"Erran? No. He got no chance. Did she show you the way,

the old tunnel under the mountains? Yes, certainly she must have done. How did she bid you farewell? Did she kiss and cling, did you have her again, in the green slime of the passageway? Or did she curse you?"

"Get on," I said. "If you will tell it, tell."

"I will tell. She set you on your road. After this, she went to her chamber in Erran's palace, and unbound the velvet cord from the draperies, and hanged herself with it."

He was weeping. He was not shamed to weep for Demizdor.

I thought, *I have surely known it all this while, known she was dead.* At our parting did she not call to me and say, "You are my life"? But I could see her only as she had lived, riding her horse, steady as any brave; in our bed at sunup, golden with sleep; how she had lain with me, crying out my name; her skin, the living warmth of her. Cold now. Empty now. Rotting in some tall tomb in Eshkorek, shut in by diamond-headed nails.

Orek had turned on his side in the grass to get on with his sobbing.

The cat, too, had begun to cry, wailing in inhuman spasms over Hwenit's body.

And I, caught between two griefs, like corn between the millstones.

The sky cleared. The wood soaked in a sallow sunlight, winged over with damson scud, promise of more rain to come.

I had changed ground. Taking up Hwenit's body, I had carried her into the black tent and set her on her rug bed there. And found she lived. It was the remnant of a pulse. Zrenn's knife had pierced up through her breast, yet it must have missed the heart. But, though she breathed, it would not be for long. The cat had followed me, meowing and rubbing on my boots, apparently thinking I meant to help her. But she was past help.

A little after, someone came to the doormouth. Orek, knuckling his eyes like a whipped boy, said, "I and the slave will bury my brother out there."

"It's free soil," I said. "Do it."

I had realized for some while he would not try for my life;

his passion was squandered in tears; besides, he had had a surfeit of slaughter.

He turned and went away. They had only knives to dig with, and the slave scrabbling with his hands—it would be a shallow burial, and no gold to lay on the casket.

For Hwenit, she could rest among her own folk, though it would be no comfort to any of them.

Somewhere in my mind, Hwenit and Demizdor were merging. Life snuffed out and beauty turned to cold meat for worms. And Hwenit, my black witch, she had said she would die of her love, the perennial girl's lament, now proved true. She had never even lain with him, her Qwef, not once. I saw the desert of it, its yearning barrenness. Brother, sister, only words; but this, a reality, the destroyer at the gate. What could it have mattered, after all, to celebrate her hungry youth and his, before the sword fell on her? All the plots and schemes, the moralities and codes of men, seemed dust in the face of death.

The cat came and licked my hand with its rough tongue. I had seen hounds mourn and entreat in this way.

A shadow fell through the doormouth again. I looked; the Dark Man stood there, his arms muddied to the elbow—slave, guide, rower, digger of graves.

He would not speak till I asked him what he wanted. Then he nodded to Hwenit and said, with the first modicum of curiosity I had ever seen one of his race exhibit, "Unwilling, woman?"

This made no sense. I told him to use his own tongue, that I could follow it. Then he said, in a corrupt rattling speech, "The lord cannot make the woman obey? Shall I bring anything to the lord?"

He supposed that, though she was near-dead, I would restore Hwenit. I had not even considered it. I had healed a horse, a child, half accidentally, but I had not been sure with the horse, and there had been some fight in the child for the healing to work on. Hwenit's pulse was weak as the flickering of a moth's wing. Yet when I reached and put my palm on her neck, she was still warm; she had seemed a century cold. Irregularly but continuously, her heart beat. How had she lived this long? Perhaps she clung to her shred of life, waiting for the magician to cure her?

She had helped me, taught me something of my Power.

I owed her a debt. Maybe there was only one way to pay her.

It frightened me. Before, during those haphazard healings, I had not thought. Now the nerves ran on me. What must I do? And, more, dreadfully, what was the consequence?

"See to your master," I said to the slave.

The slave stretched his mouth. I had never observed any of them smile before.

"You are all my masters. Lord Orek, the buried lord, Zrenn. You." He shut and tapped his left eye. "I am called Long-Eye," he said. He moved sideways and was gone.

Westering red lights began to fleck into the tent.

I tried too hard to reach Hwenit. I tried to knit blood and flesh with hammer strokes.

At last, sitting bathed in sweat in the black exhalation of nightfall, it came to me how unvigorous and silent it had been before; the poisoned stallion in Eshkorek, the choking baby in the village, when I had not even felt the virtue go from me.

So Hwenit's pupil smoothed his slate and began afresh.

The sun rose. I left the tent, and the slave was at his grave-digger's office a second time. This second grave, out of synchronization with the other, seemed oddly superfluous, an afterthought.

"Who is this for?" I asked him, using his own wretched speech.

"My master Orek," he said.

You harness death; you harness life. You can kill or cure. A grave becomes a symbol, one weak branch fallen from a flourishing tree.

The sun, clear of the wood, swam red and golden in front of my eyes.

I had not expected much else of Orek. Though he was young. I had no compulsion to pity. The slave clamped down the clay to cover the blond face, over which a scrap of cloth had been laid.

"How?" I said.

"His knife," said the slave, responding to me with a weird vivacity I had not formerly noted in these slave people. "He wedged it among the tree roots and threw his body on the blade. He did it wrong. It took a while."

I recollected gold-faced men lying on their swords in a crimson pavilion.

The sun was dividing, a blackness down its center. It would split in twain and fire the sea. Then I saw it was a black man against the sun, standing over me where I had sat. Qwef.

"Tell me if Hwenit is slain," he said to me.

"Why should you imagine so?"

"I felt it," he said. "Yesterday's dusk. I felt she was near death."

"There was magic between you after all, then."

"Blood speaking to blood. Yes. I felt it. I could not sleep. In the night I went to look where the boats are kept through the winter. One boat was missing. I guessed then that they had come seeking you. I took my own boat. I rowed through the darkness. Is she dead?"

I got to my feet.

"Look in the tent and see."

He turned and ran.

Presently, I went to look too. She had been lying sleepily, nursing the red cat. Now Qwef kneeled by her, his face buried in her neck, and she stroked his hair, murmuring. I heard the cinnamon triumph in her voice, ever so soft.

There was a white scar on her breast, like a sickle moon.

The fluttering heart beneath it had faltered, then drummed. She had come back easily from her sleep—the dark ocean, cheated of her, falling away as the waves had fallen from her body that night I lay with her.

The white bitch had healed Peyuan after the dragon's blow.

I, sly as she, had healed Peyuan's daughter.

The circle ended and began.

3

I went to the beach on the other side of the island. Zrenn's stolen boat was aground on the sand, and gulls were swooping and picking about on the waves. Otherwise I was alone.

It was a fine pale day, without storm or much heat.

I had gone beyond sleep, and sat like a shipwreck there, trying to come to terms with my own self.

It was very hard.

Certainly, I was not as I had known myself. For all Hwenit's teaching, I wondered what new wells lay untapped within me. What of those strangest of all strange things she had mentioned, the priest gifts: the summoning of fire, the control of elements, the power of flight?

Each thing, perhaps, was there to hand in me, would come at a need. Yet, as the priests had done, surely I must prepare myself, train myself to be a vessel for such talents.

My thoughts went around and around, availing me little. Mingled in them was the image of the white woman, and the dark man, my father. Here was my destiny. I might look no further. I had sworn an oath to him. Find her and kill her, the enchantress who had harmed both him and me. When I thought back to my dreams, to Kotta's story, to Eshkorek, it was very natural to me to hate her. So my debate crystallized. The tangle of mysteries was simplified to that one aim: his vengeance, my vow.

I stood up, then, discarding the rest.

If I had Power, I would use that Power to achieve my goal. Let me use it, then.

I cast about. How? I had no idea. It was laughable. Here was a baby who could smash mountains, and did not know where they were to be found.

At that moment, I saw the Dark Man, Long-Eye, standing

at the edge of the wood, looking at me. I called to him, and he ran up at once, like my dog.

"Lord? How may I serve you?"

I perceived he had made himself over voluntarily as my chattel, having lost his other two masters, and assuming my anticipation of a slave. About a yard off, he kneeled down, and obeised himself. I recalled he had named me a deity, and apparently believed me so. He showed no fear. It seemed that, at the commencement, his race had known gods and no other. Gods had bound and ill treated and slaughtered and played with them. Gods were a fact, as were the sun and the shaking of the earth. Just another terrible reality.

I was not sure if I had summoned him for aid or merely for human conversation, but I said, "To find a witch, what do your priests do?"

"We have no priest. The chief is priest. We do not worship."

I had begun remembering the krarl, but I knew nothing of the complex inner rituals conducted by Seel and his like in their stinking dens. It was indicative of my mood that next I said, idly, to Long-Eye, "A bitch mothered me. I am her kin but I must find and destroy her; the flaw in the scheme being that I don't know where she might be."

"In himself, Lord Vazkor will know."

"I do not," I said, "though I will suppose she is no longer in this land or continent. I think I would know, now, if she were that near. I think I would be guided to know it."

"There is a big land to the south," Long-Eye said. "East, then south. Across the great ocean. Perhaps there."

When he spoke, it was like a summons. I glanced beyond him, at the curve of the sea. Why not that way? For sure, I could not go back. All was trouble and enmity behind me. I had no hearth, no kindred, nor any service to bind me, and my road had been paved with dead women. I had run toward the shore, had I not, as if it were my beacon?

"Who told you of this southern land?"

"Old maps of the lords show it," he said. "There was trading once."

I narrowed my eyes against the glare of the sun, and inside my lids suddenly saw a ship, fat-sailed, black on silver light. Precognition or self-deception? No way to learn but to risk the throw. Hwenit would live because of me, I was that much of a magician, and Long-Eye thought me a god.

In my current situation, I was prey for risk, and for any symbol.

To leave the island for the blank wideness of the sea was symbol enough of what I had felt in myself.

Before the lovers roused in the tent, or the boats of the black krarl came from the mainland, Long-Eye and I had put out onto the ocean.

THE BIRTHGRAVE

Tanith Lee

Tanith Lee's first venture into the world of heroic fantasy is a big, rich, bloody swords-and-sorcery epic with a truly memorable heroine.

Alternately warrior, witch, goddess and slave, she travels through a barbaric world, sometimes helped, sometimes betrayed by her lovers, searching for a way to free herself from the taint of her vanished race.

'A feast of excitement and adventure . . . filled with rich, alien names, half-sketched barbarian societies, ruined cities, decadence and wonder.' *Marion Zimmer Bradley*

BROTHERS OF EARTH

C. J. Cherryh

The sole survivor of a skirmish in space manages to touch down on the nearest inhabitable planet.

There he finds one of his hereditary enemies, a woman of outstanding beauty, dominating the planet with her advanced weapons and gadgetry.

Grudgingly she permits him to live and to be adopted by one of the Great Houses which rule this feudal world.

Gradually he learns the language and the intricate ways of the humanoid natives, and finds himself, to his utter disbelief, the centre of a murderous civil war, which only he can bring to an end.

In her second novel, startlingly different from her earlier GATE OF IVREL, C. J. Cherryh has given us a picture of an alien society which has known no equal since DUNE.

ROBERT E. HOWARD OMNIBUS

The fantastic worlds of Robert E. Howard . . . join the master of fantasy and adventure in a dozen stories featuring Conan the Barbarian, Solomon Kane, Kid Allison, the mighty Cormac and many others.

Journey to the voluptuous barbarism of the East, to the perils of Outremer, to the bloodstained Northlands of the Vikings, to the lawless days of the Old West . . .

A feast of jewelled splendour, black enchantment and savage death.

Also available by Robert E. Howard in Orbit: